SALEM COLLEGE
LIBRARY

The Burton Craige
Collection of
North Caroliniana

The Congregation of the Dead

Max Childers

The Congregation of the Dead

A Novel

Max Childers

WYRICK & COMPANY

Published by Wyrick & Company
Post Office Box 89
Charleston, South Carolina 29402

Copyright © 1996 by Max Childers
All rights reserved.
Printed in the United States of America

Library of Congress Cataloging-In-Publication Data

Childers, Max.
The congregation of the dead : a novel / Max Childers.
p.   cm.
ISBN 0-941711-32-3
1. Fathers and sons--United States--Fiction. 2. College teach-
ers--United States--Retirement--Fiction. 3. English teachers--
United States--Retirement--Fiction. I. Title
PS3553.H4855C66   1995
813'.54--dc20   95-38203
CIP

The Congregation of the Dead

1

"And you wish to stand by every word in this...this document?"

Walter Loomis, never-to-be-tenured assistant professor of English, nodded and blinked. His eyes, behind the thick lenses of his glasses, were large and had a perpetually startled cast. He wanted to appear calm and commanding, but his eyes, and the slight smile that played across his lips from time to time, gave him away.

"Howard, what do you think of Professor Loomis' observations?"

Albert Ransome, Dean of Arts and Sciences, shifted his attention to Walter's chairman; or rather his former chairman. Howard Farwell, Dryden specialist, cleared his throat. He did not look at Walter as he spoke.

"I've never...read anything like it."

"Do you find this amusing?" Ransome gently asked Walter, who had broken into a toothy grin.

"Perhaps...yes. I do." Walter said, his voice hitting a high note of glee.

Ransome picked up the letter that Walter had composed the previous afternoon.

"Dear Dry Rot," Ransome read. Ransome was slight and pale. He reminded Walter of one of those translucent fish that live in the deepest part of the sea—at depths that would crush a submarine's hull. "This is (the letter read) just to let you know that I quit. As of today. You might say that

1

I've had a better offer. But then again almost anything is better than working for you and Fish Ransome..." Ransome paused and underlined something in the letter. Farwell cleared his throat again, then emitted a series of choked, rumbling noises. Walter stared out the window. He noticed that it was snowing again. It snowed frequently at Altgeld College; a total, white blankness. He grinned again, glad that he had come to the meeting with Ransome and Farwell. He could have left town earlier, but the scene was worth waiting for.

"...I leave here with a great sense of relief and escape. The students are awful. As for you, my dear Dr. Farwell, and my esteemed colleagues, the less said the better. I see now, by the way, that I was fortunate in being rejected for tenure. A stroke of good luck. Altgeld College and Wetumka, Illinois are at the very heart of the land of the dead. Today, I count myself among the living. So good-bye and fuck you. Sincerely, Walter Loomis, Assistant Professor, Department of English (retired)."

Ransome tossed the letter on to the desk.

"*Fuck you.* You put that in?"

"That's right," Walter said.

"I'll see that you never teach again!" Farwell choked. His round, midwestern country boy's face had turned a dangerous shade of scarlet, the same color that had enveloped him the day before when Walter had handed him the letter and watched as he read. "No one, *no one* quits in the middle of the goddamn semester."

"I just did," Walter said, almost giggling.

"You're on contract," Farwell said, calming down slightly, speaking to Walter as if he were a naughty child. "For the entire academic year. And I'm going to see that you abide by those terms. And when this semester is over, I hope to never hear of you again!"

As he spoke, Farwell worked himself halfway out of the

chair. He wanted to go on, but as was his habit, he lapsed into another series of rumblings. Walter smiled at him. Those rumblings had served as a kind of aural and temporal punctuation during endless departmental meetings. After a certain number of rumbles, the meetings would grind down and finally end.

"Now Howard," Dean Ransome said, motioning for Farwell to sit down.

"You should try to maintain your self-control," Walter blandly added. Then he laughed, a jarring, almost obscene noise in the decorous calm of the Dean's office.

"I don't have to listen to that!" Farwell hissed, turning to Walter.

"Howard, please," Ransome said. Farwell rumbled again, straightened his tie, and did as he was told.

"Now Walter," Ransome went on in a reasonable, kindly way, "what's this notion about not finishing out the semester. We have nearly six weeks to go. A crucial point in the year. And it seems to me that you should feel some obligation to your students. You can't simply abandon them."

"I won't finish this term," Walter said. Yes, he thought. This is all very, very good.

"That's your final answer? You realize that a replacement will have to be found for your classes. And that will involve any number of headaches—including other professors doing your job..."

"I don't have a job. Thank God," Walter said. Ransome pretended not to notice this declaration.

"...and even if your opinion of us is low, you could still think of your colleagues."

My colleagues, Walter thought. Five to nothing against tenure. "I'm getting out of here as fast as I can," Walter said.

"You won't reconsider?" Ransome said, the gentleness sliding out of his voice. "You're actually going to do as you say?"

"You have my answer," Walter said. Then he laughed again. Ransome, never more pale and translucent, glared at him. Pure hate, Walter thought. Good.

"In all my time here," Ransome began, his thin lips barely moving, "I have never seen a more egregious breach of academic discipline and decorum. Yes. You should go. In fact, it would be in everyone's best interest for you to leave as soon as possible. You are, without doubt, the most shameless..."

Walter stood. There was a peculiar lightness in his limbs and head that he had never felt before.

"Where are you going?" Ransome said. "I haven't finished."

"But I have," Walter said.

"I've got one question, Loomis," Farwell said. "What could've made you decide to do this?"

"Opportunities," Walter laughed, closing the door behind him.

Walter Loomis was a large, resigned-looking man in his early forties. Despite his height—he was nearly six three— he was stooped; his shoulders sloped at a steep angle and his neck was bowed so that his chin swayed close to his chest. He moved with a stumbling gait; as if each step required a tremendous amount of energy. He enjoyed conversation, but he seldom spoke unless spoken to. On first meeting him, many, especially his fellow academics, pegged him as simple—perhaps even oafish. It was as if an invisible wall existed between Walter and the world at large; it was a wall that he ran into at regular intervals. Those who did get to know him—professors at Altgeld or the other places where he had taught, his ex-wife, and a few students—tended to view him with a kind of tolerant pity. They thought that they were granting him their affection despite his shortcomings; that they had the compassion to accept Walter in spite of himself, and to recognize his small talents. When they wanted to be kind, they said that he was easy-going. When they decided to be brutally honest, they said that Walter was a guy who would never get anywhere. Valerie, his former wife who had secured a position as a feminist critic at Penn about the time she decided to divorce Walter, had told him, on the day that she ordered him out of the house, that he reminded her of a child on a tricycle. He would just lurch along until he ran into something. Then he would lie there in a confused heap for awhile before recommencing his lurchings. She was delighted with her analysis, which she eventually decided to be true of most men. She related her version of Walter at academic conferences and at feminist lit-crit seminars all over the country. Invariably, she got a laugh.

Actually, buried beneath his exterior, Walter Loomis was not much like the prevailing impression of him. He sensed, rather than knew, that there were other versions of Walter Loomis. Occasionally, as in Ransome's office, those unexpected versions would spring forth—to the consternation of others, and to Walter's surprise.

The Walter Loomis who walked out on Ransome and Farwell, the Walter Loomis who had composed the letter of resignation, had manifested himself the previous day. Walter had conducted his normally bleak fiction workshop. The class met twice a week, and some of the students, juniors and seniors, had in the past month or so taken to indulging in almost open insolence. Altgeld was a small school, and the students, like everyone else, had heard that Walter had failed, for the second and final time, to gain tenure. He had also failed to be granted tenure at three other colleges, all in a descending order of academic excellence. The reasons for his rejection were invariably the same, despite the fact that he had published a novel and two collections of short stories (all, however, with obscure houses) and had sat on his share of dull, mind-killing committees: Walter did not have what

it takes. He appeared distracted, lost, somewhere else—
often in the midst of students and professors. The tenure
committee had found it easy—even if they felt sorry for him.
Walter's an unfortunate case, they said. His next stop would
probably be a community college in Northern Montana.

Walter's main problem in the fiction-writing workshop
was a young man named Brent Malone. When the class
started in January, Walter had informed the students that
they should never submit certain types of stories: Dungeons-
and-Dragons fantasies, westerns, true romance, imitations
of television shows, or any sort of homage to Stephen King.
Most of all, as Walter put it in the class syllabus, he did not
want to see any science fiction submissions, or "Bug-eyed
monster yarns" as he put it, plagiarizing from Edmund
Wilson. Walter's syllabus was direct and emphatic on this
point. Indeed, all that he wrote, fiction, book reviews, and
various types of scholarly sweepings (including his letter of
resignation) was forceful, direct, vivid, and often brutal. The
reviews of his only novel, *Dancing at the Abattoir*, had said
as much—also noting that the author had an unfortunate
inability to create positive, life-affirming characters. Valerie,
who found Walter's fiction but another example of late
modernist cant, had told him that the voice in his work,
despite being filled with the very sound of masculine oppres-
sion, was considerably stronger and more interesting than
the Walter she had to wake up to each morning. Walter had
tried to think of a snappy reply, but, as was often the case,
nothing came to him.

As for his writing career, lately he encountered a terrible
lethargy each time he sat down at his desk. His volume of
stories, *Lunar Follies*, had come out the previous year to virtually no recognition, and he had managed to take only a
few notes toward a new novel—one that he knew would be
no more successful than his other work. After he had been
denied tenure, he seldom even took notes. Whatever gifts he

had were drifting away from him, and he was filled with a kind of dull self-pity.

He had been stewing over his work, or lack of work, as he read through the student stories before class. He composed a short, conscientious critique for each manuscript, patiently pointing out omissions, failures, and absurdities in careful, non-judgmental language. *This character needs better development,* he would write. *Or this scene doesn't quite grab the reader as it should.* He would also provide praise for the most ordinarily competent elements. In this way, he hoped to keep the students off his back. He sometimes regretted overrating the small hope of future success in their work. None of them had the patience, or the willingness to fail, that he thought was required by the writer. The main thing, though, was to keep them quiet and shove them further away toward a degree.

Walter had saved Mr. Malone's story for last. Mr. Malone—Walter refused to call students by their first names—insisted on science fiction. Malone was a fashionably skinny, MTV-type who wore jeans with holes in the knees, sported Nirvana and Sonic Youth T-shirts, played in a local alternative band named Pussy Boy, and every two weeks turned in a new cyber-punk story. He submitted more work than any other student in class, and the stories were all the same: androids and humans shooting it out in a desolate, futuristic landscape. Walter had written extensive notes on the stories, encouraging Malone "to try something new. Explore your options in fiction. Perhaps something autobiographical?" Despite the gentleness of Walter's remarks, Malone would rush to the office after his work had been discussed, and after he had read Walter's suggestions. "I write what I *feel!*" Malone would sneer. "The rest of the class thought it was great!" and so on. Walter would nod and smile sadly until Malone wore himself out.

On that day, the day that saw the emergence of a new

Walter Loomis, there came the moment when Malone's work had to be considered. It was called "The Machine as Child, the Child as Machine" and it was twenty-three pages long. Walter sighed as he began to read, noticing that only fifteen minutes remained until class started. He had put off reviewing Malone's latest effort a bit too long. He quickly scanned the first ten pages. A cyborg couple adopt a fully human child and train him as an assassin. Walter skipped to the last few pages: the child, now a man, is the vocalist for a cyborg band which has changed the consciousness of both cyborgs and humans, uniting them in an oversoul which projects, video-like, into the mind of every inhabitant of the Earth. The story ended at a gigantic, violent, sexual world-wide concert, with the hero being consumed by his followers. Walter briefly pondered the last page, then, not quite knowing what he was doing, wrote a single word in large capital letters on the back of the manuscript. PUTRID.

He smiled at the word, then slid the story to the bottom of the stack of manuscripts before going off to class.

Of course he was immediately sorry for having written the comment. And—with class starting—it was too late to do anything about it. He felt that he would look ridiculous scratching out his evaluation in front of the class; and even if he had removed the word, he could not think of any bland or ambiguous comments to insert in its place. Then he could see Malone's reaction to the word. He decided to save Malone's story for last. Perhaps he could even postpone giving the story back until the next class meeting. By then he would have summoned up enough energy to think of new, pointless comments.

But it was not to be. After Walter and his students had critiqued two transparent imitations of Raymond Carver, a story about a boy becoming a man during a deer-hunting trip in Northern Michigan, and an unbearably cute tale of campus romance, Walter, wearied and appalled anew by all that had passed before him, turned to "The Machine as Child, the Child as Machine." As he opened the discussion, he noticed that Malone and two of his friends, a boy named Will Hanks and a girl named Mandy Slotsky, who always wore black and had lately dyed her hair a shade of metallic red, were staring hard at him. This had become their habit since news of the tenure decision had come down. Sometimes they would laugh at Walter behind their hands. In this, they differed little from Walter's colleagues.

"Perhaps we could have some comments?" Walter asked tentatively.

"It's the best story of the semester," Mandy Slotsky said. She also wore a good bit of pale make-up and wrote semi-literate stories about nihilistic characters in upscale bars. To Walter, it appeared that her make-up grew thicker at each class meeting—as if at some point she might be transformed into a mime. "Brent's other stories were definitely good," she said in a thick Chicago accent. "This one is definitely the best."

"I think the beginning's strong," Miss Unger said. She was a large girl, packed into stirrup pants and a Harvard sweat shirt. With slight alarm, Walter realized that she could be mistaken for a life-size bratwurst. He nodded a thanks for her observation.

"It's so *violent*," Miss McCantry said. She was a blond, well-dressed sorority girl, the author of the campus romance.

"Well...like...it's set in a violent time, you know. And the guy's an assassin," Will Hanks said. Will Hanks played bass for Pussy Boy. Walter had seen him stapling advertising flyers for the band on the departmental bulletin boards. He had not turned in a single word of fiction since the semester began.

Without any participation from Walter, Mandy Slotsky, Miss McCantry, and Will Hanks argued back and forth about violence in fiction, movies, and American culture in general. Walter listened, at least grateful that they were consuming time. The debate had the fitful rhythms, received opinions, and canned insights common to most class discussions. He tried to remember how many years he had spent presiding over such nonsense, but quickly gave up. The thought depressed him almost as much as Mr. Malone's fiction.

They kept going for a good ten minutes, with Miss Unger and another student joining in. The rest of the class doodled in their notebooks and yawned. Walter glanced at the clock above the door: only eight minutes remained in the hour. Maybe, he thought, I won't even have to talk about Malone's story at all.

"What do *you* think, Dr. Loomis?" Miss Unger asked. Walter, who was still gazing at the clock, requested that she repeat the question. Malone laughed and said something under his breath to Will Hanks, who nodded. Both of them grinned.

"What do *I* think? About violence in art? Or about this story?" Walter was instantly sorry that he had brought up the story. The best thing would have been to keep everyone sidetracked. And then came a familiar feeling, entropy, fatigue, as if he were coming to an absolute halt. It isn't just the tenure committee, he thought. The feeling was strongest in his classes, where he had come to fear the possibility of falling asleep, or losing muscular control, or becoming incontinent.

"Ah...about both," Miss Unger said.

"Yes. That would cover it." Walter did not know what he meant by these words, but for some inexplicable reason, Miss Unger nodded in satisfaction. His eyes lifted toward the clock—like a martyr searching for impending signs of eternal, heavenly reward. Only four minutes remained. They will talk about this after class, he thought. They will snicker again. Malone will imitate my frozen state for Mandy Slotsky.

"Just what does that mean?" Malone rasped as if on cue. Walter smiled beatifically at the boy, whose throat was apparently raw from howling and spitting away the previous evening at some bar. The lad has suffered for his art, Walter thought. He noticed the cluster of pimples on Malone's chin, and that his hair was slicked back with grease. An affectation, Walter thought.

"It means, Mr. Malone…it means…," Walter trailed off. Malone's smirk filled the room and Mandy Slotsky laughed. She did not even bother to hide it.

"What the hell does it mean, Loomis?" Malone said. Miss McCantry's mouth formed a pretty, perfect oval of astonishment. Walter smiled again.

"It means," Walter began, the fatigue magically evaporating, "that your story is derivative in its conception. And yes. There is violence, and there will be more violence—of all sorts. It is, if used in an artistic way, a necessary, even a moral element. Think of Hemingway, Swift, Flannery O'Connor. All very different artists, but all showing us violence as a kind of end, a logical end of vanity, and cruelty and…"

He paused and looked back up toward the clock. Class was officially over, but the words kept coming.

"…but considering your 'story' Malone, I don't think of great writers at all. I think…of Bugs Bunny cartoons, and assembly line sludge. Books and stories extruded like hot dogs and being swallowed by the mindless, perpetually-adolescent public. This piece of *shit* you call a story isn't even a good imitation of something that was moronic to begin with…"

He paused again, and laughed. He had not planned to say what he had said, any more than he had planned the one-word evaluation of Malone's manuscript. The words had charged out of his mouth by their own volition.

No one moved or spoke. None of them, in the whole of their short, suburban, middle-class lives, had ever had anything that they had undertaken described in such terms—at least by a certified adult authority figure, even one so battered and compromised as Dr. Walter Loomis.

Walter stood and announced that class was over. He took advantage of their momentary paralysis, especially Malone's, who sat working his jaw. He left the manuscripts and jerked down the hall. He made a quick stop by his mail box, grabbed what was there, and made straight for his office. He locked the door behind him, and tossed the mail toward the desk—most of it landed on the floor. Breathing heavily, he listened for the approaching sounds of his young scholars. Soon, apparently recovered from their astonishment, they arrived. First came the knocking, and Walter held his breath for fear that they would hear him. Then there were the mutterings, Malone's rock and roll rasp rising above the voices of his accomplices.

"What a fucking asshole...you know how long I worked..."

"I'd like to see *his* stuff." It was Mandy Slotsky.

"A big yawn, I heard," Will Hanks said. Walter had suspected him of never having read a book.

They continued to grouse and mutter for a few minutes. Then, to Walter's relief, their voices drifted down the hall.

He had one window in his office and it faced out on the red brick wall of the opposite wing of the building. The sun was making a feeble, early afternoon effort to cut through the overcast. Gray, exhaust-defiled snow was piled up around the perimeter of the parking lot below. The weather report that morning had called for more snow, six or seven inches, during the next two days. Walter imagined the snow lathering down on Wetumka in great, willowy gouts, smothering the college, the ugly town, and the unrelieved prairie that stretched north to Lake Michigan and south toward the equally emptied-out landscape of western Kentucky. He closed the blinds. What lay beyond the window only made matters worse. And besides, he thought, Malone might see me and come back.

A year, five years, perhaps six months earlier, he knew that he would not have been quite such a coward. He was never the sort of professor who would inspire excessive respect, much less fear in his students. But at least he might not have run away. I give up, he thought. I surrender, too tired. It was just like it had been in Georgia and New Hampshire and where was that school where I lasted only a year? Texas? Yes. Right after graduate school. I've been driven out again, and without even the dubious glory of a howling mob at my heels.

Tired of his self-pity, he picked up the mail from the desk and floor. There was a letter from a college in Missouri. He had, upon realizing that his time at Altgeld was coming to a close, sent out a dozen resumes. The message, from Mid-Continent Nazarene University, was one of regret that Walter's qualifications did not meet their present needs. He tossed the letter, along with three advertisements from textbook publishers and a copy of the minutes from the last curriculum committee meeting, into the trash can. Then there was another letter and the return address startled him: Helmsville, North Carolina, his parents' old home town. The envelope also bore the name of Roy A. Bunch, Attorney-at-Law. The letter could not have been any stranger or more unexpected if it had arrived from Mars. Cautiously, with a sense of dread and revelation, he began to read.

Mr. Walter Loomis:

I am sorry to inform you that your father, Edgar Dawes Loomis, passed away on February 8th of this year. Believe me, I made every effort to contact you, and it was only through the discovery of a collection of short stories by you (*Scenes From An Interstate Laundromat*) that I could get any bearing on your present residence. I contacted the publisher, Nightwood Press in Los Angeles, and they were kind enough to pass on your address. I do want you to know that I regret having to tell you about your father.

To get down to business, I was retained as your father's attorney about a year before his death. On a personal note, he told me that he had not seen you since you were a child, and he was, I believe, still somewhat reluctant to contact you. I would not hazard a guess as to why, since my dealings with Mr. Loomis were on a purely professional level.

At any rate, your father's will has been probated and you have been left a half interest in his real property. This property includes a 600-acre tract in Darden County, North Carolina which consists of farm and timber land. There are also numerous pieces of farm equipment, several outbuildings, as well as acreage fronting the Reedy River. You are also to receive, alone and outright, a house of 2500 square feet in area and liquid assets, again yours outright, in the sum of $897,015.21.

This is, as you can see, quite a sizeable estate. I hope that you can contact me at your earliest convenience. You may reach me by telephone at 704-822-0531.
Yours,
Roy A Bunch, Atty at Law

Walter quicky read through the letter. Then he read it over more slowly, staring hard at the words. The longer he looked, the more the words did indeed seem to constitute a transmission from another planet. Stupidly, he thought that he would never present such a preposterous turn of events in his fiction. He laughed at himself, leaped from his chair, and launched into a clumsy, shuffling dance around his undecorated, austere, paper-bestrewn office before it came to him that his father, a figure so distant as to be non-existent, was dead.

"Father," he said. He was trying to remember his father when the knocking began again—a loud, revenge-filled banging. Malone was back.

"He's in there for sure," Malone said, no doubt addressing Mandy Slotsky. Walter danced over, turned the lock, and flung open the door, catching Malone in mid-knock. Mandy Slotsky and Will Hanks were right behind him.

"AAAARRRRGGGHHHH!" Walter roared, raising his arms above his head and advancing on Malone and his fan club like Frankenstein's monster turning on the mob of tormenting villagers.

"AAAARRRRGGGHHHH!"

Malone stumbled backwards, nearly knocking Mandy Slotsky to the floor. Walter kept coming, his teeth bared, his eyes bright, and pursued them until they vanished down a stairwell. Then he hurried back to his office. There was much to do.

Farwell, two secretaries, and the Chaucer scholar had rushed into the corridor at the second of Walter's triumphant bellows. But all was empty and as it should be, a dead, academic silence. For once, Walter Loomis had been too quick for those who sit in judgement.

2

Walter did not rejoice in his father's death, even if he felt no sense of loss. He had not seen Edgar since he was eleven—when his parents divorced and he had gone away with his mother. They left his father in Washington where, at the time, he ran some sort of consulting business. Prior to starting his firm, Edgar had spent many years with the CIA. This much Walter knew. Margaret, Walter's mother, had seldom spoken of Edgar after the divorce. Once or twice, however, she had mentioned that Edgar had been in the O.S.S. during the war, and had been one of the first agents hired by Allen Dulles when the CIA was organized. "He thought it was like being present at the creation of the world," she said. Edgar had apparently been a real company man—right up until the time he was linked to the group which took the fall for the Bay of Pigs. Walter had sometimes wondered if the Bay of Pigs had caused his parents to split up. There had been scenes when Edgar returned from Florida, cursing and stomping through the house, drinking and quarreling with Margaret, raving all the while about Kennedy's betrayal. The divorce came quickly after Edgar's resignation from the agency.

Walter's memory of that time, like his memories of his father, were jumbled and, he knew, probably unreliable. Edgar had been gone much of the time, leaving Walter and his mother to their own devices. On those occasions when

Edgar was home, he brought presents from Guatemala, Iran, and other places Walter had never heard of. Edgar also brought a thick, lunging tension with him, and Walter soon learned to stay out of his father's way. When he was big enough to ride a bicycle, he often avoided the house until nightfall. It was that way until Edgar escaped and set forth on another mission.

An image of his father had remained with him from that time: a big man with a mass of curly black hair who distilled an overpowering, bullying strength—all poorly masked behind courtly manners and a slight, but noticeable, southern accent. Whenever Edgar had regarded Walter, his only child, it was with an air of ill-concealed analytical contempt—as if his son was a project that had gone wrong at the beginning and could not be turned into anything profitable or useful.

After the divorce, there had been a hurried departure from Washington and a meandering drive south. It had taken Walter a day or two to understand that his mother had no final destination in mind. To keep moving was the only apparent goal. They drifted through the hot summer from Norfolk to Raleigh to Charlotte, staying in cheap motels while Margaret studied the want ads in the local papers. She was propelled by a quick panic—like an emigré from some grand, fallen dynasty attempting to maintain a sense of aristocratic dignity as she ran out of money and time. Margaret had, as Walter learned as he grew older, studied the examples of the great ladies of film and fiction: Melanie Hamilton in *Gone With the Wind* and the heroines of the Brontë sisters. She had learned how to be noble, tragic, and enduring. During their destination-less voyage, she became so immersed in her role that she paid him little attention. She let him eat whatever he wanted in the roadside restaurants, and bought him toy Confederate soldiers, as well as cheap games, miniature checkerboards and pinball machines, specially designed to occupy a child during a cross-country trip. She drove with great deliberation and maintained a quivering, transparent serenity.

After more than a week of this, which Walter enjoyed immensely, they came inevitably to Helmsville—her old home town. She never spoke of the place without condemnation in her voice. It was a medium-sized town by the standards of the North Carolina Piedmont—close to the state line and not far from Charlotte. It was a mill town too; feudal and stratified in those days, with an ugly, impermanent appearance. "It was built for money. Nothing but money," Margaret would say. She did not object to money. She only wanted a little grace and beauty to go with it.

They stayed at her parents' house for what, to Walter, seemed like a long time. Walter's grandparents, who would be dead before he finished prep school, lived on one of the few attractive streets in Helmsville. His grandfather, by then retired, had earned the house on the tree-lined street by faithful service as an executive with the North State Spinning and Finishing Company. No doubt he had looked forward to a peaceful, unworried retirement after all those years in offices and board rooms. He found little of either when his daughter showed up unannounced in the middle of a gummy June afternoon.

There had been extended, quarrelsome discussions among the adults. Walter had eavesdropped, crouching just outside the dining room when there was nothing good on television, or when he had grown bored with his soldiers and games. "I expected such behavior out of Edgar," his grandmother said over and over. She would say this until Margaret told her to stop. Then they would argue over Margaret's lack of respect for her parents. Later, they would make up and Margaret would begin a determined assault: She wanted money so that she and Walter could "start their lives over," as she put it "in a beautiful place." She meant

Charleston, which Walter had heard mentioned often even before their arrival in Helmsville. She would repeat the name of Charleston as if it were as romantic and enchanted as Paris—or perhaps Oz. When Walter was older he would smile when he remembered her enthusiasm. She got what she wanted, he thought: Rhett Butler's home town.

His grandfather, at some point in the discussion, would observe that Margaret and Walter had a home: that they could stay as long as they wished, and that he could find good, steady work for Margaret right there in Helmsville. Margaret would raise her voice at that point and say that she could not see herself working the first shift at North State's textile labs. Nor did she want her son turned into a cotton mill aristocrat. "And besides," she would finish, "Helmsville reminds me entirely to much of that damn Edgar." After that, the three of them would natter listlessly into the summer night. Walter would usually return to the TV—even if there were only two channels in Helmsville and not ten like he was used to in Washington.

In the end, Margaret wore them down and got the loan. The car was loaded, the grandmother weeping softly the whole time. And they headed south again. Margaret became serene—and even more talkative—as they made their way down through South Carolina. "Charleston is a *real* place," she said. "A place I can really live in." She was almost giddy by the time they reached the Lowcountry. "Never underestimate the value of flight," she said, as they entered Charleston. At the time, Walter did not understand.

They seldom spoke of Helmsville or of Edgar. Within a year of the divorce, she had remarried. Walter's stepfather, Simmons Tarrant, owned the antiques store where Margaret had found work the week they arrived in the city. Before she became a wife again, she had become the store's best salesperson, and Simmons, a properly courtly and distant Charlestonian, had found himself married to her without quite knowing how it happened. His friends and family could not believe that Margaret was not from Savannah, or even Charleston itself, so gracious were her manners and so lively her disposition. And she eventually came to know as much about the antique business as Simmons, who had been raised to honor the artifacts from the past. The business prospered as never before. Everyone said that Simmons had made a good match. Walter suspected that Margaret never let it be widely known that she was from a red-dirt mill town. It certainly would have compromised her greatest, her only creation.

They—Walter, Margaret, and Simmons—settled into the old Tarrant house, which was located on the Battery. They led a pleasant, calcified life and Walter was glad to be left alone. When he was thirteen, he was sent to an Episcopal prep school in Virginia, where he first settled into his own role of affable, befuddled alienation. His teachers were invariably surprised at his excellent essays, and he took both the history and English prizes his senior year. He never showed them the short stories he worked on when he had finished his tiresome academic chores. He cultivated solitude up there in the Blue Ridge at his fake-English school. He did not form a single lasting friendship from those years, or from the years that followed at the state university in Columbia. Simmons, who seldom required anything of Walter, had insisted that he go to school there. The university was his alma mater and it was cheap. Walter had shrugged. Anywhere was fine with him. He spent his time there loafing, reading, and writing: he liked the university better than his old prep school. It was large enough for him to disappear into the faceless student crowd. In his senior year, two of his professors urged him to go to graduate school, so he did. There did not seem to be much else to do, and teaching would give him a chance to keep on writing. By happy coincidence, he failed his draft physical, after building up his blood pressure with salt, nicotine, and meat, on the same day he was given a fellowship at Texas. His professors congratulated him, but he almost regretted leaving Columbia. It had all been so nearly perfect—a place of few expectations and no regrets.

In his second year in Austin, when he was working on a degree in American literature and starting to get a few stories published in the smallest of the literary magazines, he received word of the deaths of Margaret and Simmons. They had been incinerated on a cruise ship named the *Nordic Princess*. The name struck Walter as ridiculous—almost as ridiculous as the fact that Margaret and Simmons were the only casualties.

They took a cruise or a vacation to Europe every year. Margaret had insisted, and Simmons, who loved peace and quiet above all things, did as she wanted. That year, she had decided to do the Caribbean and South America. "I expect to come back wonderfully tanned," she wrote to Walter just before they sailed, "and wearing feathers and pearls." Her flourishes gave him a laugh. It was as if she were finally secure enough to parody the role she had worked so long and hard to perfect.

The fire had broken out about three a.m. in an electrical panel next to their stateroom. Naturally, they were sailing on the first-class deck. They were found in bed after the crew had brought the fire under control. The Coast Guard had praised the ship's company for its prompt action, and the cruise was only interrupted long enough for the bodies to be landed at Miami for shipment to Charleston.

The funeral had been High Church Episcopal with closed coffins. Walter knew that both Margaret and Simmons would have appreciated the tastefulness and poetry of the occasion. The house and antique business had gone to Simmons' nephew, a pasty-faced sort who had never missed a chance to suck up to his rich uncle. A wise decision,

21

Walter thought. The joke, as Walter told the unbelieving nephew, was that he did not want any of it. "The less the better. And may God help you," were Walter's parting words. And he meant it too, even in the midst of grieving for Margaret. And he had also grieved for Simmons. The man had had the good grace to leave him alone—and the sense to bequeath his worldly possessions to someone who cared for such things.

Following the burial, Walter had tried to contact Edgar. He called the Washington number, and he wrote to the old address. The call never went through and the letter came back. Walter felt that he had done his duty and left it at that. He could still, despite the passing of the years, summon up that one memory: his father's calculating gaze and his own sense of flimsiness and failure. Silence and distance were to be preferred.

3

After vanquishing the students, and before the meeting with Ransome and Farwell, Walter had called the lawyer down in North Carolina to announce that he would be in Helmsville as soon as he could wind up his affairs in Illinois. Bunch, the lawyer, had a tired, permanently irritated voice, and seemed surprised at Walter's plans.

"I understand that I've been left a house. I intend to live there," Walter said, slightly insulted. Bunch whistled, then assumed a more business-like tone.

"Call me when you get in. I'll get the keys for you and see about the money too. If it suits you, we'll switch the account names at your father's old bank." Walter thought this made sense and Bunch excused himself, claiming that he had to be in court in fifteen minutes.

Once he hung up, Walter happily went about the task of evacuating himself from Wetumka and Altgeld College. He quickly cleaned out his office, boxing up books and hauling them to the trailer that he had rented that morning. No one offered to help him, and once, as he was huffing his way down the stairs with a particularly heavy load, he ran into Farwell who rumbled, turned red and brushed by him. Walter smiled broadly.

It did not take him long to clean out his duplex either. The furniture was rented; he had never owned much more than the card table where he typed out his manuscripts. He left behind his collection of mismatched plates, cups, silver, and utensils—a gift to his landlord or the next tenant of his borrowed space.

With a stronger sense of purpose than he had known in some time, he taped and sealed the cartons that held his manuscripts. He had, throughout an otherwise sloppy life, taken a great deal of care with his writing. As he worked, he contemplated the unlimited time that would be his for writing, or whatever else he might decide to take up. Hell, he thought, I can publish it myself if I want to bother with it all.

He wedged the manuscript carton into the already crowded back seat of his old Volkswagen and made a quick job of the rest; more books, clothes (his wardrobe, as Valerie often said, was pure minimalism), an electric typewriter, and a few pictures; framed posters and a copy of a Jasper Johns flag. As he went back and forth from the duplex to the curb, he mulled over the notion of purchasing new things once he had taken possession of his inheritance. He would have more money, he calculated, than he would make in decades of teaching at Altgeld College. And what would he buy? He did not require much, and had taken a secret pride in sticking to the basics. What had been a necessity when he left home as a boy, had become a habit since. He had an image of his father's money beckoning to him, calling him. Only, he told himself, what Edgar left me won't be transformed into things, but time. He could live without working, or doing the kind of work he had been at all of his adult life. Except for the writing, the possibilities are endless, he thought as he closed and locked the trailer doors. God help me—God bless me.

With the packing completed, he walked the three blocks to his bank and closed out his checking and savings accounts. Together, they came to $914.35. This amount, even when added to the few thousand he had in the Altgeld retirement plan, appeared puny beside what awaited him. I could spend all of it right now, he thought as he strolled back to the duplex. Ah, but that would never do. Keep the money and travel light. This insight delighted him, and if the sidewalk had not been so icy he would have broken into the same little dance he had performed when he read the letter from Roy Bunch.

As he turned the corner onto the street where he lived, the sun broke through. Wetumka, and the rest of Western Illinois, was experiencing one of those rare warm March days. The temperature had shot up to the mid-forties and the newest snow had begun to melt, overflowing the gutters with brook-like noises. The streets were fine for driving and he hoped that the roads were clear for the fifty-five mile trip to the interstate. A good day to get out of here, he thought.

He took one last look around the duplex before he left, celebrating his departure from the rooms he had barely inhabited for seven years by swigging down a Budweiser he had discovered when he cleaned out the refrigerator. My farewell party, he thought. Only it's like I never lived here. All I know of this town is the few streets that lead to banks, supermarkets, and the college and what I knew of the college was my office, the library, the classrooms. Despite the years at Altgeld, he could not recall the names of the buildings, and only those of a few students, mostly bad ones. They had, for Walter, achieved a separate identity from the undifferentiated mass that had paraded before him from one semester to the next.

He opened a road atlas and traced the routes he would follow. The destination was still mostly a name. There had been his mother's contempt for Helmsville and its environs, although when very young he had learned to be skeptical of her opinions. He had received many of his impressions of his father from the same source. He did not own a single photograph of the man, and the only image that he trusted, that gaze which was an evaluation, had ceased to hold much power. Edgar was a clean, white blank—a mystery without any apparent solutions.

Walter had, despite the rush of events that had transpired since he first learned of Edgar's generosity, tried to figure out why so much had been handed to him. There it was, though: the money, the house, the land, too—a half interest with a person, or persons, unknown. Another mystery, he thought: the unnamed other. The other might have skill in operating a farm. And the other might be as stunned by Edgar's generosity as I am, he thought. Guilt is a possibility: the other could've been injured by Edgar; bequest as atonement. He had no reason to make atonement to me. Edgar was an absence only—an absence that did less harm than his brief presence. In any event, Bunch, the man with the dead-tired voice, can tell me when I reach my new home.

He turned up the beer. *Home:* the word hovered around him like a living thing. He had never really wanted to lay claim to a specific place. Trying to live in his own skin had been enough of a problem. Have I ever lived anywhere? he thought. Where I was never mattered much before.

There came a rising in his chest, a flutter that alarmed and excited him. He closed the front door and dropped the key in the mailbox. The Volkswagen started on the first try, which was unusual: Walter took it as an auspicious sign. As he pulled away from Wetumka, he did not even bother to glance in the rearview mirror.

With the road atlas on the seat beside him, Walter followed the red line that pointed downward from what midwesterners like to call the Heartland. This term had amused Walter, although he had never revealed his amusement to anyone in Wetumka. He drove steadily, the weather in his favor. All through the morning and afternoon and far into the night, he was content to ride the slow lane, with the eighteen wheelers and the rest of the traffic blasting past. Now and then he checked the radio for weather reports, but most of the time he was perfectly content with only the tinny rattle of the engine and the highway's hum. South of Louisville, he checked into a Holiday Inn. He ordered dinner in the motel restaurant, and the waitress told him that he was just in time: the kitchen was about to close. She did not bother to hide how sorry she was to see him; Walter guessed that she had planned on finishing up and going home early that night.

The dining room was deserted; Walter liked it that way. The food, packaged in a distant location and microwaved for warmth, tasted uncommonly good. Walter ascribed the taste to the occasion; he was almost half way to Helmsville. He lingered, slowly eating the dessert cheesecake, the music of the band in the lounge next door muted and plaintive. He gave the waitress a big tip and she thanked him twice. Apparently, she forgave him for spoiling the evening.

In his room, he took a shower and crawled naked into bed. He had not slept without some type of clothing since the first year of his marriage. The sheets were smooth and sensuous. In a few minutes, he was snoring, his lips slightly parted, in the warm, stale motel air.

Late the next morning, between Nashville and Knoxville, it came to him that he was in the South. He had pulled into a truck stop for gas and a pair of sunglasses. As he hit the interstate entrance ramp, he realized that the air had a new feel to it. A chill hung on, but nothing like the crunching cold of where he had been. Beneath the chill was a smell—a fecundity, an odor of things about to grow that lived even in the atmosphere of the interstate. Later, farther down the road, he crossed the French Broad River and the green of the banks, mixed with the tawny, receding colors of winter, unfolded below him. Well, he thought, there it is: The Good Old Natural World. A fact to be sure, and a cliché in the hands of many.

He had never held an allegiance, an affection, for nature;

or the South, for that matter. He had lived much of his life in cities, or else small towns that he never ventured far from. As for the South, he had put it behind him when he left college. The South had belonged to his mother, and she had acted as if she were a sole proprietor. His stories and his novel were set in malls, apartments—flattened, claustrophobic spaces in nameless cities and suburbs. He wrote of the hemmed in, those ringed and squeezed by a tasteless, vacuous culture, all rendered up in the dead pan of late modernism. The perfect setting, he thought, for the terminally ironic; the home of the deracinated.

Valerie, not long before they split up, told him that his work exhibited "an oppressor's attitude." She found it "too detached, formal" and, finally "immoral." He wanted to tell her that she sounded like an old-time Soviet cultural commissar, but instead he whined that "No one reads my stuff anyway. Or at least not many people do." "That's beside the point," she would answer with impregnable and absolute certainty, breathless at the triumph of her argument, "You offer no hope."

Yes, he thought, as the river slipped behind him and the Blue Ridge reared up in the distance. Deracinated. That's what the famous southern novelist, the one whose book I panned in an obscure west coast journal, called me. I wasn't sure if he knew what the word meant. By the kind of chance that Walter later grew to take for granted, he and the novelist had appeared on a panel together at a writer's conference. It happened fifteen years earlier, when Walter's first work was just out and the novelist, Milton Collie, had recently published his sixth novel in seven years, all from a house in Chapel Hill which had been founded by his old writing professor. Collie's prose was called "lyrical" and "evocative of time and place" by those reviewers that he had charmed, either in person or in print, over the years. Walter had called the novel, entitled *Ringgold's History,* turgid and bloated, despite being less than three hundred pages long: a piece "of standard issue Dixie Lit. Such novels are not written—they are assembled like model airplanes." Walter was a bit stunned that Collie had read the review, since the *Fresno Quarterly* was hardly a big-time operation. But Collie quoted the line about the model airplanes before the panel discussion started; and at the cocktail party that evening, he, and his much younger wife, who also published with Collie's old teacher, had drunkenly confronted him. "You nothing boy. You...*de-rac-in-ated,*" Collie had loudly breathed into Walter's face. Walter left the cocktail party, sure that he and Collie had provided the highlight of the conference. Naturally, Walter ran into Collie at breakfast the next morning. Collie, badly hung over, and through a mouthful of eggs, greeted Walter, shouting, "There he is *again!* That boy that don't know where he's from!" Walter settled for a quick cup of coffee and a quicker escape from the conference.

It had been years since he had had cause to consider the insights of Milton Collie. It's this trip, he thought. He had reached the mountains, climbing toward the Tennessee–North Carolina border. It was much colder there and, as he swung the Volkswagen and the trailer around the curves on I-40, he had an acute awareness of the space and mass that dropped away on one side of him and rose on the other. Milton Collie territory, he thought. I must be trespassing.

He pulled off at an overlook, which presented a postcard-perfect view of the world below. The wind punched at him, whipping his fine, dry hair into a sort of halo. There was only one other vehicle in the parking lot, a motor home with New Jersey plates. A family—parents and three children—ate a Kentucky Fried Chicken lunch at a picnic table. The father, barrel-chested and hairy, wore shorts and a New York Giants cap despite the mountain wind. The mother and children, two boys and a girl, were similarly dressed—

as if being in the locale designated as the South required warm weather clothing. The man waved at Walter, who waved back. They probably feel compelled to practice southern hospitality too, he thought.

He went to the far end of the overlook. The sky was blindingly, perfectly clear—just as the radio stations between Cairo, Illinois, and East Tennessee said it should be. He stretched, trying to loosen the road tightness and the memories.

And what awaits me in Helmsville? he thought. How would Margaret like it? Her son stumbling to rest in the only spot in the world that she detested? She could not have predicted that Helmsville was the only place left to go; and that it had been provided by the mythic and hated Edgar.

He breathed deeply, sucking down the cold. As I drop lower down the road, he thought, it will turn warmer. And as time itself turns, on through April and May and summer, I will have some place to be.

"Thank you, Daddy!" he shouted over the rock ledge, toward the valley. "To hell with you and thanks!" The words boomed out, despite the wind, before fading and dying. As Walter danced back to the Volkswagen, the man from New Jersey and his goose-pimpled family stared, their mouths full of chicken.

Three hours after shouting from the mountainside, Walter arrived in Helmsville and called Roy Bunch, who gave him directions to Edgar's bank. The bank, Carolina Citizens, was on the west side of town. As for Helmsville, to Walter it consisted entirely of strip malls, apartment complexes, aging mill villages, fast food restaurants, and car lots. And it was warm, as he had hoped it would be. It's one big New South cliché he thought, even as he understood that he had yet to see all there was of Helmsville. The ramshackle temporariness provided him with a curiously pleasant sense of alienation. I'm here, but I won't be long, he thought. My place is further off—and it stands alone.

Bunch was a solid-looking, sloppy man of about fifty. In person, he was as tired and irritated as he had sounded over the telephone. He had, however, done his job and Walter was satisfied. The bank manager had already seen to the paperwork, and he too appreciated that Walter had decided to stay with what he called "his institution." Since Bunch and the manager had taken care of all of the preliminaries, all Walter had to do was sign the appropriate documents and accept a box of checks and a passbook. Walter turned them over in his hands. There was sixty-eight thousand in checking, seventy thousand in savings, and the rest in CDs— accumulating interest. One week before he had been grading essays, and trying to find ways to endure his colleagues and students. I was numb, he thought. And now I'm not.

As they left the bank, Bunch said that he had not had time to eat lunch and would Walter mind joining him at the McDonald's next door. Walter agreed. He had no choice, since he depended on Bunch for directions to his new home. Bunch ordered a salad and a Diet Coke. He ate automatically—apparently without tasting. Walter figured that Bunch would have preferred a double quarter-pounder, but his wife, or doctor, or both had decreed that he must stick to salads for the rest of his days. They made small talk about the weather and the drive down from Illinois until Walter asked how his father died. As he spoke, he was puzzled as to why he had not asked sooner—almost as if Edgar was not the real reason for having come so far to sit in a plastic booth with a harried, balding lawyer. Bunch swallowed a chunk of iceberg lettuce and a few slivers of carrot before he spoke.

"Heart attack."

"Was it quick? Was he alone?"

"I don't know how fast it was, but he was by himself. He

was out in one of his fields, ramming his pick-up truck into a stump. Or at least that's what we figured. The stump was halfway out of the ground."

"Why would he do that?"

Bunch shrugged. He smelled faintly of sweat and Aqua Velva.

"It's cheaper than calling a removal service. Farmers around here do it all the time, if the stump is rotten enough. This particular stump was full of wasps—or hornets hibernating for the winter, I'm told. I forget which. They must've swarmed him. He was stung fifty or sixty times. The doctors said that might've brought on the heart attack."

Walter, who had no clue as to his father's appearance in life, could not picture him in death. Swollen, he thought. He must've been enormously swollen.

Bunch drove slowly, making it easy for Walter to follow. In a few minutes, they were out of the strip mall and fast food district and, after passing through several blocks of restored Victorian mansions—like the kind once owned by Walter's grandparents—they were beyond Helmsville.

Bunch's Ford heaved along over the rough, potholed black top. Out in the open country, there were a few houses and store-gas-station-game-room combinations; for the most part, there was nothing but fields and woods. Flowers, yellow ones that Walter could not identify, had blossomed. For no reason, Walter had a sudden, ridiculous surge of happiness at the sight of them and the fields and the trees. Don't get all gooey inside, he told himself, laughing.

His happiness grew as he moved further from town. I will be truly isolated, he thought. I could disappear there. Bunch's round head bobbed along before him. Bunch lit a cigarette and tossed the match out the window. I'll bet he smokes constantly, Walter thought.

The black top ended at a T-intersection, where Bunch

took a left, followed by a sharp right down a gravelled road that was canopied by a thick overhang of oaks. The road dipped and rolled for more than a mile, and Walter followed so cautiously that Bunch slowed to a stop and waited for him. The columns of trees gave way to fields, just budding with rows of plants. Before Walter had time to speculate as to what grew on his land, a house came into view.

It was not at all what he expected. Back from the road stood a large, brick ranch model, complete with concrete driveway, carport, and a yard full of ceramic deer, donkeys, sombreroed Mexican gnomes, white chickens, ducks, and a birdbath. The grass was freshly cut, and the carefully tended dogwoods and azaleas would be putting forth blooms in the coming weeks. Across the meadow stood a big white barn or stable and a cluster of outbuildings in varying stages of repair. Oh well, Walter thought, at least it looks like it's in good shape. He had imagined a rustic frame house—like Robert Frost might have lived in while composing his earliest poems.

Bunch did not stop there, though. The road wound up another hill before it flattened out through another large pasture, where half a dozen horses, still shaggy in their winter coats, grazed against a backdrop of more pines. After a short straightaway, the road curved away from the pasture. Then there were more trees, pines and oaks mixed together, a final steep hill, and Bunch rolled to a step in front of something that, at first glance, actually resembled Walter's Robert Frost fantasy.

Trees surrounded the house, which despite its ample, wrap-around screen porch, two stories, and acutely-pitched roof, had a smallish, almost miniature appearance—more like a house in a fairy tale than the setting for *Mending Wall,* Walter thought. As Walter drew closer, however, the fairy tale image dissipated. His new home was like any number of old farmhouses anywhere; the white paint had peeled badly, and the roof, even to Walter's untrained eye, needed work.

"There you have it," Bunch said from the front porch. He opened the door as Walter climbed the creaking front steps.

It was dark inside—even after Bunch turned on the lights in the living room and the central hallway which led from the front porch back to the kitchen. Silently, Walter followed Bunch from room to room. The darkness was due to the surrounding trees and the colors of the rooms, mostly somber shades of blue and brown. What also struck Walter was the lack of furniture and decoration. The living room held only a couch and an old cabinet model television set whose screen was furry with dust. Two other downstairs rooms were not furnished at all, while the kitchen was no better than functional. It smelled of bacon grease, and the appliances were at least twenty years old. So this is where Edgar came to rest, Walter thought.

"Was any of the furniture removed after he died?" Walter asked.

Bunch, who had taken a seat at the sticky-surfaced kitchen table, blinked at the question.

"Not that I know of. I was out here a few times in the last year or so. Your father didn't like to come into Helmsville, and he actually said we were to do business here. Like when doctors used to make house calls. There's probably more stuff upstairs. I had the impression that he spent most of his time up there. Why do you ask? Furnishings not suit you?"

"They're perfect."

"Is that right? You and your daddy have similar tastes, huh?"

"I'm serious."

Bunch opened his briefcase and laid out some papers. Without asking permission, he lit another cigarette. Walter did not mind. Bunch was his tour guide and, at that moment, he could forgive him his vices. He's taken me to my home, he thought. Here I am. He went over to a window, which, despite the trees, provided a clear view of the driveway. He could see and hear whatever might approach the house from that direction. He hoped that no one would approach it at all.

"We've got one more little transaction," Bunch said. Walter sat down.

"You're pretty satisfied?" Bunch asked, flipping ashes into a thick, enamel mug.

"I suppose I am."

"Your father would be satisfied, too, I suppose. Say, I jacked up the thermostat—it's down the hall. It should get warm in here pretty soon. The nights'll be cold up through the end of April."

"I'll be fine."

"This place might not look so great, but Mr. Loomis had central air and heat put in last year. Makes it pretty comfortable. Of course, our winters are nothing like what you're used to."

Walter nodded without quite listening. This may be what I've been searching for without knowing it, he thought. Insulation, protection. Bunch shoved a piece of paper across the table and explained that when Walter signed the deed of trust, he would take full possession of the house and also of his interest in the land. Walter found the appropriate lines and scratched out his signature. Then he remembered something else from Bunch's letter.

"Who owns the other half of the farm?" Bunch, who was sliding the deed of trust back into the briefcase, paused and stared hard at Walter.

"Ricky," he said slowly. "You know? Ricky Loomis."

"Ricky Loomis?"

"Yeah. You've never heard of him? Didn't he call you? I gave him your number as soon as we finished talking the other day. Hell, he was sitting right there in my office. He *said* he would call. See, I thought it was important for the two of you to get acquainted. That's funny. Are you sure he didn't call?"

"I never...I would know if someone called me. Who is...?"

"Ricky Loomis?" Bunch rubbed his forehead, kneading the tight flesh while Walter waited for an answer.

"He's your brother. Or your half-brother."

"I...didn't...realize...that...I had...a...brother." The words sounded as if they were being torn out of Walter's throat.

Bunch seemed nearly as stunned as Walter. "He said that he'd call. Knowing Ricky, I should've..."

"Just a minute. Please. My brother. That's what..." Walter stopped.

"You've never heard of him?" Walter shook his head. "So you didn't know that you had a brother?" Walter continued to shake his head.

"So besides me having to tell you that your father's dead, and how he died, I'm the guy who springs it on you that Ricky's your brother. I *am* sorry. That's the truth. If Ricky had only..."

"Why is he named Ricky?" All that Walter could think of was Ricky Ricardo. Bunch paused, carefully regarding Walter—as if seeing him in a new light.

"Probably," Bunch finally said, "Ricky was the name Mr. Loomis and Beatrice..."

"Beatrice?"

"Ricky's mother. That's probably the name they wanted. Ricky, that is. Seems like a perfectly normal name to me. I had a client once named Tinka. That's what I call an unusual name."

"I've never heard of Beatrice either. Until now."

"That makes sense—if you think about it."

"I didn't know they existed. I hadn't spoken to my father since 1961. Did Ricky know about me?"

"He *said* he did. Said that your father mentioned you from time to time. Mr. Loomis had found out that you're a writer."

"All of this is...quite a shock. Quite a shock."

"I can't see how it could be any other way," Bunch said.

"Any other way?" A half-brother, he thought. And a woman who could pass as my stepmother. Most of a family.

"What's that?" Bunch leaned closer—as if he had not heard Walter correctly.

"Never mind. How can I reach...Ricky and..."

"Beatrice? You can't—at least not right now. They've gone to Atlanta, and they didn't tell me where they were staying. And they mentioned New Orleans for when they got through with Atlanta. A holiday trip to get over the funeral and all that. They waited three weeks—until the will was probated and they got their share. They said they were distraught, completely distraught. By the way, Ricky's liquid inheritance is smaller than yours."

They've gone, Walter thought. Perhaps I won't even have to meet them. If they would only keep going. But that won't be the case.

"They all lived together? Edgar too?"

"In a manner of speaking. Do you remember the house we passed after turning off the paved road?"

"The ducks and chickens?"

Bunch smiled. "That's the one. Very tasteful. Anyhow, your father lived here, and Ricky and Beatrice, and Ricky's girlfriend Star lived with the deer and chickens. And the Mexicans too. Don't forget the Mexicans. Beatrice has been buying that stuff for years. As for your father's...living arrangements, I don't have any explanations. He fell out with Beatrice years ago and built the house for her and Ricky. I believe Ricky was about twelve when that happened."

"How old is he now?"

"I don't know. Twenty-eight? Twenty-nine? You don't resemble him much. He looks a lot like Mr. Loomis. I sure wish he had called you before he ran off to Atlanta."

"Perhaps he was shy about it. Uncomfortable."

"Ricky? Wait until you meet him. And you should see Star. She takes up a lot of his time. And right this minute, she's probably taking up his money. You'll meet her too. She never strays far from Ricky. Neither does Beatrice."

"I never expected any of this."

"Yeah. I understand." Bunch lit another cigarette. "So, I'll file the deed first thing tomorrow and the family homestead will be bound to you. And you'll be bound to it."

"Tell me. What have you gotten out of all of this?" Bunch laughed, and the laugh turned into a hack, which soon subsided.

"What lawyers always aim to get—a nice, fat fee. Your father paid me well in advance—and at about four times the rate I normally get for this kind of work. I mostly do criminal and personal injury, but wills and trusts are nice and steady. Since he paid me up front, he insured that all of my legal expertise would be brought to bear on his problems." Bunch laughed again and cleared his throat.

"Money is a great focusing agent," Walter said. He had decided that Roy Bunch was in almost as great a need of Edgar's bounty as he had been.

"It didn't take you much time to get to Helmsville once you got my letter."

"That's true," Walter smiled. Be careful, he thought. Don't underestimate Roy Bunch, Attorney-at-law. Bunch's briefcase clicked closed.

"Time to get going. I took the liberty of bringing a load of groceries out here yesterday. That way, you won't have to drive back to town. Just basic breakfast stuff—milk, bread, bacon, coffee."

"Thanks. What do I owe you?"

"Nothing. Someday you can buy me thirty dollars worth of food."

"I would like to talk to you again. When we have time."

"I got an office in the Commercial Building, in the heart of greater downtown Helmsville." Bunch opened his wallet and handed Walter a card.

"Take care, professor."

"I'm no longer in that line of work."

"Quit, huh? And in the middle of a semester. And a writer, too. I've never dealt with a writer before except for a couple of expert witnesses. They didn't write fiction—or at least they didn't think that they wrote fiction."

"I'm not sure I'll stay in the fiction business."

"Take care anyway. A famous writer, right here in Helmsville. At least almost in Helmsville."

"Not many people read my books—or buy them either."

"A shame. Maybe you'll be famous when you're dead."

Walter could not tell if Bunch was putting him on. Bunch's large, worn out face was without expression.

"A prophet is without honor in his own country."

"That's the truth."

From the front porch, Walter watched the tail lights of Bunch's Ford fade down the road. Darkness had arrived in a rush, and except for the dull glow from the windows behind him, the rural night was an utter totality. He hurried inside and locked the door behind him.

4

There were no dreams that first night; not of Ricky, or Bunch or Edgar. There was no past or future, only the blessed, benumbed present. When Walter awoke, he had that same feeling as in the Holiday Inn near Louisville—of not quite knowing who, or where, he was. He sat straight up, awash in the benign nothingness, shivering naked in the cold of seven o'clock. He pulled on his shorts, padded down the hall, and turned up the heat. He found the nearest grate, straddling it as the furnace made faint hissing, rushing noises and the heat blew upwards to his thighs and genitals. After awhile, the house had warmed sufficiently, and he shaved, showered, dressed, and made coffee. The kitchen was colder than the rest of the house and the bacon smell that had greeted him the day before was a permanent element of the atmosphere. As he finished a second cup of coffee and spread an English muffin with strawberry preserves, he decided that he would have to open all the windows in the house for a good airing. If there're going to be smells around here, at least they'll be my own, he thought.

He finished a third cup of coffee and another muffin before he got around to inspecting the upstairs. He pushed open the first door that he came to and found himself gaping into a blue-black hole. There was some kind of covering over the lone window, and he stumbled heavily against hard, unyielding shapes until he found the light switch.

The room was cluttered with wobbling totems of papers,

40

books, notebooks, and files. In a couple of corners the materials were stacked evenly, waist-high, and in his search for the light switch, he had toppled one of the largest piles, which had cascaded and spread against the bases of the others. He edged his way toward an impressive, ornately carved desk, the surface of which was covered by small, neat stacks of computer printouts. The computer, along with a printer, stood on a simple, functional table, along with a mug bearing the name of the Helmsville High Stallions. Walter picked up the mug. Old coffee sloshed around the bottom and dark green mould crept up to the brim. Walter carefully put the mug on the window sill, and parted the draperies. After the darkness, the morning light was vivid and strong, and the view was more spectacular and revealing than that available on the ground floor. Fields and woods, the backside of Edgar's domain, stretched away below him. The sky was cloudless and through a far stand of willows, Walter could make out the glint and sparkle of the sun on moving water. That would be the Reedy River, he guessed. His mother had said that the Reedy was a public bath for lintheads and coloreds. It struck Walter as lovely.

He sat down in the blue swivel chair behind his father's old desk. The chair was comfortable, but Walter was less aware of comfort than of the realization that Edgar had been in the seat that he now occupied. And not that long ago, Walter thought. He probably drank from that mug as he...did what? The papers and books, profusion and disorder. Might be part of a code. But to what? Would it be worth it to go through all of this? What would he discover? He could seal the room off and proclaim it the Edgar Loomis Memorial Study.

It occurred to him that most of the papers were probably concerned with money. He had no idea how Edgar had made his money—only that he had made an extraordinary amount of it. That fit with what Walter had known of him.

Truly a devotee of the bottom line, Walter thought. He
picked up the computer sheets that lay closest at hand, leaning back in the chair as he did so. He was glad to see that
the sheets had been detached along the perforated edges. He
disliked the confused, snake-like way that they uncoiled
from the printer. His students used to hand him such sheets
and expect him to put them in some sort of order. And he
disliked computers too. He wrote long hand and typed out
final drafts on his old Royal electric.

The sheets contained financial records, totaling up profits and evaluating farm expenses for 1991. He quickly ran
through the pages, not really knowing what he was supposed to look for. In the past, Walter had never had any reason to be informed about money, profits, and the various
bottom lines. Despite his ignorance, he understood that
1991 had been a good year, with a large income and moderate expenses on "upkeep and improvements." That
explains part of my financial miracle, he smiled. Financial
miracle was the term used by television evangelists. They
had entertained him at night after he had finished grading
papers or writing and while he was waiting for sleep.

He leafed through two more sets of sheets—more testi-
monials to Edgar's sound management skills. The room
bulges. And it has to do with money. Edgar liked money.
And I'm fortunate he did.

There were also the books. Walter rummaged around in
those closest to his chair. There was *Six Crises* by Richard
Nixon, and *Heart of Darkness,* and *The Information Please
Almanac* for 1973. And there was his own name as well—
his first collection of stories, *Scenes From an Interstate
Laundromat.* The volume had a slim, insubstantial feel to it,
and his younger face, staring glumly back from the dust
jacket might have belonged to an absolute stranger. He
could barely recall the stories, except that most were brief
and snapshot-like, that being the most fashionable style of

the times. The very last occasion upon which I was fashionable, he thought. One reviewer had written "Mr. Loomis' stories have two qualities. First, they are brief. Second, they are not brief enough." The review had appeared in a magazine nearly as obscure as the one in which he had pilloried Milton Collie's novel. The other reviews, all six of them, had been favorable—at least noting that *Scenes from an Interstate Laundromat* showed "promise." Whatever the hell that means, Walter had thought at the time.

Edgar's copy showed signs of having been read, which made Walter uneasy. For virtually all of his life, Edgar had shown no interest in him; as far as Walter knew, his father had never thought about him until he made a will. Edgar had never telephoned or written, never asked how Walter was doing at school or in his jobs. He had never asked if Walter was happy or psychotic or both. A genius or a ranting imbecile or a stolid, good citizen. He had never given any evidence that it mattered to him whether Walter was dead or alive.

And he got to judge me through my books, Walter thought. Judging me secretly, covering himself so that he could not be judged in return.

Walter opened the front cover and leafed through the pages. There were notes on almost every story, all recorded in a tight, beautifully controlled handwriting. "This is sound enough—almost," read a line on the last page of the longest, most ambitious story. Walter closed the book.

Edgar could have arranged the entire tableau, he thought. The lost son in the father's study, discovering the father's critical judgement, the father's words commingling with and commenting, upon what the son had produced. And the son would experience an epiphany that would reveal how the father had watched over him all along. The judgement *and* the money would make the scene complete. Practically a work of art—or something like that.

Walter tossed the book to the floor. That's one scene I won't go through with, he thought. He flushed, slightly wobbly and off-center. I'll put it away, he thought. I'll shut his words away without reading. He closed the study door, slightly puzzled with and ashamed of his feelings. He had never fully blamed Edgar for their common past—had never cared enough to do so. And he laughed at the current trendy therapy by which adults blamed their parents for not making their childhoods models of grace and perfection. And Edgar had, at most, been an image—coupled now with notes on a page. Which is even less of a reason for feeling like this, he thought, almost ashamed by this impotent gesture. He nearly went back into the study, but changed his mind without quite knowing why.

He concentrated on inspecting the second floor, figuring that he needed to know as much as possible about where he was to live. There was a second bathroom that, unlike the one on the first floor, was in poor shape. The sink and shower were marked by long, rusty water stains and the floor had a mushy feel to it—as if the wood beneath the bleached-out tiles was soaked and rotten. And the room had a damp, fungus-thick odor as well, like a decayed hotel room in a tropical country. He came to Edgar's bedroom. A dozen or so suits, some dating back to the 1940s, were neatly arranged in a walk-in closet, along with shoes and ties from earlier eras. Stuck in the back was a cardboard box full of khaki trousers. Underwear and socks were carefully packed in a chest of drawers and the single bed was made to military perfection. Like the rest of the house, Edgar's bedroom was without decorations of any sort. Walter made a fast tour and got out as quickly as possible. He felt like an intruder, and knew that the feeling would not pass until the closet was cleaned out.

There was one last room, and Walter had to force the door with his shoulder. A small hawk, compact, lethal, and dead, was wedged atop the lower half of a dirty window. Its wings were crumpled as if it had beaten itself to death in an effort to escape. Even from the doorway, Walter could see that the hawk, dusty and mummified, had been there for a very long time. What was left of a smaller bird lay on the bare, hardwood floor, its beak opened in a perfectly preserved cry. A breeze, slow and gentle, beat through a broken window pane: the point of entry for the hawk and its thrashing, cawing prey. The room had been shut up for a good while, perhaps even years. Walter pictured the hawk, having eaten its fill, circling the constricted space, bumping against things that were beyond its power to name, incapable of knowing where the escape route lay. Circling and calling until all of its strength and all of its life was gone.

Walter stepped over to the window. The hawk's eyes were wide, as if searching for subsistence among the vagrant flocks of starlings and robins. Walter touched the feathers, which were as dry and brittle as last spring's flowers, shuddered and jerked his hand away. He felt the breeze and listened to the groaning of the house. As he backed away, one foot came down on the stick-like remains of the smaller bird, which splintered and shattered. The sensation, and the light, clicking sound of the delicate breaking bones, unnerved him. He soon found himself at the bottom of the stairs, sucking in air in great, dry gulps.

He told himself that he had been silly. After all, he thought, the study and the birds and the rest of the mess upstairs only needed to be eradicated. And they could wait. He set to work, relieved at not thinking. In less than an hour he unloaded the trailer, the biggest part of the job being the stacking of book cartons in one of the empty first floor bedrooms. As soon as he had arranged the rest of his belongings, he made a list of all he had to do. The list took a while to compose and covered two pages. Doing all of what he had written down would, he knew, take weeks. The cleaning of the study and the removal of the birds were not included. The making of the list calmed and satisfied him, and so did the sweat that he had worked up while unpacking. He had never had many reasons for using his body. When he was teaching he had been physically inert most of the time— a state brought on by his profession and what he had come to think of as ordinary dread—perhaps even daily terror. He was always waiting: the end of the semester, tenure decisions, the arrival of the galleys for his next obscure, unprofitable book. In that life you could wait forever. He folded the list and stuck it in his shirt pocket. "The best piece of writing I've done in years," he said.

Without Bunch as his guide, the drive to Helmsville was confused and lengthy. The roads all looked the same, and he kept doubling back and forth, the empty trailer rattling and weaving along behind him. Once he crossed over into South Carolina, and he stopped for directions three times at country stores. The clerks, identical in their jovial, pussle-gutted malice, provided directions that he later understood as elaborate practical jokes. Eventually, at a crossroads not far from where he started, he found a state trooper. The trooper, who never moved from behind the wheel of his cruiser, drew a map which turned out to be very accurate. He had the carefully cultivated aura of a marine drill instructor, complete with the fascist-style haircut and mirrored sunglasses. The trooper spoke in a compressed, tight-lipped way—as if the use of words induced pain. Walter thanked him for the map and the trooper nodded curtly before returning to the contemplation of the traffic-less crossroads. The storekeepers and the cops around here are out of a bad movie, Walter thought.

Thirty minutes or so after the trooper handed him the map, Walter dropped the trailer off with a U-Haul dealer in Helmsville. Then he went to a copying service and had half a dozen of the maps run off. They would be useful in connection with his other chores, and he would keep a couple of copies in the car until he was more familiar with the territory. I should drive the backroads until I know my way around, he thought. In the past, he had seldom shown much interest in where he lived. In Texas, after he had taken his first teaching post, he had rarely visited the center of the small city where the college was located. There was, he was sure, nothing there that could possibly interest him.

Without too much trouble, he found Carolina Home Improvement World, which he had spotted the day before when he was going to meet Bunch. It was one of those large, hangar-like places that sells paint, lumber, light fixtures, lawn mowers and everything else needed to stoke the home owner's mania for rebuilding, remodeling, adding on, and making new. Never before did Walter have a reason to visit such an establishment, but he soon caught the spirit. Happily, he pushed his shopping cart up and down the aisles: tool sets, interior latex paint, rollers, brushes, plastic sheeting—all went into the buggy. He was not actually sure about how to paint, although he had watched once as his ex-wife expertly redid the kitchen and bathroom of their apartment in Austin. She had been emphatic about his not helping her in any way.

As the buggy's load increased, and it became harder to push, he experienced a childish pleasure: he was buying things. He was sure that he would put all of it to good use. There was not enough room in the Volkswagen for all of his purchases, so he put in a delivery order: six book shelf kits, a chain saw (he had no idea how to use it, but it was one of those things needed around a farm), a swing for the front porch, and a Black and Decker power drill. The clerk who rang up his purchases whistled at the total, which came to more than seven hundred dollars. Walter smiled as he wrote out the largest check of his life.

His next stop was Furniture Heaven. The name pleased him, as did the enormous sign, which was complete with stars and a benevolently grinning quarter moon. Inside, Furniture Heaven was like Carolina Home Improvement World: huge, cavernous. The concrete floor went on for what seemed like acres, and was spread with the sort of comfortable, tasteless furniture that Walter had often given to the characters in his stories of tasteless suburbia. Life doing more than imitating art, he thought as he surveyed the love seats, floral print living room suites, Spanish Colonial coffee tables, French Provincial dining tables, recliner chairs and imitation mahogany bedroom suites (pronounced suits by the priest-like owner who eagerly waited upon Walter).

Walter was the only customer, which in part accounted for the owner's enthusiasm. And Walter had an even better time than when he was buying paint and chain saws. He was entranced by the startling, innocent ugliness of the merchandise of Furniture Heaven, although there were problems in making selections. It was not that Walter cared particularly for good furniture—his mother's obsession with it had seen to that. But he did understand the truly tasteless, having studied the subject for much of his life. Appreciating the ugly allows you to fully understand where, and how, you live; an axiom that he took pride in.

After a careful search, he found a fairly plain and subdued bedroom suite, a sober, dark blue couch, and a solid easy chair. In the appliance department, he bought a twenty-five inch television set, a self-cleaning range and oven, and the single remaining white refrigerator in Furniture Heaven, if not in all of Helmsville. The owner tried to interest him in half a dozen other pieces, but Walter turned him down with a smile. How would Margaret and Simmons react to my selections, he thought with glee. They who spent a good portion of their adult lives treating arrangements of wood, cloth, and leather as icons of breeding and class.

He wrote an even larger check than that which he had presented to the Carolina Home Improvement Center—over four thousand dollars. The owner introduced himself as Carl F. Smyre.

"Come back whenever you need me, Mr. Loomis," he said, his voice shaking in what Walter was alarmed to identify as genuine emotion. It *is* love, Walter thought, shaking hands with Mr. Smyre. A kind of love I never knew existed.

Mr. Carl F. Smyre pulled himself together as Walter handed him a copy of the trooper's map. Walter told him that without the map, he could not find his way home, and Mr. Smyre shyly inquired if Walter was new to Helmsville.

"I arrived yesterday. Actually, as you can see from the map, I don't quite live in Helmsville. I inherited a farm from my father."

"Oh...I'm sorry. Not about the inheritance. Your father."

"You might've known him. Edgar Loomis?" Walter had, without intending so, inserted a grand, English aristocratic clip into his speech.

"No, Don't think so. Wait a minute. Was he kin to *Ricky* Loomis?" The name brought Walter up short, and Mr. Smyre's tone had changed. It was no longer full of love.

"Ricky. Yes. My half-brother."

"He is, huh? You don't resemble him—in the least." Mr. Smyre cast a furtive peek at the check, which he still held in his hand—as if he was not at all positive that it would go through the bank.

"That's what I've been told. We have different mothers," Walter said evenly, more haughty, more aristocratic than ever. "And what is *your* relationship with Ricky?"

Mr. Smyre stuck the check into the cash register. He looked down at his shoes, then up at Walter.

"Let me put it this way. He owes money. He still owes me money on a bedroom suit he got for his momma..."

"Beatrice."

"I never met her. Ricky said it was for his momma. So he just stopped paying about six months ago. I took him into small claims court, and he still won't pay. Won't even discuss it with me. Hangs up when I call, or has his momma say that he's not there. Twice, I heard him tell her this in the background. Like I'm not there or something." Mr. Smyre's litany had taken on a sad, whining edge that gave Walter an idea.

"How much do you have coming to you from my brother? I mean my half-brother."

"What for?" Mr. Smyre turned suddenly and inexplicably wary. Before Walter could reply, Mr. Smyre went back to his office. When he returned, he handed Walter an official-looking document that bore the seal of the Darden County small claims court. "That much," Mr. Smyre said.

The amount was only a bit above two hundred dollars, which to Walter did not merit Ricky's refusal to pay. He could've paid that before Edgar died, he thought. He opened his wallet and offered Mr. Smyre some of the money he had taken away from Wetumka: money from the old life. Mr. Smyre was beaming once more as he took the bills.

"Say, Mr. Loomis," he said as he handed Walter the change, "that's a mighty classy gesture. It sure is."

"Family debts." Hell, Walter thought. I'm coming across like a true lord of the manor.

"Yeah? Ricky oughta be grateful that he's got kin like you. I tell you."

Walter gave a dignified nod and Mr. Smyre extended his hand once more. Walter felt as if he had spent the entire day shaking hands with Mr. Smyre. Mr. Smyre escorted him out to the Volkswagen. For a tricky moment, Walter thought that Mr. Smyre might even get into the car with him.

"I want you to know that it's been a real treat doing business with you. Yessir it has."

"A pleasure on this end," Walter said. Mr. Smyre leaned in the window.

"And I want you to consider Furniture Heaven for *all* of your home needs." Mr. Smyre's voice once again throbbed with love, but it had also taken on the rhythms of a commercial pitchman. Walter assured him that he would come first to Furniture Heaven, and Mr. Smyre promised delivery no later than three that afternoon. His two helpers were not doing much that day so he would see to it that Walter received "fast, dependable service." Walter gunned the engine and Mr. Smyre, all love and salesmanship, was forced to back abruptly from the window. Walter could think of no other way to get back on the road. Mr. Smyre waved wildly as Walter turned into the traffic. Damn, Walter thought. That was fun.

The supermarket was Walter's next and final stop on his first expedition to Helmsville. He stocked up on anything that struck his fancy, growing more excited as he dumped steaks and anchovies and Bibb lettuce into yet another shopping buggy. He felt born to push buggys, but he no longer played at being a landed English aristocrat. Now he was a content, self-actualized American consumer. In addition to the security promised by a full larder, he had time to appreciate the astuteness in paying Ricky's debt. While Ricky remained a pulsating blank, Walter could, nonetheless, picture the potential responses. There might even be gratitude, he thought. Or Ricky could offer to pay me back, which I will generously refuse. Or he may become sullen, thinking I have shamed him. Walter concluded these fantasies in the checkout line, as two clerks heaped the bags high with more things that belonged only to him. Ricky, money, whatever, he thought. Family and leisure can certainly take up a man's time. He laughed and nearly did his little dance, startling the teenaged cashier and the two middle-aged bag boys.

About the time Walter finished unloading the groceries and the rest of his purchases, the delivery men from Carolina Home Improvement World arrived. After they left, Walter ate a sandwich and drank a beer, and contemplated what he should do next. As he went over the list, he saw that he had omitted a number of important tasks, such as disposing of the old downstairs furniture.

He stripped the two musty, slightly-damp mattresses, dragged them to the edge of the porch and tipped them into the yard. The mattresses were easy compared to the box springs, which took a good fifteen minutes of hard effort before he could get them through the front door and push them onto the mattresses. He flung the rickety bedside tables from the porch and left behind a chest, which looked too heavy to move. He came across an old but serviceable Electrolux in a hall closet and vacuumed the bedroom. He hummed as he worked, settling into a pleasant thought-free state. The leaning forward, the motion of his arms and back, did not begin to hurt until he had vacuumed most of the downstairs and realized that he had cleaned space that he would probably not even use; space that was not particularly dirty. He ceased whistling, and, breathing heavily, went to the kitchen for another beer. His shirt was wet through with sweat, and the chill of the morning had been replaced by midday heat. He remembered the windows then. Shuffling tiredly, he went around the first floor, jerking open the few windows that were not painted or jammed up. The breeze was gone and the still, warm air brought only small relief.

He had a hard time dragging the furniture from the living room, but he finished the task before Mr. Smyre's truck arrived. He was standing on the front porch, surveying the jumble of furniture below him—which looked like a set for a surrealistic film—when the truck crunched up the final few yards of the driveway. Two men, indistinguishable from those who worked for the Carolina Home Improvement

World, asked him where he wanted his stuff put.

They worked with efficient speed, accomplishing in minutes what would have taken hours for Walter. The only difficulty they had was with the old refrigerator, which Walter had, without thinking, filled with food. They took the old range out, then silently waited as an apologetic Walter heaped the kitchen counters and table with groceries. After they carried the old refrigerator away with the hand truck and dumped it with the oven in the weeds out back, one of them, a muscular black man somewhere between twenty-five and fifty years old, told Walter that he ought to take the door off the refrigerator because a child or drunk might crawl inside and suffocate. Walter, feeling foolish and inept because of the business with the food, asked if such persons might be found in the neighborhood. The man shrugged and handed him an invoice.

When Mr. Smyre's truck left, the silence settled back in. Observing the delivery men made Walter aware of his inability to manipulate the concrete objects of the world. He thought about this as he sat on the porch. It had always been that way. He did not know how to use his new chain saw or drill. He could not go ahead with painting the house because he did not know how to get the lids from the cans. The mound of furniture and the appliances had created a mess that he could not eliminate. Earlier, when he was full of energy and purpose, when he had turned from the study, he had not anticipated any of this. Now, the sight of his labors induced a stagnant lethargy. He was rooted to the porch, contemplating the ugly, dilapidated couch, the old television set, the scarred tables and spring-ruptured chairs. All of it. And it was depressing. So much for the grand strategy, he thought.

It was at that point that he remembered the food and bolted, as well as he could with aching legs and swollen joints, to the kitchen. The frozen vegetables and Stouffer entrees had already started to melt, the water trickling down from the counters and pooling upon the floor below. In a slow panic, Walter shoved all of it into the refrigerator. When he was nearly finished, he realized that the refrigerator was still warm inside. Mr. Smyre's efficient, military-style delivery men had not bothered to plug it in. After much wrestling and grunting he worked the refrigerator out from the wall. He gave it a great, final pull, and nearly turned it over before throwing himself between it and the floor. He moaned under the weight, steadying himself as he pushed it back into position. Then he had to work the refrigerator back away from the wall again in order to get the plug in. He did not even experience relief when he heard the steady hum of the condenser.

The battle with his new refrigerator sapped him further: then he could not recall if his new, self-cleaning range was plugged in. Grimly, he tugged it from the slot in the counter far enough to see that the prong was where it was supposed to be. After he slid it back, he experienced another domestic revelation: he could have turned a burner on and saved himself from pointless, half-maddened labor. I hate the damn thing, he thought. God knows I hate it.

He resumed his seat on the porch steps, not wanting to go inside for awhile. But the old furniture sat there—waiting. I could burn it, he thought. There might be a law against burning. Could there be a specific law against burning furniture? I would have to pull all of it away from the house, and I can't face that. Can I burn a refrigerator? An oven? The grease might make a really strong fire.

As Walter considered all the possibilities, he took no notice of the figure that emerged from the woods. He was squat, husky, squeezed into tight jeans and sporting a cowboy hat, boots, western-style shirt, and work gloves. His face, however was smooth and child-like—nothing like the weather-beaten cowboy of movies and commercials.

"Howdy," he said in a high, piping voice. Walter, deep in contemplation, leaped to his feet at the greeting. He could not tell from which direction the voice came, and he scanned the trees and yard until he saw the cowboy, who had advanced closer to the porch.

"Who...?" Walter began. The cowboy grinned, his teeth small and yellow.

"Didn't mean to scare you. Just checking up. I'm Obie Waldrop."

Apparently the name was supposed to have some significance to Walter, despite his never having heard it before.

"Opie?"

"Naw. *Obie.* Lotsa folks make that mistake. Opie, he's the kid on *Andy of Mayberry.*"

Obie seemed an apparition, and as such he made Walter suspicious. His sense of suspicion grew as Obie grinned at him.

"I've never heard of you. I don't mean to be rude."

"You ain't. Rude that is. Somebody forgot to tell you. Ricky can be like that. Course, he's got a lot on his mind. Thinking and going like he does."

Obie Waldrop continued to smile. Walter had the feeling that he might smile all day. No matter what he was doing.

"So you know Ricky."

"Sure do. And Mr. Edgar, too. Going back twenty, twenty-five years. Ricky was a kid when I came here."

"From Texas?" Obie laughed and slapped his thigh. Whooping it up at a hoedown, Walter thought.

"Naw. Not Texas. Helmsville born and bred. I run the stable back down the road. Live there too."

"I'm Walter Loomis."

"I figured. Ricky mentioned you."

"What did he say?" Walter meant to sound casual, but failed badly. Obie cocked his head to one side, like a small bird observing something interesting in the tall grass.

"What did he say, huh? Just your name. That you're his brother. Shoot, I can't even recollect *how* long ago he told me."

"Half-brother. Did he know that I was moving down here?"

"Moving? Like moving in? Naw. Least I don't think so. I ain't seen him since him and Star and Miss Beatrice took off on that trip. All Ricky'd talk about was that trip. After Mr. Edgar got buried that is. You hearda Star and Miss Beatrice?"

"Do you want to come in? Have something to drink?"

"That'd be real nice."

As Obie ambled up the steps, Walter checked for spurs on his boots. None were there.

Walter had to have another beer, while Obie drank milk. Obie kept his hat on and smacked like a small boy at the milk's goodness. He had a white moustache on his upper lip.

"So you worked for my father." Walter was not quite sure why he had invited Obie in. He was tired of worrying over the old furniture, as well as all the things he had bought that day. Obie's presence gave him a break.

"Sure did." Obie swallowed another slurp of milk and the mustache grew thicker. Walter waited for him to say more, but Obie was content to slurp away.

"What sort of work did you do?"

"Same as I do now. Tend the stable. Take care of whatever else needs taking care of. Look after horses. People board them with me. Stable's been full all winter."

So that's why you dress that way, Walter thought.

"Does that bring in any money?"

Obie narrowed his eyes. "Enough."

"You know that I'm part owner of this farm now?"

"Naw. Is that a fact? I'm working for you." Walter detected the slightest note of insolence in Obie's tone, but let it pass.

"It is...a fact. That you work for me. And Ricky too, of course."

"I about raised Ricky, even if I am only nine years older than he is. You could say that we're sorta like brothers and father and son mixed, if you follow me."

Walter did not, but he nodded and asked Obie if he wanted more milk. He put the jug on the table and let Obie help himself. Obie filled the glass right to the top.

"So I work for you too, huh? Got something for me to do? Anything special?"

Walter brightened at the question.

"There's that furniture in the yard. I'd appreciate it if you could help me get rid of it."

"Throwing out all of Mr. Edgar's belongings?"

"Not all. Only those that I don't need." Walter felt that he was engaged in conversation with an extra in a grade-B western. From what he could remember of Texas, the accent was right—flatter and meaner than what could be heard in the Carolinas. He was conscious then of his own, hard-to-pin-down inflections. Deracinated? Yes, he thought.

"Right." Obie finished his second glass of milk and softly burped. "I got to get my flatbed from that first pasture off the road. And I could take that couch off your hands and put it in the stable. People'll have something to sit on while I saddle up their horses. Rest of it, we can carry out to the landfill."

"There's an oven and refrigerator too."

"Yeah? I can use that refrigerator myself."

"Thanks. For the help."

"Don't mention it...Mr. Walter."

"Walter will be fine. Just Walter."

Obie smiled. He looks like the oldest kid in the world—all dressed up in his cowboy suit, Walter thought.

Like Mr. Smyre's delivery men, Obie had a hand truck.

His flatbed had a homemade but effective loading ramp, so Mr. Edgar's old things, as Obie continued to call the furniture, were soon loaded and ready to go. Obie lived in a three-room apartment that was joined to one side of the stable. The stalls were full and the horses, big and uncontrollable-looking, stamped and neighed as Obie called their names and made soothing tongue-clicking noises in their direction. The horses made Walter nervous. He had never had the slightest desire to be near horses, much less to ride one. The closest I want to get to livestock is a cheeseburger, he thought.

Obie's apartment was not quite what Walter expected. Instead of the rough-and-ready bunkhouse decor which would have suited Obie's get-up, there were diaphanous white curtains, lavender walls, Danish modern furniture, and a reproduction of a Mark Rothko print. As they switched the refrigerators and situated the couch in the stable, Obie worked and moved with a scurrying, small animal-like energy that impressed Walter—mostly because of his own fatigue.

He felt better once they were on the road to the landfill. Obie found a radio station and his choice of music was more surprising than the style of his living quarters: the local public station with *Scenes from a Childhood.*

"Schumann?" Walter said. *Scenes From a Childhood* was familiar from repetition.

"Is that who did that one? I never pay attention to the names. If it's pretty, I'll listen to it."

"I see."

"Mr. Edgar, me and him worked together a lot, and he were in this truck a lot too. He kept the radio on this kinda music. He said it was civilized. I just thought that it sounded nice."

They turned onto the main road, Obie expertly shifting gears and nodding to Schumann.

"Your Daddy was something," Obie said after a couple of miles of empty, sun-dappled country.

"So I've heard."

"Heard?" Obie narrowed his tiny eyes and lit a cigarette.

"My parents divorced when I was very young."

"Yeah. I didn't even know that Mr. Edgar had another boy besides Ricky until three, four years ago." That fits, Walter thought. And I didn't dwell too much on Edgar either.

"Did he say much about me? I was eleven the last time I saw him."

Obie blew a cloud of smoke out the window. They passed a sign that ordered motorists to seek Jesus. Obie appeared to be thinking.

"Not much. No sir. Me and him were together all day sometimes. He talked. Loved to talk. At least to me. But your name came up right out the blue one day. You could say it was a shock. He said that you're a writer and a teacher."

"That's what I did."

"Give it up?" Walter did not answer. He did not want to engage in a discourse on his past.

"What did he say about himself?"

Obie laughed and tossed the cigarette butt out the window.

"The most amazing shit. And I don't doubt that lots of it was true. Like how he was friends with Nixon and Reagan. About being in Cuba. He'd raise hell about politics, too. I never paid much attention to that part. Politics don't interest me none."

"He had strong political views."

Obie laughed again.

"You can sure say that he was for taking some people and shipping them to Alaska. Weirdos and pinks he called them—Jake-Leggers. He loved the army, navy, marines, and air force too. Sometimes generals came down here to see him. He'd have me cook pigs and had real big parties. Hardly anybody'd be from Helmsville. The best ones, the biggest anyhow, was on the Fourth of July. Foreigners would come down, too. I couldn't tell exactly where they was from, but I believe that most of them spoke Spanish. Some of them Spanish-type guys would stay two or three weeks."

"My father had a number of...international connections," Walter said slowly. And what might have gone on with Reagan, Nixon, the generals, and...Spanish-type guys, he thought.

"There were women too. Mostly after he split up with Beatrice. Do you mind if I tell you about that part?" Obie was clearly warming to the subject of Mr. Edgar. Walter glanced out the window. The country was uniform and unfamiliar. He had the feeling that he was moving in a far-off and unknown direction.

"Hey," Obie said. "Do you want to hear that part? If you don't, I won't say another word."

"Ah...no. Go ahead." Why not, Walter thought. What harm could it do?

"They used to come out regular. Not so much in the last few years, but different ones every few months back then. Good-looking women too. One of them fixed my apartment the way it is now. I never bothered to change it. Too much trouble. She was from up north. Mr. Edgar wouldn't let her fool with his house. Said it was to stay traditional. He grew up there, you know. So he told her to decorate my place. Mostly to get her off his back."

"My father must've been a man of some...vitality."

This time Obie's laughter irritated Walter. Every other utterance of mine is a goddamn joke, he thought.

"Vitality," Obie barked. "Sure. That's the right word." The last notes of *Scenes From a Childhood* faded, and Obie pointed the truck down another dirt road.

"Landfill. You got the dumping fee?"

Walter paid the man at the gate and they were waved through. A few minutes later, Obie backed to the top of a dirt mound. There he and Walter shoved Mr. Edgar's goods into the pit below. The dumping, unlike the loading and shifting, agreed with Walter, and he liked watching the oven bounce down the muddy walls of the pit. Back on the road, Obie lit another cigarette as the radio played *The New World Symphony*.

"That's a good one," Obie said.

"Did my father like it?"

"Oh yeah. He liked all the pretty ones."

Obie dropped Walter off and told him to call if he needed any more help. It was nearly dark before he could rouse himself from his new chair. He took a long shower and prepared a meal of steak, salad, and baked potato on his new range. He ate in front of the television set, watching whatever came on. Later, he opened one of his book case kits and was immediately dismayed. All these parts, he thought, as the screws, shelves, and poles slid out on to the floor. What did I buy all of this for? Why did I spend all that money and waste all that time in pointless going and coming? He did not have any answer. He jammed the parts back in the box and returned to the television, which he watched without seeing or hearing.

Time, the evening, dribbled by. At the foot of the stairs, he took one step upwards, then stopped. He backed away and went straight to bed.

5

He walked. The first hikes were short, only a mile or two from the house. He stuck to the riding trails that criss-crossed the land, occasionally encountering horsemen who nodded pleasantly as they crowded him off the track. Eventually, he grew more ambitious, ranging far from the house, sometimes returning only in the last hour or two of daylight. He took to bringing a sandwich, and a small thermos of water looped to his belt.

The first few days left him sore, worn-out; but as he drove himself along the trails his body resisted less. He sweated freely, the salt running into the corners of his mouth, and his muscles tightened. His breathing was deeper and clearer than he could remember. He was pleased to find that he was actually getting into shape—the best condition since phys ed classes were forced on him in college.

Besides the horsemen, the only other person he ran into was Obie. One afternoon, he found Obie hacking away at a mass of Virginia Creeper that had worked its way across a trail. They greeted each other cheerily and Walter went on his way. That evening, as Walter finished dinner, Obie showed up. He drank two glasses of milk and asked Walter if he needed help with anything. This seemed to be Obie's standard question, and he had probably asked it every day of his life. It gave Walter an idea. He offered Obie five hundred dollars to assemble the bookcases and paint the downstairs rooms. After inspecting the now dusty purchases from

the Carolina Home Improvement World, Obie shyly pointed out that [Mr.] Walter had neglected to purchase sandpa-
per and primer. Walter pretended that this failure came not
from ignorance, but from mere oversight. Obie then said
that a light-weight sander could be had for a hundred bucks,
and that it would make the job go that much faster. "Of
course," Walter said. "A lifetime investment." He wrote out
the check and Obie started work the next evening after he
had disposed of his daily chores.

Obie was as expert as Walter had been incompetent. He
put a smooth finish on the walls, the jackdaw buzz of the
sander blending with the classical music from his radio.
Walter, relieved of his burden, holed up in the kitchen,
drinking beer. Obie, like his journeys about the farm, had
temporarily relieved him of thought, or at least the intellectual obsessiveness that had once plagued him. I'm getting
healthy, he thought. And that is enough. He took to his bed
almost as soon as Obie finished for the night, ignoring the
new television, the books arranged on the shelves, and all
else that was immediately outside of himself.

The land—his land—was marked with a variety that had
not been obvious on his arrival, or from the window of
Edgar's study. There were large sections of free standing timber: some oak, but mostly pine. He liked the oaks best. Some
of them were a hundred feet or better, and had been there
before Edgar or anyone else had claimed them. Walter took
a child-like pleasure in the trees. There was one special place
among them that he had come upon early in his walks; atop
a ridge that gradually fell away against the Reedy River. He
would halt there, lingering, napping now and then, his head
wonderfully empty for hours. The spring was half advanced
into summer, so the weather was not as hot and uncomfortable as Obie said it would be by late May and June. Nor
were the ticks, snakes, and mosquitoes out yet. "Don't

worry," Obie said during a milk break in the kitchen, "it gets real nice again in the fall. Shoot, you can camp out down there and nothing'll bother you." Yes, Walter thought.

The oaks rustled and swayed in the breeze, and Walter was glad for their music. The forest floor was cool and uncluttered. The height of the trees and their interlocking branches blocked most of the sunlight, so there was not much secondary growth. Along the trails, the Virginia Creeper, the blackberry bushes, the laurel and the sumac threatened to swallow all else that grew there. The oak stand, however, was free and clear.

There were many more pines than oaks. Some were old, thinly towering trees, but most had been planted within the last three decades. Obie, who was the unofficial historian of the farm, said that Mr. Edgar replanted after every harvesting of the pines. Weyerhauser came in every two years to cut, taking the pines for newsprint and a few oaks from other, more distant, stands for what Obie called "real high quality toilet tissue."

The pine forest spread out in every direction below the ridge where the oaks stood, marking the contours of the land, broken here and there, with untended thickets. There were cleared fields too, like those Walter had seen when Bunch led him to the house; fenced grazing land and a small herd of white-faced Herefords that Obie took care of, as well as three large meadows where the riders exercised and galloped their mounts. According to Obie, the cultivated fields were rented to Washam and Speight, the big farming outfit from near Winston-Salem. Their crews came in to plant and harvest corn and soybeans. "Between them and Weyerhauser," Obie said, "Mr. Edgar made a smart bit of money."

Walter rested his back against an oak and squirmed around until his rear was comfortable. He had come a good distance, eaten his lunch, and was drowsy. He was proud, too. It was two weeks to the day since he had taken possession of his patrimony, and his gait was loosejointed, ground-devouring, almost countrified. He guessed that he had covered four miles and, after time in the oaks, he could do four more without feeling it at all.

The trees were not silent, but there were none of the human noises that had once filled his life, and the lives of most others. Branches snapped, limbs creaked agreeably in the wind, birds called, and bushes rustled with rabbits and squirrels. There was nothing, however, of that other world which he had thought was *the* world.

Here I am, he thought. Walter in nature. He disliked the fact that when he saw himself it was in the form of some ironic, manufactured image. It's like I've the lead in an uplifting film about Thoreau. Like Obie is a salt-of-the-earth extra in *The Searchers,* or Edgar starring in a made-for-TV version of *Citizen Kane.* Or, if Edgar was young, a cheap spy thriller. But it could be that I'm learning how to see.

The natural world had been a postcard to him—as it is to most people. Years before, not long after they had married, he and Valerie had taken a trip west from Texas. They had done the usual things tourists do, (assumed the expected stupid roles that he had secretly laughed about.) Valerie was in her youthful, transcendental stage then, and she thought that she was really seeing the Grand Canyon or the Painted Desert with fresh, original sight. It had all bored him, to her irritation. We can't see any more, he had argued across the interstate through the Mojave to the Pacific. We can't see nature, or ourselves. The words we have to use, the vision of our senses, has been appropriated. It is sold back to us, and we are convinced that it is our own. Valerie was angry [and rightfully so] at his arrogance. She called it aesthetic nihilism, modernist game-playing. He called it reality; the reality of our own filmed, taped, filed, and forgotten age. "What we think is ours is really owned by all the image corporations" he had blurted in triumph as they hit Needles, the western edge of the desert. "Los Angeles is next. The greatest repository of all of our second-hand dreams." She had told him to please shut up, but he tricked himself into thinking that she had gone at least halfway toward believing him.

And now, he thought with an agreeable sense of distance from what he had been, she is at Penn, promulgating the doctrine that a consumer, media-drenched culture is a conspiracy to marginalize the unempowered. Or words to that effect. And I no longer give a shit. Systematized thought has never been my strong point, and never less so than now, especially among these trees and my final, concrete world.

He was sleepier than when he first sat down, despite the dampness of the earth from a pre-dawn storm. He closed his eyes, turning off memory and light.

Nothing woke him up, but he came to anyway. He blinked rapidly, not sure of what he was seeing. But it was there. Twenty yards away, a fox, like the red fox from his childhood book about Henny Penny, drank rainwater from a stumphole where a small tree had been ripped out. Its muzzle was dripping, its long pink tongue lapping the wet soil. It's like I'm not here, Walter thought as the fox raised its head, its eyes on Walter's. It showed neither fear nor curiosity. It was not looking for anything. Then the wind shifted, carrying Walter's scent, and the fox flashed away.

He did not move. The fox filled the space around him. He had never been that close to a living wild thing. He tottered to his feet, filled with all of it.

He never saw the fox again—at least up close. He had glimpses of a fox from afar, foraging on a tree line, vanishing back into its secret fox life. He knew that there had to be more than one; perhaps there were dozens. Dozens of foxes and other unseen things darting and feeding in unsighted places. That afternoon, following his return to the house, he removed the dead hawk and the scattered bones and feathers of the chewed bird. He patched the broken pane with strips of wood and vacuumed the floor, leaving the door open to air out the tired, musty odor. He did all of this without planning to, rushing breathlessly into the task. When he finished with the hawk's room, he paused by the study door, but could not enter. When Obie arrived to put the final touches on the living room, Walter mentioned neither the fox nor the hawk.

A few days later, he found a road that he had not known of. It looked like the other logging roads that criss-crossed the land. He picked it up beyond the ridge where he met the fox. The road's surface was well maintained, and it appeared to have been freshly graded and graveled. It was not hard to picture the Weyerhauser trucks yanking themselves up the incline, stuffed with skinny resinous pine trunks.

The downhill grade pulled him along, and he calculated that he could reach the river at a point that had been unknown to him. On other days he had worked his way along the banks, where the water, like the earth, was red and brown, clotted with clay and silt. The road went around, then through a large thicket—a mixture of blackberry bushes and scrub pine. The dense foliage held in the afternoon heat, muffling all sound. But he heard something: a faint bubbling beyond the road. A well-marked path wound away through the thicket, and a few yards later he found it.

The stream was clear and unmuddied, fed by a spring. The water percolated noisily up from the earth, forming in a rock pool, before cascading down a natural flume into the stream bed. He undressed quickly, leaving his sweaty clothes in a heap, and slid down easily into the pool.

The bubbles rose around him in regular, rhythmic intervals from some distant point far below him as the chill enclosed him, and grabbed at his breath. He ducked down below the surface and popped back up, gasping. He went under again and again, splashing like a child in a wading pool. Satisfied, he splayed himself across the pool's sensually comforting bottom. The bubbles ballooned around him as he adjusted to the cold. As he relaxed, the chill gradually disappeared. He urinated and watched the yellow and white foam drift, then plunge, into the stream. And on to the river, he thought. Within which I leave my spoor.

The sun climbed higher; it was beginning to be one of those hot days that Obie had told him about. Hungry and naked, he retrieved the sandwich. He ate it in the water, gobbling it down in three or four bites. He wished that he had brought more food. A full course dinner next time, he thought.

He lolled about in the water. Later, he sat beside the spring as the warm air dried him. Finally, he dressed, but his clothes had a coarse, crude feeling to them after the silkiness of the water and air. I may come down here and stay naked, he thought. Conduct a royal, naked progress across my domain.

He laughed, laced his shoes. Although hours of daylight remained, he would go home. The discovery of the spring was an important occasion. A point on the earth without past references, he thought. A reverent moment. And I'm not trying to be ironic, either. He took one last look around. There was no doubt that he would find his way there again. He reached the path and saw that it continued on, away from the road and spring. The bushes and vines had been recently trimmed, and there were at least a dozen spindly scrub pine stumps, the trees themselves tossed back into the underbrush. He was sweating again, considering turning back, when he spied it; bone-white, man-made, at least ten feet tall. Its dimensions, its purpose became more obvious with each step.

A tombstone, a monument—complete with a freshly

painted iron fence. He knew who was there before he saw the name. There was an inevitability to the entire scene; the son splashing and pissing and eating at the site of the father's remains. Walter read the inscription from top to bottom—as the stone so directed.

Edgar Dawes Loomis
November 10, 1920   February 4 , 1992
Diplomat, Agronomist, Patriot, Entrepreneur
Father
Under his hand the land grew fruitful, with bounty for all.
This be the verse you grave for me
Here I lie where I long to be
Home is the sailor, home from the sea
And the hunter home from the hill

The lines from Stevenson were without attribution. He probably wanted the world to think that he wrote them, Walter thought. The locals would probably believe that. Why didn't he add the title of poet to the inscription, the final personal advertisement?

The earth was still fresh and red, with a few shoots of grass sprouting above the grave. Obie tends it, I'll bet. The faithful retainer, Walter thought.

He rested against the fence. Did he do this with me in mind? Probably not. And yet there is the coincidence of the spring. The inheritance itself. It all seems so improbable. Does Edgar reach out from beyond life? Be careful. You'll develop into a conspiracy nut.

He backed away from the monument and began his weary hike. It would be uphill most of the way, and there would be no meetings with foxes, no idylls among the oaks.

He did not cease his walks, but he did not return to the spring either. It would be too much like a pilgrimage. Perhaps Edgar envisioned his grave as a holy place, he

69

thought. If only miracles could be arranged. Perhaps too I should be ashamed of my ungrateful ways. Maybe I'm shameless. As he is—or was.

Walter started a journal, putting down his impressions of the farm and the land, as well as his views of Edgar—both past and present. He wrote at night, and the parts about the land were the best. He had traversed a good portion of it; or at least those parts connected by trails and logging roads. Larger, wilder sections lay as yet unseen. As Obie said, they would have to wait until the fall. As he scratched out his observations, the line from the monument about the fruitfulness of the land seemed true. Edgar had arranged his chunk of the world to suit his desire, his design. And Walter was forced to admire him for it. There was a balance, a symmetry between the untouched and the cultivated.

It must have taken him years to make the farm take on even an approximate version of his image of it, Walter wrote, seated in his easy chair, sipping at a Budweiser and scribbling down the page. And he surrendered that other world that he had starred and preened in—Washington, the CIA, all of that. It had died for him. He came here and started over. I will have to grant him that.

The sessions in the easy chair lengthened from a few minutes to three or four hours. He slept later, and his treks were shorter, in part due to the onrushing heat. In the past, journals never held much appeal for him. When he wrote, he had directed his language outward, into the end result—the stories and the novel. The rest of what he put down was only notes. Then, too, he had a mild disdain for those who thought their lives and their journals were literature. "Look at me," they said. "I'm having an insight." The journal made him consider other possibilities, too. For instance, he became convinced that the old adage about writing providing coherence and meaning amidst the chaos was so much comforting nonsense. The words appear orderly. But as I read over these lines, when I project what I say beyond this notebook, the order vanishes—consumed by all that lies in wait beyond the page, beyond myself.

As he finished, he crossed out these lines. Then he wrote all of it out again without changing a thing.

There came a day when he did not leave the house at all. Nor did he open the journal. Mysterious Edgar, he thought, squatting on the porch until the sunlight got to be too much for him. He napped in the air-conditioned darkness, despite having slept until eleven. When he woke up, the phrase returned, burning away at him. I must get up and move, he told himself. He remained in bed, however, until late afternoon. There is mysterious Edgar, he thought. And there are words. Have I been too much alone? That has always been the case. And what is the case—my case—at present?

Eventually, he forced himself under the shower, running the water very hot, then very cold, hoping to jar himself out of where he was. His state, his case, was not new; there had been plenty of times when he had ground to a dead halt, when he could not figure out how to go on in his own skin. He dressed slowly, pausing between the underwear and the pants, between the deodorant and the shirt. Fully clothed, he resumed his seat on the bed.

He flipped open his wallet. Nearly four hundred dollars. And the week before, his retirement money had arrived from Altgeld. He had not bothered to open the envelope. He calculated that he had spent less than fifty dollars, excluding Obie's fee, since his big buying spree.

"And what would mysterious Edgar say to that?" he inquired to the empty house.

With the aid of the state trooper's map, he drove into Helmsville. He had made the trip in record time. The more he dwelled upon his father, and his father's attendant enigmas, the faster he drove, pushing the Volkswagen as hard as it could go.

Feeling business-like, he deposited the retirement check in savings just before the bank closed. The manager who had arranged matters on Walter's first day in Helmsville was professionally friendly and solicitous. Walter had forgotten, or perhaps had yet to fully learn, the pleasures of money. The manager first ushered him past the other customers, then personally saw to his deposit. The man was disappointed that the check was not larger, but remained fawningly gracious. As he left the bank, Walter considered visiting Mr. Carl Smyre at Furniture Heaven. No, he thought. That might be overdoing it.

He ate dinner at a Mexican restaurant, El Rancho de Casa, because it was the first place he came to that served food. He put away three margaritas, chiles relenos, tacos, and a cube of flan that shimmied obscenely as the waitress dropped it in front of him. The food and the margaritas, heavy on the tequila, went down well enough. He had eaten his own cooking for too many days, although he never cared too much about what he ate; he was satisfied if there was a great quantity to be consumed.

He drank a Carta Blanca after he inhaled the flan, and gave the waitress a big tip. I'm a man of means, he thought. Goddamn right. The margaritas and the beer did not have an immediate kick, but Walter sensed that he should put a temporary halt to his intake. The patrons of El Rancho de Casa were not particularly interesting so he left, heading for what he did not know. It was an old mood. While he had seldom paid attention to where he lived, he had carefully watched others; their voices, gestures. He cut away the portions of their lives that would be of some use to his writing. Have I grown weary of solitude, he thought as he slowly cruised the twilight streets. Have I forgotten that the world is a show that I need to attend now and then? He laughed. Prowling is a necessary evil. I should write that down when

I get home.

After a series of random turns, he came to the old business district near the courthouse. The stone soldier on the obligatory Confederate monument stood guard over the deserted streets. A few loafers, or refugees, hunched and sprawled on the courthouse steps. They watched Walter as the Volkswagen chugged past, then lapsed back into their torpor. Every other store was closed down, boarded up for years. Through a diner window, a single customer could be seen, his head bent low, shoveling away at his meal. A waitress and the cook smoked and gaped off into space. A classic scene, Walter thought, his belly rumbling with cumin and alcohol. *I must be getting sentimental here in the American dusk.*

Up the street from the diner stood an old office building—right on the corner of the main downtown intersection. The name, The Commercial Building, was carved in dirty, pigeon-spattered Georgia granite. Walter parked at the curb. *It must've been distinguished in its day,* he thought. *Late 1920s, most likely. Does the interior have those Art Deco flourishes so adored by the chi-chi set? Symbols of playful grace and local corporate aesthetics.*

The lobby was as dingy as the outside, and whatever decorative touches that may have been there in the past had been erased by successive remodelings. The plain, cheap paneling, the dull red carpet over what was probably a marble floor, and the light green institutional paint, were too-obvious signs of surrender. The name on the directory beside the elevator jumped right out: Roy A. Bunch, Attorney at Law, Suite 311B.

Naturally, Bunch was not in at that hour, and the creaking elevator shook up the offerings from El Rancho de Casa. Walter broke out in a greasy, filmy sweat. The pebbled, translucent glass, with Bunch's name in flat black letters, gave off little light from the darkened office. Walter did not

73

bother to knock, and as he took the stairs down to the street, he could not determine why he had sought Bunch out.

Slowly he strolled around the eight blocks that constituted the former center of Helmsville. Any life that had once existed there had migrated to the interstate and the malls. The land of the dead, Walter thought. My grandparents, both sets of them, went up and down these streets. And my mother and father too. And so did I, as a child. Margaret and Edgar. They must have courted here, as it was said in those days. Catching Dick Powell and Myrna Loy at the movies. Hearing about Pearl Harbor on the way home from church, is what Margaret said. And they pledged their troth as Edgar, dashingly arrogant in his second lieutenant's uniform, commissioned and certified by Franklin Delano Roosevelt, marched off to war. To be a spy, to arrange for other men to be spies. At least that's what I imagine, since he never told me what he did in the war. No heroic charges through French hedgerows against panzer grenadiers, or landing on atolls amidst the precise, killing fire of doomed Japanese gunners. Oh no. That wasn't Edgar's style. Or mine either, pumping up my blood pressure to stay out of Asian rice paddies. Edgar's duty never kept Margaret from praying and counting the days until his return. Like in the movies. The movies made them and they trimmed doubt from their lives to fit their roles. They had a marvelous time.

He passed the Tar Heel Hotel, where a person who may, or may not, have been a woman sat in a lawn chair by the entrance knitting what might be the longest scarf in history. An enormous ball of acrylic yarn sat beside the chair, while the person's hands worked rapidly with the knitting needles. Her, or his, hair was styled in a baroque beehive. The body, bulging in a soft, mushy way, spilled and lapped over the sides of the chair. The knitter glanced up at Walter, and returned to the scarf. The face was devoid of even animal curiosity, as if Walter was not part of any equation of consequence. Walter nodded and went on. And could you, he thought, assume a role in Mom and Dad's movie? There was no room for such creatures in those days.

He heard the noise as he rounded another corner—onto the deadest street of all; a place where all the stores were ruined, where the vacant lots did not seem capable of supporting growth of any sort. The noise was human, more or less, like a child attempting to imitate a howling dog and a train whistle at once. The noise had fearful powers of penetration, shoving its way directly into the forepart of Walter's consciousness. He whirled about and looked from where he had come. The knitter gave no sign of hearing, and seemed to be outside the waves of the noise. When Walter turned again, he found the source.

The street ran straight to the courthouse, the Confederate soldier in full view. A lanky boy in drooping shorts that dropped below his knees stood upon a bus stop bench. His head was shaved, and as Walter drew closer, the ear ring, the acne, and the make-up became apparent, along with the fish-belly pallor of his bare legs. His body did possess colors, however; in the form of swirling arabesque tattoos they spun and danced down his arms and back.

The boy's head was thrown back, his mouth opened so wide that his jaw seemed unhinged. The noise originated from deep within him, and had no beginning and no end. As Walter listened, the food and alcohol did further contortions in his lower tract. He became lightheaded, and his legs weakened. He halted a half a block from the boy who, perhaps through some sort of instinct, recognized Walter's presence by inclining his head and nodding slowly. As if by signal, the head swung back to its original position. The noise ceased as the boy took a deep breath, then accelerated to a higher, unbearable pitch. Walter slowly backed away, pausing once to steady himself. An old purple Pontiac, driven by a large, wall-eyed woman, crawled down the street. The car was filled with jostling, shouting, fighting children. There may have been only four of them, but their flailings made their number appear much larger, their baby fists falling upon one another, their shrill infant voices mixing with the song of the howling boy and the deep, unmuffled throb of the Pontiac's engine.

He retraced his steps to the Volkswagen. With the Pontiac's departure, it was the only car on the street. And I'm the only one who doesn't seem to know what he's doing. I've re-entered the world. To be certain.

At a topless bar on the edge of town, he gulped down two quick beers. The air conditioning was in top working order, and Walter sat close enough to the stage to count the goose pimples on the luminous pale breasts of the small dancer. She was young and concentrated with a lip chewing intensity upon her movements—which were clumsy, without spontaneity. She could not quite find the groove in the song's beat. Walter ordered a third beer, the song ended and another dancer, who sported a tattoo of a weeping cross on one shoulder, took her turn. Vaguely, Walter took note of the tatoo. Perhaps she is in league with the boy who howls downtown, he thought. I've always known that anything was possible. Only I forget now and then.

The beer was very cold, and Walter complimented the bartender, a heavy-set, scholarly-looking young man. The bartender nodded thanks and collected dirty glasses for the sink. Here too, Walter thought, they know what they're doing, or at least what they're supposed to do. Even the men at the tables. They're sneaking out on their wives, or buying a fantasy to carry with them into the night. That may insure more solace than howling, but I can't be sure.

There is a question. I have money. I have land. Physically, I'm stronger than I've been in years. So what is the question? His guts heaved. I'm nearly drunk, he thought. And when was the last time I could make that statement? Years past. Time gone.

Without too much effort it came back to him. Valerie had left him two weeks before his novel came out. He accused her of planning it that way to spoil the publication. He cringed at the recollection of his petulant voice over the telephone, shouting in the general direction of Philadelphia. He had downed half a quart of scotch, squatting in his apartment, the carton of books, the complimentary copies of his novel, having arrived that day. When he hung up, he flipped the carton onto the floor, his novel cascading and thumping about his feet. The books stayed there for two days.

There had been other, more joyous drunks. With a friend who owned a TR-6, nipping at vodka, ripping through the springtime country night around Columbia. The friend had disappeared years before. And I suppose he could claim that I had disappeared too, Walter thought. Oh, there were other times, besides. At a faculty party—the time in New Hampshire when I vomited off the back porch of the chairman's house. I was so self-conscious and put away too many gin and tonics. A tenure situation again. Many years ago. Why does everything seem to have been many years ago?

A writer. Unannounced, the word came to him. He shuddered. The bartender caught sight of Walter in mid-spasm, shrugged and passed a pina colada to another customer. His shudder having ended, Walter again considered the word. A writer is bound...to gather the evidence. To be unafraid. It was, and it still could be, a noble, but halfcrazed calling. In my case, I must tell people what they don't want to hear. Unpleasant. They chant about how they want to feel good about themselves. What a concept. Most of them should be alarmed, disgusted about themselves. And not only the howling boy of Helmsville. If I were at home, I could put that one in the journal. Aphorisms for one and all. My last will and testament as a writer.

And what do I not want to hear? His glass was empty and he held it up for the bartender. The new draft, golden and promising, was placed in front of him. To put it more succinctly, what don't I want to see? He shuddered again and drew in the suds. The foam stuck to his upper lip, and for the first time, he noticed his face in the smoky mirror that hung behind the bar.

"Let there be no more avoidance!" he loudly declaimed.

"Hi," a small voice said at his elbow. It was the small dancer. She wore the skimpiest of skirts and a Hank Williams Jr. T-shirt.

Walter was not sure of the origin of the voice. Before he could reply, she took the stool next to him and lit a cigarette. She held it gingerly, like smoking was new to her, trying to smile through the haze. Why is she sitting there? he thought. There are plenty of other seats. As she kept on trying to smile, he understood that she wanted to come off as alluring, seductive. He wanted to tell her to stop, that it was all right. But he could not without making her feel worse than she probably already felt.

"You from Helmsville?" she asked. Her accent was what Margaret would have called pure linthead.

"No and yes." And that's the truth Walter thought.

"Huh?" She gulped out the word and he smiled at her.

"I live nearby. My family was...native to the region."

"Where're they at now?" She was obviously bored with her own questions.

"Dead. For years." He heard the odd staccato hack of his own voice. Am I angry? Surely not angry at this child.

"You buy me a drink?"

Walter knew the question was coming, but he laid a twenty out anyway. The bartender pounced on it as if by signal. In a single motion he gave Walter a ten in change and handed the girl a drink; as if it had been prepared beforehand.

"Thanks," she said. "What's your name?"

"Conrad. Joe Conrad." One of Edgar's favorite writers. He remembered that *Heart of Darkness* rested beside his own first book up in the study.

"I'm Kelly."

"Like Grace Kelly."

"I guess." She had obviously never heard of Grace Kelly, but Walter could not hold that against her. He was also slightly ashamed that he had given her a false name, despite the fact that she was hustling him, despite the ten dollars for a glass of club soda.

"Your dancing, Kelly, is special. You possess grace and verve. Or verve and grace. Like Grace Kelly." From her expression he could tell that she was conscious of his mockery. I can't help it, he thought, his sense of shame growing stronger.

"Excuse me," he said. "Yes. A fine dancer. That's what you are."

"Thanks...Joe. "

"What about your life?" he said, not able to stop himself.

"Huh? I don't know." She sipped her club soda through a straw. Her eyes were big, filled with light.

"I don't have a firm appreciation of my life either. I've been contemplating the past, present, and future. No. Wait. Not the future. At any rate, when an answer has been received, evaluated, and...fully digested, I'll give you a call."

"You trying to get my number?" She made a small, but obvious gesture of drawing herself away from Walter. He laughed, a little too loudly, a bit uncontrolled.

"No. Not at all," he finally said. He tilted his head back, pouring the rest of the beer down his throat.

"I just work here," she said. "Dancing is all."

"It's been a pleasure." He picked up the ten from the bar,

took her small, damp hand, and pressed the bill gently into the palm. "For you. A drink, or whatever else."

"O.K.—Yeah." She folded her hand over the money.

"Certainly. By all means. Good night."

As he started the car, his head was clear, as clear as that moment when he plunged into the spring. And clear despite his drunkenness.

"Let there be no more avoidance!" he chanted as the started home.

Map or not, he was lost. He had envisioned himself at the study door in no time at all. Instead, he slowly rolled down a two-lane black top in darkness that was as total, as complete, as he had ever been immersed in. He wanted to weep at it all, but he did not, clinging hard to the wheel, confused at how the countryside all seemed different in the night. He pulled over more times than he could count to read the map, berating himself for not exploring the roads of Darden County as he said he would.

"A miracle!" he yelped as the headlights revealed the drive. Beneath the archway of oak boughs, the darkness remained absolute, but it no longer frightened him; he was there. He slowed and rolled down the window, the air all scented with clover and cut grass and faint smells he could not name. And then he came upon it. He had forgotten, deliberately, but never completely enough. The time had arrived.

The lights, their number and power, made the brick ranch house look like an ocean liner encountered on a midnight voyage. A van was in the carport and figures moved behind the draperies as country and western slammed out across the fields. Walter recognized the song; Kelly had danced to it with such unskilled determination. And there were floodlights too—illuminating the deer, the ducks, the Mexicans and the burros.

He had expected the moment, but he was astonished that it had come. He slowed almost to a dead stop, transfixed, his gaze darting from the windows, to the van, to the smiling brown face of a ceramic peon. Then he smashed down on the gas.

Without a light of his own, he slipped through the dark house, undressed and got into bed. He lay there for a long time, listening to his own beer-scented breath, until he fell asleep.

6

"Man, New Orleans was special. Something special."

Walter nodded, still under the greasy, iron hand of the hangover. The hangover was bad; not the worst of his experience, although seated at the dining room table at the ranch house that had glowed so in the night, it seemed to be.

"You ever been to New Orleans?" Ricky asked. He was not as tall as Walter. He had a sturdy, athletic build that he probably worked reasonably hard to maintain. His hair was dark blonde and curly—cut short on the sides and kept long and flowing in the back. Like a professional wrestler or high school football player, Walter thought. And his square-jawed, pugnacious face touched Walter's vague memory of his father's visage. There has to be, he thought, a photograph that would fill out the comparison. If I wanted to find it. Ricky dressed like Walter's students—or at least their springtime garb of baggy shorts and T-shirts. Ricky's shirt proclaimed the NCAA basketball championship of the North Carolina Tar Heels.

"Hey, you ever been to New Orleans?" Ricky asked again, chewing at his dinner.

Walter nodded again, with slightly more emphasis. He had been nodding regularly, speech being a bit arduous for him. But Ricky persisted.

"I'll bet you had a good time, didn't you. You go there for Mardi Gras? Mardi Gras is some scene."

"I can't remember why I was there." Walter lifted a fork full of lima beans to his mouth. He had never disliked lima beans, but these beans, like the ham, the potato salad, the corn bread and the rest of the dinner, were repulsive.

"Can't remember! Man, you must've had a good time!" Ricky laughed as he reached across the table and scooped up two more pieces of cornbread. His all-consuming appetite, blooming health, and country boy table manners made Walter sicker—almost as much so as the food-packed table. Beatrice laughed too. Walter smiled and his face hurt.

Beatrice was as large as her son, with brutally swept back black and white hair—like a skunk's pelt. Like Ricky, she was deeply tanned. She lacked his booming, slightly bullying manner, however. As Walter pushed the food around his plate, he was conscious of her calculating, measure-taking gaze. She and Ricky also had the same large, shining white teeth—only her tight lips covered hers most of the time.

And there's Star herself, Walter thought. While she was somewhat younger than Ricky, she resembled both him and Beatrice because of her smooth-skinned tan. She wore gym shorts and a tank top, her small, tight breasts firm against the fabric. She daintily, but voraciously chewed her dinner and had not spoken to or glanced at Walter since they began to eat. He seemed not to exist for her, which reminded him of those southern girls he once tried to teach in Texas and Georgia. They had moved in distracted orbits around Daddy, money, and clothes. They were of the suburban new rich, most of them. And if she sticks with Ricky, Walter thought, she'll keep right on being rich.

Ricky had called that morning, his manly, happy voice cracking over the telephone, boring insistently into the tenderness of Walter's ear. "Come to supper!" he shouted. Walter was too broken and groggy to think of an excuse. This is how he came to be with Ricky, enmeshed in the preposterous, immense implications of brotherhood. Without the hangover, the burden would have been large enough—this yammering stranger with his name and the stranger's women. He wished, as he had wished all day, heaped up in his bed in sweats and bad dreams, that they could have remained strangers. But that was not possible. Beatrice passed him a platter of smelly ham. He did not take seconds and suspected that his refusal was viewed by her as further incriminating evidence; too good to eat our food.

He contemplated the ache that enveloped his being as Beatrice went on about the grandeur of an outlet mall near Birmingham. When she had the opportunity, she would turn the conversation back to their pilgrimage to the South.

"...and the prices. I couldn't believe them. Especially the shoes."

"You musta bought fifteen pairs." Ricky grinned in Walter's direction.

"Only nine. You get a chance to buy quality, you take advantage of it."

"Take it easy, Momma," Ricky said.

"Those shoes are nothing compared to that motorcycle you got before we left," Beatrice said, an edge in her voice.

"Hell, money ain't no object. Right, Walt?"

"I suppose not." Kept it noncommittal, Walter thought.

"A motorcycle's necessary?" These were the first words that Star had spoken since Ricky introduced her to Walter. After the introductions, Walter had been guided directly from the front door to the table, and the meal had commenced with a purpose.

"For my image," Ricky said, grinning once more at Walter. "A wealthy young man with charisma and potential. Say Walt, Obie tells me that you're fixing up The Old Home Place."

Walter dabbed at his mouth with his napkin and appeared to contemplate the question. The less they know, the better off I'll be, he thought.

"Only a few touches here and there."

"You're figuring on staying, then," Beatrice said, shifting a ball of food around in her mouth like a cud. Let's get right down to brass tacks, Walter thought.

"*Of course* he's staying!" Ricky yodeled, compounding what Walter had come to accept as permanent headache. Ricky then reached over and squeezed Walter's arm in a gesture of jock buddy-hood.

"That would seem to be so," Walter said, as Ricky released his grip.

"What do you plan to do here?" Beatrice asked. Walter knew that his plans would not make sense to her—or anyone else. Should I say that I will some day have the courage to re-enter my father's study? That I will walk, or else pass from waking to sleeping all day in bed? That I will have strained, elliptical conversations with topless dancers? That I will write ambling, yet terrified prose in my journal?

"Walter plans to be rich. Like us, only richer. Take care of the farm and be rich and live real good," Ricky said in a kind of litany—as if the phrase had been repeated countless times.

"I'm settling in right now," Walter said.

"Walt's a writer. Daddy showed me your books. Only I ain't had a chance to read them yet."

Before Walter could tell him not to bother, Beatrice resumed her interrogation.

"You make much money off those books of yours?"

Walter laughed, startling the others. They stopped eating.

"What living I made came from teaching."

"I heard," Beatrice said. "College professor. What subject?"

"English." Or foreign languages, Walter thought, recalling ancient departmental jokes.

"My favorite subject," Star said. Walter noticed, for the first time, that her voice was low and throaty.

"I wasn't so good in English," Ricky said. "I did read...what's that book about dogs at the North Pole?"

"The Call of the Wild," Star said. She smiled—a small, slight smile.

"Yeah," Ricky said. "That's a good one."

"Your Daddy was always reading," Beatrice said. "Had his nose in some book or another."

"Now me and Daddy mostly talked about practical things," Ricky said. "Running the farm and all. He raised me up to be a man of action." What a quaint and curious turn of phrase, Walter thought.

"Lord that's the truth," Beatrice said. "Edgar had enough energy for ten men."

"He sure did," Star said. She languidly rose from the table and disappeared through the kitchen. A door closed in the back of the house. A strip of ham fat congealed in Walter's plate, nestled against the nearly untouched mound of lima beans.

Beatrice cleared the dishes and said that dessert would be served after supper had a chance to settle. Walter offered to help, but she pointed out that she could handle it herself. "She's the boss of this house," Ricky belched. He then suggested that he and Walt should relax in the living room "and get to know each other better." Again, Walter could not think of a reason to refuse. Limply, helplessly, he went.

The living room, like the other parts of the house that Walter had glimpsed on his way to the meal, was packed with things, much of it being the most extreme and arresting examples of Furniture World's wares. Instinctively, Walter understood that it would be best not to mention the payment of Ricky's old debt; it might lead to fulsome declarations of brotherhood—or perhaps personal injury for Mr.

Carl F. Smyre.

Walter dropped into a gold velour wingback chair. The cushions exhaled noisily. Ricky pushed the lever all the way back on his recliner so that from Walter's angle of vision most of what could be seen was chin and feet. Ricky found the remote and the television came on. A quiz show blared forth, the shouting, clapping contestants dancing about as they competed for a Bermuda vacation. The quiz show was quickly replaced by a baseball game. Ricky flipped from channel to channel, seldom pausing for more than a minute or two. The motion of the garish, shifting images made Walter dizzy. He closed his eyes, trying to think of the best time to get away.

"I'm gonna get me a satellite dish," Ricky said, settling on the Weather Channel where a young woman described the arrival of a low pressure system in Eastern Oregon. "A real good investment, and the depreciation ain't as high as you'd guess."

"I don't know much about it," Walter said, daring to open his eyes now that Ricky had satisfied his urge for channel-surfing.

"Yeah? It would cost you an arm and a leg to get cable. It was pretty expensive here, and you're even farther out."

Why am I listening to this? Walter thought. Because I came here. Almost voluntarily.

"I'll just stick to plain old television."

"Whatever. To change the subject, Walt, there's something I've been meaning to apologize for." As he spoke, Ricky jerked himself into an upright position and lowered his head—like a small boy caught in some forbidden act.

"Apologize?"

"I shoulda told you about Daddy. And not left it up to Roy Bunch. Only it was hard to get the right words and I didn't have a handle on what to say. It was my duty and I blew it..."

"It's fine, Ricky. Really." And it's pure bullshit too, Walter thought.

"You mean it? I've worried about having this...confrontation. Ever since I found out that you were going to live here."

You probably hoped that I would be an absentee landlord, Walter thought. Just a name up north.

"I've wondered a lot about what our first meeting would be like. And I wanted it to be good. Talking face to face like we are now. Why outside of Momma, you're my only living blood kin."

And what an alarming situation that is, Walter thought. Ricky stared at him, his large brown eyes moist with blood kinship.

"I understand," Walter said, lighting on the first innocuous phrase that came to mind.

"You mean it, Walt?" Walter was afraid that Ricky might weep, which would do nothing to help the hangover.

"Yes, I do." Stop, for God's sake, Walter thought.

"Good." Ricky flipped the lever back into position and Walter was no longer forced to view his face.

Ricky absorbed himself in more weather reports—local, national, and world-wide. Walter dropped lower into the gold velour, his stomach pumping and moaning. He had to leave, but he could not move, despite the powerful supplications from his gut. To keep his mind off his lower tract, he catalogued the contents of the living room. For my next journal entry, he told himself. After noting the three couches, the four chairs, the two coffee tables, the five lamps, the various figurines of birds, bear cubs, and comical cows, the three clocks and the two Polynesian masks above the mantle, he gave up. There's too much, he thought. And not just in this room either. It's endemic. A plague of too much. His bowels burned, flaming suddenly with the most raging demands yet. With his face pulled back into kind of a death's head smile, he managed to stand.

"Say, you don't look so good," Ricky said, solicitous with brotherhood.

"Bathroom," Walter huffed.

"Back down the hall. Third door on the right. Can I get something to settle you down? Alka-Seltzer? A beer?"

At the hint of alcohol, Walter's bowels screamed at him. Without answering, he broke for the hall. It was dark there, and he could not waste time searching for a switch. He pressed forward, colliding with the unseen mass which filled the darkness around him. Things rustled, snapped, and toppled over each other as he tried to feel his way along. Until there was light. Beatrice, her hands in yellow rubber gloves, stood at the far end of the hall.

"There's a switch down here," she said flatly. "And at your end too."

Walter tried to look normal as he strained against himself, seeing for the first time what he had tried to fight his way through. The hall was jammed with bags and parcels, many of the contents having piled up in drifts across the floor. He gaped down at a purple sundress that still bore a price tag.

"What..." he began, dazed by all that lay before him—more clothes, shoes, a set of steak knives, a bag of compact discs. He was compelled to ask despite the deep and abiding burning.

"From our trip. We haven't unpacked all of it yet. How come you're back here?"

"Bathroom."

"You don't look right."

"No...I." Mercifully, Beatrice expertly navigated through the clutter and opened a door. Without a word, she returned to the kitchen. Walter heard the dishwasher start as he slammed into the bathroom.

In the isolation, Walter did not have to speak to or look

at anyone else. All he had to do was surrender the molten richness, the excess that he had consumed and grown heir to. He giggled as he flushed away the first load, the choking scent filling the air. Yes, he thought. A yielding up of the inner essence of the outer world, a turning inside out to match myself to the abode of Ricky, Beatrice, Star and the rest of humanity. Could this olfactory manifestation of all that *is* creep beneath the door, pierce the walls, and merge with them? Would they notice?

After depositing two more loads, he remained in position, temporarily content. I can put this in the journal too. That famous Los Angeles writer has parlayed his shits into a substantial reputation among those deluded enough to confuse life with writing.

I must objectively consider Ricky, he thought. A good-natured distance would seem to be the best avenue for developing our relationship. Perhaps I was momentarily frozen by his resemblance to Edgar, or at least as much of Edgar as I can summon up. Be friendly, but stay away as much as possible. I can do that. He may even mean well. Who am I to say?

He perched on the toilet until his buttocks and thighs ached, postponing his return as long as possible. There came the time, however, a half hour or so after his flight, when he had to move. He cleaned himself carefully, gladdened by the new, dry tightness of his lower tract, and washed his face and hands. After he dried off, he examined the contents of the medicine cabinet. It was a pleasure he had occasionally indulged in while in the houses of friends and strangers. With blood kin, it was almost appropriate.

A set of very old dentures, yellowed and chipped, grinned at him. Prescription bottles occupied the rest of the space, arranged row on row with military precision. There were antibiotics, decongestants, and vitamins of every sort. Walter could not identify the other medicines. However, that did not stop him from speculating upon their uses. There were Ricky's tan pills, and Beatrice's hair supplement. And there was Star's tit medicine, a special unguent for pertness. They accumulate like evidence, he thought. Like the contents of a shopping mall tumbled into a hallway. Like satellite dishes and all the suites from Furniture World.

The strawberry shortcake actually tasted very good. Another sign, like my massive, cosmic stool, of the waning of my hangover, Walter thought. The berries were fresh and chilled, and the whipped cream as rich as those who consumed it. Ricky had seconds and thirds, slurping with innocent gluttony. Walter was quieter, less demonstrative over the goodness of the earth, but only because he forced himself. Star had a tiny portion, and Ricky kidded her about her weight. She did not laugh.

They sat in the backyard, which was not nearly so animated by Beatrice's decorative figures as the front. A birdbath stood beside a statue of St. Francis and a doe and her fawn lingered nearby. Walter was glad there were no floodlights in the back. The stars were there, out in full force.

"Pretty night, huh?" Ricky said after he had stopped sucking on his spoon.

"Sure is," Beatrice said. Star lit a cigarette.

"You ever heard of secondary smoke?" Ricky asked. "Had to stop the van every twenty miles going down to New Orleans so you could suck on a cigarette."

"We're outside now, Ricky," Star said. "It'll blow away."

"All right, all right," Ricky said expansively. "As long as it don't bother Walt."

"I've no objections." Soon I'll make my excuses, he thought. And get the hell out of here.

"You feeling better?" Ricky asked. Walter remembered to keep his answer good-natured and distant.

"Much. Thanks."

"You looked pretty bad there in the hall," Beatrice said. Walter sensed that Beatrice was the sort who derived sublime pleasure in discussion of explosive bowel movements, constipation, goiters, boils, carbuncles, fistulas, and other corruptions of the flesh.

"This is the kind of night Daddy loved," Ricky said. "He'd stay out til morning some times. When I was a kid, he told me about the constellations and the Milky Way and all that. We lived at The Old Home Place then. It's funny: I don't remember much of what he told me—just him telling it."

"The man knew all kinds of things," Beatrice said. "You should've heard him talk. His mind..."

"His mind wasn't like anybody else's," Ricky said with a hint of reverence as he completed Beatrice's lines. "He was one of a kind." Walter had the feeling that Ricky and Beatrice had repeated the conversation many times. One of a kind is right, he thought, recalling Obie's story of the women who came and went to The Old Home Place. And he arranged for Beatrice and Ricky to stay right on. Edgar kept it all.

"There was more to him than other people," Beatrice said. "Thinking all the time. And so much energy."

"He was active all right," Star said. Walter heard a doubleness in her tone again, even if Ricky and Beatrice appeared not to.

"The body and the mind, thought and action united," Walter said, half-absently. Ricky sat up in his chaise lounge. For a man of action, Walter thought, he spends a lot of time on his backside.

"That's it, Walt! That's him. And you haven't seen him since you were a kid. It's...it's like there's a part of him that's with us."

"There sure is," Beatrice said with an utter lack of conviction.

"The body and mind united. That's brilliant, Walt. How did you think of that?"

"I'm not sure." The question is why I said it, Walter thought.

"You were right on the money," Ricky said.

"Have you seen his grave?" Star asked.

"No. I haven't yet." Walter felt well enough to lie now—even if he was not sure why he had to.

"Close to the spring, down toward the river. He said he wouldn't be in a cemetery for anything. Not with those dead people. Like he wasn't gonna be dead himself some day."

"He's *not* dead," Ricky said. "Of course you gotta say that his body is dead, but he lives on. In us. In all that we do."

"And what did he do?" Walter asked.

"He got it all down on his head stone," Star said. "Wrote it years before he died. He had it all rigged up the way he wanted it. Only I got the feeling that he thought he would never die. Like he was exempt."

"Come on, Star," Ricky said. "Daddy was special, but he was down to earth too. You got to give him that. Remember how he used to work as hard as I did, right up 'til the end?"

"He worked lots harder than you did," Beatrice laughed.

"So you say." Ricky and Beatrice glared at each other. The stars blinked on and on. Walter shifted his weight, seeking comfort in his lawn chair. His mouth was suddenly too sweet with shortcake. The last waves of the hangover rose and fell.

"Roy Bunch told me that Edgar was working when he died—trying to uproot a tree stump," Walter said.

"That's right. Bunch got the story from Ricky. Old Edgar was just working away," Beatrice said with odd and unexpected satisfaction.

"Ramming something," Star said.

"I found him. I was supposed to meet him at The Old

93

Home Place so that we could go over some accounts..."

With restraint and dignity, Ricky told of Edgar's death. How as the sun began to set behind The Old Home Place, he grew worried. How he called Obie, who did not know where Edgar could be. How he dispatched Obie to search part of the farm, while he saddled and mounted Hickory, his Palomino stallion, and went seeking his father. And how with unerring instinct he and Hickory made straight for the spot where Edgar had gone down. Miraculously, neither he nor Hickory were stung by the swarming hornets.

"And I took my father in my arms, laid him across the saddle, and brought him, led him home." Home from the hill indeed, Walter thought even as he heard the unmistakable pain in Ricky's voice.

"Lord I miss him," Ricky said after a suitable and dramatic pause. "Now and then I hear him calling me, or I think I can see him off in the distance, moving in and out of the woods. Walt, he loved the woods. He'd spend days out there. He must've known every inch of this farm."

"Is that right?" Walter said, envisioning an encounter with Edgar among the oaks on the ridge—or at a bend above the rapids.

"Why wouldn't it be right?" Beatrice yawned.

"Oh, he loved the land," Ricky said, his voice steadier. "How did he say it? 'The land abides and you must hold it against all forces.'"

"He said that," Beatrice yawned again, gathering up the sticky bowls and spoons.

"Biblical," Walter said. He could not tell if he was being ironic.

"Yeah. He coulda been in the Bible," Star said.

Walter locked the front door, a precaution he had not taken in some time. The Old Home Place, as Ricky my blood kin calls it. This came to him as he climbed the stairs and pushed open the study door.

It's only another spot, he thought; the only place around here I have yet to really come to. He found the light, secure in the fact that the hangover had died away, that he was flushed and cleansed. I'll get started now, he thought. It could go on all night.

7

Whatever he thought might be there, did not seem to exist. He worked until nearly daylight, beginning with the books. He thumbed through each one before tossing it down the stairs. He liked the splatting, bumping sound, and it was satisfying when an old biology text—with Edgar's name and Chapel Hill dormitory address for 1937 on the first page—burst and rained out its innards. He threw almost all of them. There was a wonderful sensation in the act of hurling. He saved his own books—just barely, going through them in search of more of Edgar's literary judgements. He found none, except in the single volume he had examined during his first visit to the study. The other two appeared to have been untouched.

There must have been five hundred books: *Information Please* almanacs from the 1950s, political tracts disguised as history, chronicles of World War Two from Time-Life, Conrad, Hemingway, Thomas Wolfe, more old college texts, and an unread set of English and American classics—Dickens, Twain, James, Melville, Hardy. All fake Morocco binding and gilt-edged.

When he finished with the books, he started in on the papers. If Edgar is here, Walter thought, this is where he is hiding—waiting for me. What Walter encountered were accounts, bills, receipts, and tax returns. He divided them according to those categories and stacked them in the boxes left over from the move. Halfway finished, he grew dizzy with paper. He set the clock for noon and went to bed.

After washing and eating, he was back at it. By four, he had shifted the boxes to the room of the dead birds. There was still no sign of Edgar, so he tried the desk. There were pencils, fountain pens, matches from the One O'Clock Diner in Helmsville and the Officer's Club at Fort Myers, Virginia, paper clips, an ancient pack of Lucky Strikes, and a yellowed grocery list. There was no knowing the age of the list, although it seemed to have been written in a male hand. He then went through the computer discs. As he watched the blue screen, the records that he had so laboriously sorted and packed appeared before him, all in perfect order, perfectly organized. He could almost admire whoever had done such a thorough job.

He ate a quick meal, his stomach and lower tract now in more dependable condition, and took a beer back to the study. The bareness of the room, like its earlier, threatening clutter, in no way satisfied him.

And why not? He considered the question. Besides a grocery list and a single cryptic comment in one of his books, there was nothing. There were no letters, notes—nothing that would indicate that Edgar was more than a throbbing void. There is nothing here, he thought, the beer flat and metallic in his mouth. And I've spent weeks cowering before the door to this shabby, now empty room. A fool. I'm a goddamn fool. He laughed and threw the beer can against the wall. It rebounded, draining out across the scuffed hardwood floor.

He considered his foolishness, past and present. His ignoble days in the withered groves of academe; his marriage to a woman he could not speak to, and who, in any case, did not want to listen to him; the various masks he had tried, unsuccessfully, to assume; the various jobs that he had ruined. He laughed again when he considered that in his foolishness he had also become motionless and as empty as the room in which he found himself. And now I have money, that great liberator, and I cannot conceive of how to use it. And I am in this room because it is the last place to come to and because there is no place else to go.

He thought along these lines for quite awhile. He could not help it. He liked it better when he did not have to think at all, like when he was throwing books. In sadness, he found some towels downstairs and mopped up the beer. When his self-pity had abated slightly, he went to sleep. He left all the lights burning in the house—like when he was a child.

The knocking awakened him. It was a little past seven and despite being out for nearly ten hours, a listless, sapped-out fatigue clutched at him. The knocking went right on as he pulled on his pants and a T-shirt. It had to be, he thought; Ricky grinned as Walter yanked the door open. It's too early to be good-natured, he thought. But early enough to be distant.

Ricky bounded into the room. He was shirtless, squeezed into jeans. And he sported a red kerchief and a cowboy hat. There was something goofy about him—like a young, untrained Labrador dog. And he's gotten himself up like an extra in one of Warhol's gay movies, Walter thought.

"Saw the lights, Walt. Thought you might be partying up here."

"It looks that way." If Edgar cannot be revealed, then Ricky will appear, he thought.

"And it's about time to get up."

"I suppose."

"Gotta get a running start on the day."

"Why are *you* out?"

"Riding. Hickory's outside. Take a look."

An enormous horse, its hide a shade darker than Ricky's hair, stood tethered to the front porch. His eyes were black-brown and his nostrils appeared to be on the point of perpetually flaring.

"Very nice." Ricky would own such a beast, Walter thought. Edgar's hearse, so to speak. I should be relieved. He might've ridden the thing into my bedroom.

"Nice? He's the meanest son of a bitch on four legs. I'm the only one that can ride him. Obie won't even get close to old Hickory. Kicked him one time. You got any coffee?"

Walter made coffee and found a block of not-too-old pound cake. Ricky went on about what great shape the farm was in, and how good he felt on his morning rides.

"Been down to the river and back. Greenest spot on the face of the earth."

Walter grunted out a response. His foolishness had gnawed at him in his dreams, leaving him touchy, overly-tender in mind and body. Ricky's presence was a test, as good health in others had always been a test for him.

"Coffee's not bad. Hey, I'll get Momma to make you a cake. Ain't no need to buy this supermarket junk. She's got a good touch when it comes to cakes and pies."

They probably stink as badly as the ham, Walter thought. A cake that exudes rot. Exactly what I need. Walter refilled their cups, sticking to grunts as a counterpoint to Ricky's babbling.

"What you got planned today?" Ricky asked.

"Planned. Oh, straightening up a few things around here." The pile of books still rested at the foot of the stairs. He hoped that Ricky would not discover them. That could produce an endless stream of questions.

"The Old Home Place. I sure do love it here. Had the run of the house when I was a kid."

"Really."

"Oh, yeah. Daddy and Momma parted when I was thirteen and I went down the road to live with her. I spent lots of time with Daddy, though. I had two houses to grow up in, but this one's special. There's been a Loomis here since 1917. Did you know that?"

"I had no idea." Walter did not remember any stories from his father's side of the family. Margaret had hinted at things, but no more than that. She did not want Walter to know, and that suited him in his indifference. And Edgar, as a father, had the aura of one sprung forth fully grown, without past or future, ancestors or descendants.

"It's a fact. Our grandfather—his name was Stamey Loomis—had the house built for his bride, Helena. And there used to be a cabin for the colored that worked here. It got torn down years ago, though."

"A regular plantation." How that must've appealed to our mutual Dad, Walter thought. A shame he couldn't own slaves.

"Stamey was an important man around here, according to Daddy. Maybe it was like a plantation. Of course, the colored folks were free and all."

"How was he important?" Walter was beginning to get interested. "Anything to do with the mills? The mills were big in this part of the country."

"Naw. His family, all of them, came from the mountains. The Loomis family got out as soon as they had the chance. Daddy told me all about it. Since you're a writer, you might appreciate the fact that Daddy could tell a great story. Could be you got all your talent from him."

"I'd bet on it."

Ricky laughed.

"What's funny?"

"You, man. What a great sense of humor. Dry as a bone. Daddy could be that way when he wanted to. You remind me of him. Never changed expressions and came out with all these one liners."

"What about our grandfather?" It's time to change the subject, Walter thought. I might not be able to bear brotherly effusiveness.

"You gotta give me lessons some day on those one liners. Anyway, Stamey got rich off gambling. He'd go into Helmsville, had him a suite at the North State Hotel, and he'd rake it in. Gambled with doctors, lawyers, rich men. Shoot, he played cards with governors, three or four of them. Daddy said that Stamey told him that he gambled with the President of the United States one time—one back in the twenties that liked having fun. I can't remember his name."

"Harding," Walter said, trying to take all of it in, realizing how it all made curious, brutal sense—even if it might not be literally true. "Warren G. Harding." Teapot Dome, he thought. The president and the president's mistress snug in the cloakroom off the oval office. The house in Georgetown full of money and cards and liquor and burlesque queens doing the Charleston. And Stamey, his son the spitting image of him, dealing cards to the president and the Ohio Gang. It made perfect sense.

"That's who it might've been. History ain't my strong point. So Stamey gambled all over: Washington, New York, Havana. Out in California, Chicago. He'd always come back here, though. Bought more land—up in the mountains. Five peach orchards in South Carolina. Poker was his game. Five card stud, Daddy said. You like stud?"

"I may have played some in college for quarters. Beer money. Nothing serious. I never got to California." All of it was a lie. Walter was never chummy with the boys who engaged in the weekend-long games. Ricky laughed again, grating on Walter.

"You're a stitch, Walt. I tell you what, you teach me how to come out with those one liners, and I'll show you five card stud. Greatest game in the world. A family tradition. I get together with a few friends every couple of weeks."

"Do you have your own hotel suite?"

Ricky whooped and playfully punched Walter's biceps. The blow hurt, but he did not wince. Just when he's telling me something I want to hear, he thought, I get to be part of a yokel slapstick act.

"That's a good one," Ricky said, as his whoops subsided.

"You were telling me about our mutual past."

"Right. So old Stamey made enough to put Daddy through college in style. And he invested really well, too."

"I take it that Edgar had a great deal of style."

Ricky thoughtfully regarded the bottom of his cup. Walter found his silence only slightly less grating then his whoops.

"I mean from what my mother told me," Walter said. This was another lie. She would hardly have described Edgar's style in favorable terms.

"*Your* momma."

"Margaret."

"Where *is* she?" The question was presented in a way that suggested that Ricky expected Margaret to appear at any second.

"I'm afraid that she's dead. It happened a good many years ago."

"Aw. I'm sorry. What carried her off?"

Does he really want to know this, Walter thought. Must be part of brotherly obligation. Our exchange of family tales over coffee—by the hearth in The Old Home Place. He told Ricky about Margaret and his stepfather and the *Nordic Princess*. He went through the story quickly, in a monotone, without much regard for dramatic presentation. Ricky wagged his head in sympathy.

"That's sad, Walt. I mean it. If it hadn't been for Daddy, you'd probably felt like an orphan."

"I was an adult when it happened. And I never told Edgar. He wasn't to be found."

"For real? Did you come here?"

"To this farm? I didn't know it existed. I was only in this part of the country on two or three occasions. And that was when I was a child."

"He was here," Ricky grinned. "With his new family."

"Did he ever say much about his earlier life, his first family?"

Ricky poured more coffee and appeared to contemplate the question.

"Not much," Ricky eventually said. "But I got this feeling. I don't want you to take this the wrong way, but I believe your mother broke his heart." The turn of phrase took Walter by surprise.

"I...never would've guessed."

"Me neither. But Daddy had some parts to him that we'll never understand."

"Did he *tell you* that his heart was broken?"

"Not in so many words. But I knew. He had her picture buried with him. Like I said, he left real clear instructions about his funeral. My momma's picture was in there too, along with pictures of other women he had known. But your momma's pictures was *placed over his heart*. See what I mean?"

"His heart. How did..." Ricky kept on grinning as if he had achieved a small triumph.

"My momma didn't care none. She ain't got a jealous bone in her body. When Daddy left her, which he didn't do until the brick house was built, and built just the way she wanted it, she accepted his running around. Like she accepted his love—Daddy always said that there were some people that got more needs and more love in them than others. He was one of those people."

"Love?" This is what Edgar would call it, Walter thought.

"That's it. Love. You know, I believe that all that he did

103

in life was through love. What do you think?" Walter tried
to envision Margaret's face flattened against Edgar's decay-
ing chest.

"I'm not in a position to know. I remember almost nothing about him. Even when my parents lived together, he was
gone most of the time."

"CIA. He told me a few things about that too. Our Dad
was a secret agent."

Like James Bond, Walter thought. With a license to kill.

"Edgar never spoke to me about his work."

"He told *me*, though. You were only a kid then, and he
had his oath and all not to talk about his missions."

"Exciting stuff?"

"That's right. Spies. Communists. All that."

"And he was full of love then?" Ricky did not catch the
irony in the question.

"Daddy was full of love at all times."

Ricky could talk for an indefinite period. It was as if he
had nothing better to do. Ricky told of the funeral and how
he and Beatrice, who had been a hair dresser before meeting
Edgar, faithfully followed the instructions. Edgar was not
embalmed, as he was specific about keeping his corpse out
of the hands of morticians. "Ghouls is what he called them,"
Ricky laughed.

Edgar was wrapped in an old army blanket, as if he were
sleeping by a campfire in his own woods, and slipped into a
simple pine box. "Like our ancestors used to have," Ricky
said. Edgar was not dressed up in a suit either. He was in his
usual work clothes instead: brogans, a farmer's denim jacket, khaki pants, a flannel shirt, and his old New York
Yankees baseball cap. "And no underwear," Ricky chortled,
delighting in their father's ways. "He didn't believe in underwear. Said that it bound a man up."

"Then we put him in the back of his pick-up and drove

as close as we could to the spring. Obie had rented a back-hoe and dug the grave. It was me, Momma, Star, and Obie. On account of Daddy just wanting immediate family there. We woulda asked you if we'd known where you were. There weren't any prayers or anything like that. He did have this piece typed up and I read it over the grave after we got him settled in."

"Do you still have it? The piece you read?"

"That got buried too. Along with the women's pictures, his old Army forty-five, and this little Cuban flag. He said it was the last flag to fly over a free Cuba. Back in whenever that was. And we had to put in some bark from an oak tree, and a hawk's tail feather, and I don't know what all."

Walter hid his disappointment at not being able to lay his hands on Edgar's funeral oration. What a document it must be, he thought.

"Tell me Ricky, what did you say in your speech?"

"I can't remember all of it. It was deep, though. And I can't say that I understood all of it either. It had in there about his life and the earth and spirits. Stuff like that. Me and Momma cried. It was real emotional. When that part was over, me and Obie and Momma shoveled the dirt over him. He was real specific about that. But we got tired after awhile and Obie finished up with the backhoe. I don't think Daddy would've minded."

"What about Star?" The reverent, dreamy tone vanished from Ricky's voice.

"Refused to help. She went off into the woods and wouldn't come back until I yelled out that it was all over. I think Daddy's dying tore her up. Momma didn't like it at all—Star's going away. They don't understand each other so good sometimes."

"That's quite a story."

"Nobody else will ever have a funeral like it. When we got back to the house, we ate this meal just like he wanted us to. Big old steaks and homemade bread and beer. Daddy put in his instructions that this was the proper meal. We buried the instructions too. It all went exactly like he said—except for the backhoe and Star's disappearing like she did. She said that she was thinking. And she probably was. She thinks all the time. More than most people I've ever known—except for Daddy." Ricky expelled a coffee-pungent breath and stood up.

"I got to get going. Hickory needs to be fed and rested. It sure has been great talking to you." He reached down and hugged Walter.

"I'm glad we're brothers," Ricky said. "You've got no idea what it means to me." His expression was guileless, wide-open. And Walter could, at that moment, believe him.

"It seems that we've been thrown together."

"And it's good luck too. Think of all that Daddy did for us."

All that love, Walter thought.

Walter did not see Ricky for awhile after that morning, although he glimpsed him several times as he cantered by on Hickory. Ricky, shirtless as usual, would wave his hat with a cowboy's flourish as he yawped out a greeting. Once he was accompanied by Star, astride a sorrel, and riding rather gingerly. She seemed to be concentrating on the management of her horse, and barely acknowledged Walter. He did not mind. They were keeping their distance too, despite Ricky's claims about brotherhood. Walter got all of it into the journal, and the part about Margaret's photo in Edgar's pine box. A romantic gesture to be sure, he wrote—one that Margaret, in all of her own genteel romanticism, would have approved of. A surprise—like Ricky himself and the family history. It's all starting to sound like a bad Southern gothic novel—with a plot by Faulkner without all the other things that Faulkner could get into a book. As for me, I am oddly calm. Am I settling in? Is that the case?

The books he had tossed from the study stayed in their heaps for more than a week and Walter was finally forced to do something about them. He considered borrowing the truck from Obie, but instead he went into Helmsville and traded his Volkswagen for a new Ford pick-up. He paid with a check and had to wait while the skeptical manager cleared it with the bank. After the truck was finally his, he smiled— amused at owning such a machine and enjoying its air-conditioning and new-car smell.

After he loaded up the books, he got lost only once on the way to the landfill. At night, as always, he returned to the journal. He found that it gave him far more pleasure than any of his fiction. He had approached that kind of writing with a mixture of dread and grim determination. He had written draft after draft, stumbling toward a state of, if not perfection, then hand-chiseled, ironic bleakness. The reviewers who had approved of his work had said that it was thoughtful and well-written. Those qualities meant nothing to him now. He wrote more about himself. He could see his existence settling into a nice pattern. Perhaps. His troubles, like his absurd behavior, had come because of the absence of patterns in this new place. His life had once been divided into semesters, summer sessions, Christmas vacations, and publication dates. He had grown to fit that particular pattern without considering whether or not it made sense.

It has taken me awhile to get used to it, he wrote. I have had to make a way to live, whereas before that way was made by the hand of others. I thought that it was life. How existential. And what a joke. And the money, now, is a kind of joke too. That habit, that pattern, will take some getting accustomed to. I still pride myself on what I don't need. Surely I can find a way to enjoy what I have. Is it really mine? Can I enjoy anything? Perhaps this will change.

He had been there for three months and the summer was

107

well-advanced. He began to sleep better, running the air-conditioner all night. The cold helped him to drop into what he still thought of as blessed unconsciousness; and the hum of the condenser and the rush of the air concealed the old creaking noises of the house. When he awoke, he actually felt refreshed, rested. He resumed walking, although the woods were hot and stewing with insects. On the logging roads, however, the air was clearer and the mosquitoes less fierce.

One morning, he encountered Obie, who was repairing barbed wire on the back side of a pasture. Walter asked where Ricky was, if he was tending to other chores.

"Ricky?"

"Sure. Or does he mostly supervise?"

Obie seemed puzzled.

"What's there to supervise? Me? I already know how to do what gets done. And the people that you and Ricky rent to, they tend to their own business. Now, I do look after the horses. A supervisor. That's some idea."

"Ricky...Ricky said that he was in charge."

"O.K. If that's what he says. This ain't the Ponderosa or nothing. There's not that much to do. Shoot, Mr. Edgar took it easy, except when he got onto one of his special projects. Like when he put in the fish ponds one year—and drained and filled them in the next. Or when he planted all those boxwood shrubs and they died on him. Ricky. He didn't even bother with big ideas most of the time." Obie removed his black stetson and vigorously scratched at his balding scalp.

"Gotta watch out for ticks this time of year. You oughta cover your own head. Else they'll make a home in your hair." Obie carefully centered his hat.

"I guess my father tended to the records."

"Somebody did. I don't know whose keeping them now. Star probably. She used to help Mr. Edgar. She studied how to do it at the community college. Mr. Edgar called her his financial consultant. I think he was kidding a little bit."

I'll bet she was a 4.0 student, Walter thought. Obie pulled on his work gloves. Walter saw that the conversation had come to an end.

The next day he was writing when he heard a car in the driveway. Through the living room window, Star appeared, still in gym shorts and a halter top, her regular, cheerleader's features as impassive as ever. She knocked briskly at the door while Walter stared at the space where she had been. She went on knocking, firmly and politely, until he got to the door.

The check, for a little less than three thousand dollars, was made out to him. "Right to the penny," she said. "With deductions for taxes and so on. Your share of the rentals." She said too that she was sorry that she hadn't gotten the money to him sooner. "Things have been a little out of whack. But they're getting back to normal now. Mind if I smoke?"

Walter got an ashtray for her. She refused his offer of coffee, beer, or anything else that he had to give her. She went into the living room and began to inspect the premises. He followed along. He was sure that she was accustomed to being followed.

"Made a few changes, I see." She held the cigarette in one hand and the ashtray in the other.

"Here and there." He was slightly breathless. He wrote this off to her unexpected appearance.

"Pretty stark. I like that." She went down the hall and Walter sat on the couch. She did not need a tour guide. He heard her enter the bedroom. Taking it all in, he thought. She started up the stairs and he followed. He had not been in the study since he cleaned it out. He found her there, hands on hips, making a careful survey.

"Boy. You really worked this room over. All those old

books. What did you do with the papers?"

"Next door. In the room where I found the dead birds."

She arched her brows and set her mouth into a mocking little grimace.

"How many? A flock?"

"Just two. A hawk and some species that I couldn't identify."

"Edgar didn't pay much attention, in the last few years at least. He had a big clean-out himself one time—about five years ago. Got rid of all sorts of shit he had been keeping around here for years. Lots of furniture. Some of it might've been antique, but mostly it was just old. Even Beatrice wouldn't have it. What I want to know is, can I take the computer?"

Walter was mulling over the fact that Edgar, too, had thrown out a houseful of things. And he did not like it when people quickly changed the subject in the middle of a conversation.

"I need it," she went on, "for records. Obie told me about running into you down by the south pasture."

"He said you were my father's financial consultant."

"Obie's a good guy. In his own way. How about his clothing style?"

"Much like Ricky's." Your beloved, Walter thought.

"Come to think of it, you're right. Only don't tell Ricky that." She smiled and he felt like a conspirator.

"If you have to keep the computer, that's O.K. since you're a writer. Can I borrow one of your books? But about the computer, I worked on Edgar's records, did the accounting and all right here. And Edgar went over all of it. Had to have it on hard copy. That's where a lot of the paper came from—like you couldn't figure that out. And I figured, what the hell. You probably don't want me running in and out all the time. I made Ricky clean a space for me in my bedroom. And if you give me some help, I'll take the computer now.

It's kinda heavy and..."

"It's yours." Only slow down. Or stop, Walter thought. She smiled and lit another cigarette.

"A gentleman wouldn't let a lady haul a PC and a printer down a flight of stairs by herself," he said.

Walter tried to smile, but by the time his facial muscles had pulled together, she was talking again. She sounded as if she seldom got a chance to talk as much as she wanted or needed. She brushed past him and went into the room of the birds. Could be medication that makes her this way, he thought.

"Hey," she called. "You did a good job with the records."

He stood in the doorway. She was bent over one of the boxes, the gym shorts pulled tight. He looked away, mumbling thanks.

"What if I left all of it here?" she asked. "I can't see how I'll ever need it—except as a back up to what I have on the discs. Do you mind?"

"No. Fine. Whatever you want. I never use this room."

"Edgar was like that. I'll bet he never came upstairs except to sleep." And I pictured him in his study, Walter thought. Passing judgement on the world. Walter shuddered slightly with a touch of foolishness.

After the van was loaded, Star thanked Walter and shook his hand. Then she reminded him about his books.

"Which is best?" she asked, as he handed them to her.

"They're all about the same."

"It doesn't matter where I start?"

"No. There's no order to them." She arched her brows again, mocking him.

"Are all writers like you?"

"I don't know. You can keep those copies. I have others." Many others, he thought. I probably sold three hundred copies all together.

"I'll bet you're an interesting guy. If I can catch you on the right day."

"Like Obie."

"No. Cool. You're cool in your own way." Walter did not know how to respond, so again he tried to smile.

"You haven't asked me about Ricky or Beatrice."

"O.K. How are they?"

"Same as ever."

And how's that? he thought. He wanted her to leave.

"I'm glad."

"I'm sure. See you around, Walter. You don't like to be called Walt, do you?"

"I don't mind." Go, he thought. She waved gaily as the van bumped down the driveway. She was going too fast.

Later in the afternoon, he took his walk. There was a little breeze and the heat was bad, but he had to move. Naturally, he had written about Star, conjecturing on how she came to be connected to Ricky. There was money, to be sure. And animal magnetism. It was all probably less intriguing than it appeared on the surface.

As he walked, he reached for and found that state of comfortable blankness. What dominated him then was his breath, his sweat, and the regular, rhythmic movement along the road that curved back around the ridge where the oaks stood, where he had seen the fox. Gradually, the road climbed the ridge, and the pull of gravity caused a pleasant but tiring ache in his legs. He paused near the ridge crest, wiping the sweat from his face with the back of his hand. He had intended to go further, but the heat had drained him and he would, instead, rest and go back.

That side of the ridge provided a good view of the heat shimmering pastures and woods. He cleaned his sunglasses on the hem of his T-shirt and repositioned them on his face. It was then that she strolled out into the nearest pasture, directly at his feet. She was probably seventy-five yards away, but he knew her immediately.

It was Star and she was naked.

He stepped back into the tree line—where he could watch her, but not be seen. She sat down, folding her legs beneath her, Indian fashion. The grass had been cut recently for hay and he winced as he thought of her flesh against the stubble. But it did not seem to bother her. She sat there, out under the hard, burnished sun, tanned all over, her hair so blond that it was hard to focus on in the light. Walter held his breath, acutely aware of the utter, baking stillness all around him. No birds called and nothing scurried through the underbrush.

She began to sing in a tuneless, child-like voice. He could not make out the words, but he sensed that she made them up as she went along. Her song went on and on into the afternoon. She acted as if the world was elsewhere.

Beneath the enclosure of the trees, Walter sweated harder than ever. He could not move. Not until the song ended. Thus rooted, the high, infant-like notes floated up to him like bubbles. Then it came to him that she could climb the ridge and bring the song to him. He began to slowly back away as she went right on in her perfect solitude. When she was out of sight, he picked up his pace, the song and Star receding. He was moving at a half-run by the time he cleared the ridge. The woods, he thought. The woods are filled with far too much.

8

The smoke, fragrant with oak and pig fat, climbed in swirls and fumes from the cooker. The party was an annual affair, Ricky had told Walter, inaugurated by Edgar. "And we're gonna keep right on with these parties," Ricky had said. "Every Fourth of July. Daddy would want it that way."

Ricky, clad in cut-off jeans and running shoes, a beer in one hand, poked at the meat—a whole hog and a dozen chickens—while one of his buddies laid a sauce-soaked mop to the gray and black flesh. Ricky had introduced Walter to the buddies, but Walter could not remember any of their names. The cooker's lid smacked shut, dispersing the smoke, which gathered around Walter's head. His eyes burned as he futilely waved away at the cloud. He was on his sixth beer, firmly planted in a lawn chair beneath a skinny elm—the only shady spot in the ranch house's backyard. Despite the smoke, he did not consider moving.

The radio said that it was the hottest day of the summer. The temperature had been over ninety-five for nearly three weeks, and a hundred and two was predicted for this, the day of Ricky's grand summer party, the celebration of continuity and tradition. At least this was how Walter thought of it.

There was a multitude summoned on that Saturday afternoon. The younger men, the buddies, went about in Ricky's style; wrestler's haircuts, athletic builds, with tattoos and earrings here and there. A pack of them tried their hand at volleyball. Golden tanned, they leaped and fell and hooted in the mowed meadow beside the ranch house.

Beatrice's friends, fewer in number, had staked out the house. The men tensely viewed the Braves-Mets game, while the women occupied the kitchen, where they smoked and fussed with the cakes, pies, and special casseroles. Walter had listened to them briefly before creeping from the house. Beatrice had introduced him, but, as with Ricky's friends, he could not remember their names. None of them had paid much attention to him either—except for a silver-haired, soldierly-looking man in a western shirt and a bolo tie. He demanded, in a parade ground bark, Walter's opinion as to the Braves' chances for the season. Walter said that he was sure that the Braves deserved to win. He left the man with the bolo tie to consider the ramifications of his statement.

There were younger women; Star look-alikes who had arrived with Ricky's buddies. Not all of them were blond, but they sported that same aerobic-generated sense of health and youth as they went at the volleyball. There were a few children too, tended by their parents with kindly distraction. The children were all between two and nine years, and were not used to so much light and space. Yelping and darting, some of the older ones had disappeared in the direction of the river. Mothers, fussy in the heat, had herded them back.

The beer, which chilled in eight jumbo-sized kegs, was drained off at a workman-like rate. The beer provided comfort for Walter as he absorbed the scene around him. And there was much to be absorbed. Rich with visual incident, he thought. He had yet to see Star. Ricky had said that she had gone into Helmsville for more supplies. "She's got a list. Lots more folks on the way. We need plenty of everything." Ricky had said this over his shoulder as he trotted off to the volleyball game.

Not unlike a National Geographic Special, Walter

thought. And here I am; a visitor from another land, an observer of alien customs. Fun and educational. Then again, who am I to put them down? All those futile evenings at faculty parties, and the irritable sadness of cash bars at writer's conferences where everyone was furtive and constipated.

He smiled as the volleyballers cheered for a spike. They have the great gift; they are unselfconscious, he thought. Despite being like actors in a chewing gum or soft drink commercial. And they have bodies. On the outside, there is nothing low and sneaking about them. As he watched the game, Star came back in what would be his permanent image of her. For the journal, he had recorded her in a flat, matter-of-fact way. The title of that segment, *The Vision of Star*, was only half-ironic. Was it desire? Yes, fool, he wrote. And fear too. His account of her and her song had forced him into contemplation of the sexual part of his life. He had put it all down with a thoroughness that amused and depressed him. When he was eighteen there was the hooker that a sophomore friend had dared him to call. It had been clinical and correct, an obsolete, coming-of-age bit of nonsense in the middle of the last golden age of sex. Then there was the nearly accidental coupling with a French major from Mary Baldwin College at a three-day party. Her date, a besuited, arrogant U. Va law student had passed out and fouled his wool Brooks Brothers trousers, and Walter had appeared as the only alternative. There was an artist in New Hampshire, a heavy woman who went about in gypsy costume and whose studio was a shrine to decorative abstract expressionism. Eight in all, not counting two more hookers, one in London and one in Rome, back when I was inclined to real travel, he wrote. They were all about the same. He assumed that all of them, except for the hookers and his wife, for the first year or two, had come away from him with varying degrees of disappointment. After the last one, a divorced economics professor with two children who had insisted upon weekly midnight visits to his apartment, he had stopped completely. She had ended it by informing him that there was nothing there, meaning within him. "Why did you come to me?" he asked. "Curiosity," she said. "And now I'm no longer curious." That had been, to the best of his recollection, in 1988.

Star's song had stayed with him; he could not shake it. Temporary flight had seemed best. As he made his preparations, packing a few clothes and buying traveler's checks, he divined that it was not simply Star and the sun. I've been squatting here, he thought. Perhaps movement will un-stick me. I will go modestly, quickly. Obie agreed to check the house, and Walter left a note in Ricky's mailbox, quickly shoving it in early one morning before anyone was awake.

He turned south. He had made a little better than fifty miles before, with a start not unlike that which had possessed him at the sight of the naked Star, he realized that he was hard upon Margaret's old route from Helmsville to a perfect fantasy. He pulled off I-77 for breakfast at Great Falls, South Carolina. My journey, an historical re-creation, he told himself—a search for bitter, dun-colored roots. South was as good a direction as any.

In Columbia, he stopped at the university, the first time he had set foot there since graduation, and the first time on a college campus since his deliverance from Altgeld. Summer school was in session, and a few students, like those Walter had attempted to teach in other places, strolled and loafed. He roamed back and forth across the antebellum part of the campus for an hour and did not see a soul who could pass for a professor. Too smart to show themselves, he thought. Back in his truck, he took a last look. The campus, the old part, was as ordered and lovely as when he had first arrived there in another life. Yet they're only buildings, he thought, as he pulled back into the traffic. I was young here.

117

South lead in many directions, but the one he locked into made for Charleston. The morning after his arrival he was on Meeting Street before eight. The pavement steamed, the vapors rose and evaporated around his ankles as he glided purposefully along. Simmons' Antique Shop was easy to find. The last time he had been there was the afternoon of Margaret and Simmons' funeral. Through the furniture-crowded window, he could see the nephew, the rightful heir, who had taken over the business. He strongly resembled his uncle, right down to the blue seersucker jacket, oxford cloth shirt, and regimental tie. The nephew, stouter and graying, berated a clerk, a slim, young woman who labored to maintain a professional mien. How unfortunate, Walter thought as he rounded the corner to avoid any chance encounters with old faces. A breach of taste and responsibility. Simmons would've been shocked.

The house on the Battery, and Charleston too, had not changed in any obvious ways. Walter could not decide whether the city was genuine, or it had, by remaining forever the same, been inadvertently transformed into a theme park. It doesn't matter, he thought. I was young too in this theme park, or museum, or city. Or whatever it is.

He did a few of those things that Simmons, with Margaret's approval, had deemed indispensable for his role as apprentice Charlestonian. He ate she-crab soup and grits. He went to the market and covered all the streets on the lower end of the peninsula. He took the tour boat to Fort Sumter and sat on the open upper deck where it was cooler and where he would have a good view of the harbor. There were other tourists in the boat, most of them attached to a fair-sized group of Germans who stuck to their own language and snapped their cameras at every solid object, including the gulls who floated and swarmed around the little boat's stern all the way out to the fort.

As he neared Sumter, he speculated upon the effect that

neon signs and advertisements for solemn, shallow Civil War documentaries would have on the overall atmosphere. Too much, he thought, even for America. Ah, but we are reverent in some places; the memorials in Washington, or battlegrounds where we turn sheep-like victims into heroes for the ages. There must be a fine eloquence in this mass of chipped and shell-pocketed masonry. A recognizable relic. A disappointment to my Teutonic comrades? I hear that they, like us, are reverent at bloody shrines.

He did not bother to listen to the lecture by the Park Service Ranger. Simmons, grave and courteous, had lectured him on Sumter when he was eleven and newly-arrived. Without actually saying so, Simmons had imparted the conclusion that Sumter was made holy by blood and fire; Charleston's shrine of shrines. Simmons believed in sacred places. For a boy, the fort was small, but still a good place to climb and run. Simmons had taken Walter to Sumter a number of times and on sailboat voyages through the sea islands—all the while behaving as if he was performing a necessary, but pleasant duty. Margaret had occasionally gone along, but she preferred the shop, the three-story certifiably Charleston house, and lunches in expensive restaurants.

After the Ranger finished, Walter and the others were free to roam. He climbed to the grassy battlements that faced the harbor's mouth and the Atlantic beyond. A destroyer made its way seaward, lashing itself across the smooth, glassy summer water like it had somewhere important to be. At the base of the flag pole, the hot, salty wind pushed in on him. Simmons, during each visit, had told the fort's story; the first shots, the Union surrender, the Yankee fleet, self-righteous and yearning, encircling Sumter and pounding it to pieces with Dahlgren and Parrott guns—but never taking it. Simmons' ancestors had been there, two brothers who served as gunners. Their names were a part of

Simmons' lesson. At precisely the right moment in his speech, he would pause and plant his pale eyes on Walter as if to say "This is important. Do you understand?" On cue, Walter would nod. It all mattered so to Simmons—so impassioned, yet formal. And so ridiculous.

There was the sea. You could get to the Cape Verdes that way, Walter thought. Then Africa. North to Europe and the British Isles. I could get my passport renewed, twenty years out of date, buy a ticket, and be gone. Like Simmons and Margaret and Edgar. They firmly and arrogantly accepted as their right the ability to go where they pleased. And they did. They owned dreams and dwelt in the sure knowledge that those dreams, gaudy and lurid, would assume corporeal form. I have seldom indulged in dreams, delusions being more readily available.

Walter was the last on board. For the return voyage, he sat in the bow, Charleston, its churches, the temple-like houses of the Battery growing larger as he traversed the placid harbor. He left town that afternoon after a short, perfunctory halt at the cemetery where Margaret and Simmons lay. He crossed a creaking, rattling bridge and followed Highway 17 up the coast. He would go with that direction for a time. Two weeks later, after nights in hotels as far north as Norfolk and days of journal writing and driving, he returned. It was nearly Independence Day.

In the late afternoon more guests arrived and the party took on a slightly manic air. The pace of the volleyball game quickened, the players ripping, laughing, and lunging with less coordination and more sloppy abandon. Cars, jeeps, trucks, and motorcycles lined the road halfway to what Walter now called, in ironic deference to Ricky, The Old Home Place. Many of the new arrivals, like those who had come earlier, resembled Ricky and Star. Others were harder to classify. They were middle-aged, anonymous in knit shirts and baggy shorts, not quite belonging in the house, and certainly not new additions to the volleyball game. Perhaps they were Edgar's retainers, Walter thought. Or they owed him money. All crowded into the yard, moving past Walter without seeing him; he was secure in his island. He had once taken pleasure in crowds, sorting faces and gestures out of the mass, perceiving the development and evolution of patterns. When he wrote fiction, he had visited malls, ball games, and flea markets in a detached, scientific state of mind; he had gathered specimens and accumulated evidence in order to make his case. What bullshit, he thought, lifting his beer. Now it's purely for sport—and so much the better. He laughed at this and a trickle of foam ran down his chin and blotted his plain white T-shirt.

Obie and a fat girl crossed his line of sight. The girl was much younger than Obie, nineteen at the most. She was decked out in a cowgirl costume. Obie ambled over to Walter, the girl tagging along. She walked like Obie too—a rolling, shifting gait that produced a minimum of forward motion.

"How is it, Mr. Walter?" Obie asked. He was drinking milk from a quart carton. Walter said that he was fine and thanked Obie for picking up his mail while he was away—six bills and thirteen pieces of junk. The girl was named Paula. She said that she was having a real good time.

"How about you, Obie?" Walter asked.

"I always like a good party. This one though—it's big. Bigger than they used to be."

"When Edgar staged them?"

"Mr. Edgar slowed down some the last few years. So the parties wasn't quite as gala. Ricky told me that he's gonna change that."

"Looks like he did," Paula said. Could she be his daughter? Walter thought. It was hard to picture Obie with children.

"Me and Paula got to get a move on. Work to do." Obie touched the brim of his Stetson in a salute.

"Work?"

"Fun-type work, Mr. Walter. The fireworks show. Me and Ricky been planning and figuring a good while on this one."

Obie and Paula rolled off into the crowd and Walter drained his beer. And it'll be some show too, he thought. Fireworks. National holidays. They love shows in these environs.

"Look here." Walter found Roy Bunch standing over him. Bunch swayed slightly. A woman considerably older than Star, but resembling her in the dedication to physical perfection, hung on Bunch's arm. Bunch wore a short-sleeved white shirt and a tie that had been pulled down into a small, hard knot. The end of the tie, which was pale pink in color, hung over the fly of Bunch's baggy, unpressed blue pants. Bunch smiled. His teeth and skin were the same yellowish-gray color. He dropped heavily to the ground, right beside Walter's chair. The woman continued to stand. She smiled with a moderate degree of doubt and resignation, which Walter assumed had nothing to do with him. Bunch waved and pointed up at her.

"This is Faye. The love of my life. And this is…You're Ricky's half-brother. Got old man Loomis' place. But I can't…"

"Walter Loomis."

"Yeah. Faye, this is Loomis. Walter. Have a seat."

"I'm afraid of grass stains, Roy. Maybe you could find me a chair."

Faye was elaborately gotten up in a silky, pastel-printed jumpsuit and high heels. A country and western singer, Walter thought. Her heavy, expertly applied make-up, and the curled and peaked hair gave no sign of wilting in the heat.

"A vision of loveliness," Walter said. He was a few degrees less drunk than Bunch.

"Hear that Faye?" Bunch asked, lighting a Winston. "This guy knows what he's talking about."

She thanked Walter for the compliment, and he offered her his chair. After the usual protestations on Faye's part, she accepted. Walter flopped into the grass next to Bunch, where the insects climbed and swarmed. Most of them were attracted to Bunch, who seemed unaware of their biting, flitting presence.

"Can I fetch food, alcohol?" Walter asked. He thought it necessary to be hospitable here on his little island.

"I'm fine. Really." Faye held up an orange-flavored Perrier.

"She likes that shit," Bunch said. "But I won't argue with her about it. I should be drinking it myself. But since I was coming to a party, a Fourth of July party at the Loomis estate, I had to get off the wagon. Hell, it's been two months. I got a right, don't I Faye?"

"You told me that you wouldn't be doing it heavy. That's what you said, wasn't it Roy, honey?" Bunch frowned up at her.

"I'm taking it easy. Or I will, maybe not right away. But soon."

"I hope so. I'd hate to think you'd get like you was the last time."

As the crowd grew, its chattering elevated itself to a level that competed with the heavy metal music that cranked out of Ricky's "great new sound system," as he called it. Walter glimpsed Star hauling bags of groceries from the van, assisted by three of Ricky's chiseled, steroid-inflated buddies. As for Ricky, Walter could hear him in intermittent blurts above the cacophony as he spiked the ball and rushed back, whooping, to examine the meat.

"A hell of a scene, eh Professor?" Bunch asked. "Excuse

me. I'd forgotten that you fell out of that line. What *are* you now? Gentleman farmer?" Walter laughed.

"If anything, I'd say a gentleman of leisure."

"Damn. I'm envious. Leisure. That's a concept."

"You have your leisure, Roy honey," Faye said. "I've watched you be leisurely for years."

"Faye believes in hard, hard work."

"Are you two...married?" Faye and Bunch laughed.

"We just go around together now and then," Faye said.

"You could, if you had to put it in words, which I'm trying to do, say that. Yes, Faye," Bunch went on. "That's as good as any way to say it. Go around together. Round and round. Like a goddamn top. Tell me Walter, what about our repartée? Good or what? You're a writer. A man of letters, besides being a gentleman of leisure. Give us feedback, please. As the saying goes."

"Thought-provoking," Walter said. "Very thought-provoking."

"I know it," Bunch said. A swarm of gnats frisked around his head, a few flying in and out of his mouth.

"A writer?" Faye asked. "Books?"

"Yes. I was a writer, but no more."

"Man of letters, retired," Bunch said. "You've given us your testament, so you're gonna stop. Like Rimbaud."

"Who?" Faye politely asked.

"A dead guy," Bunch answered. "A French dead guy. How come you'd stop writing? You got too much money now?"

"That must be it," Walter said. Rimbaud is it, he thought. And pointed questions.

Bunch wiped his mouth with the back of his hand. He was dripping sweat and rings of tiny bites covered his arms and face. Walter had bites too, but not as many. Walter scratched away. Bunch acted as if the bites were not even there.

"Fiction," Bunch spat. "It's all fiction."

Faye excused herself to feed at a table that was laden with dips, salsa, chips in various forms, and fly-molested fruit. Star emerged, marching back and forth between the ranch house and the tables, laying out provisions before departing once more in the van. The party-goers, hungry, thirsty and hot, pressed forward as Beatrice and the women from the kitchen bore forth cakes, pies, and steaming bowls. Faye, delicately, with lady-like grace, chewed a carrot, one finger crooked.

"She's a damn good woman," Bunch said. "I don't understand why she bothers with me. Must be the sex appeal."

"She's very nice," Walter said.

"Nice. That too. And it's better than some alternatives. So if you're a gentleman of leisure, what do you do—if you don't write. What are you? Thoreau without all his ideas about how to be a crank?"

"I haven't decided."

"The contemplative life. Like Thoreau. But not Rimbaud. The names rhyme. You ever realized that?"

"Some of my former colleagues could probably get an article out of that. Real precedent-setting stuff."

"As a member of the bar, I love precedents."

Ricky had begun to empty the cooker, spearing chickens, loins, and hams and tossing them onto platters.

"I haven't heard mention of Thoreau and Rimbaud in some time," Walter said.

"Not an element of the conversational fodder here-abouts. Names from college. There was Whitman and Hemingway, Virginia Woolf, and Dylan Thomas—Do not go gentle into that good night. Rage, rage and so on. These things are etched in my memory, along with lyrics from imbecilic songs and commercial slogans. I'm not quite a modern man. Most people don't remember anything. They are blessed that way."

"Blessed?"

"Think about it."

"Tell me, Ricky and Obie, he's the hired hand, say that the party is an annual event. Edgar—my father—used to put it on. Did you come to any of those parties?"

"Not me. Wasn't invited. From what I used to hear around the court house, the parties were legendary. Reagan was supposed to have been here once, but not when he was president. He was a mere patriot then, traveling the land, spreading the gospel. He made a speech, I understand. And ate only cottage cheese and fresh fruit. And there were other luminaries. Senators and other political shapes. High-ranking military men. These are the stories."

"Did Edgar say much to you about these...luminaries?"

"Our relationship was strictly business. Why do you care?"

"I'm not sure."

"Family history." Bunch drank deeply and belched with satisfaction.

It was dark before Bunch and Walter got anything to eat. At the tables, they found a mess. Crudely chopped hunks of pork, and not many of them, stained the heavy steel platters. Walter dropped a few hunks onto a paper plate, while Bunch dipped the pork into the half-inch of sauce that sloshed in the bottom of a pan. The sweets and casseroles had been consumed, leaving only gummed-up plates and spattered bowls. The cooker glowed with its last embers. The other revellers had migrated deeper into the backyard, where the band hired for the evening cranked out country and western and top forty rock and roll. Dancers stomped in the wet haze, which filled the lungs like a cream soup of kudzu and larvae.

"Good," Bunch said, wiping his hands on his pants.

"Remind me to tell Ricky what a wonderful cook he is. A hidden talent. And where the fuck could Faye be?" Bunch did not ask the question to anyone in particular and Walter did not respond.

"She'll show up," Bunch said. "Or she won't. Such is the nature of our relationship. What a terrible word—relationship." Bunch bit deeply into a piece of fatty pork. In the shadows, it seemed an unnameable mass, a blob that rose and fell from Bunch's face. Walter chewed a few gritty, coarse mouthfuls. It tasted like it had been rolled in dirt before being smoked, scorched and basted. Figures passed in the darkness, coming and going as the band approximated Garth Brooks. Then he realized that Bunch was gone.

Walter considered a search, but drew another beer instead. Those who stood by the keg laughed and joked about what a good time they were having. "We partying like niggers," a woman said to general hilarity. A shirtless muscle buddy held a keg aloft and poured the dregs over his face and into his mouth. As Walter turned from these innocent pleasures, Bunch moved into view. Through the brightness of the flood-lit front yard, amid Beatrice's animals and dwarfs, Faye supported Bunch as they inched and hobbled toward the cars. Bunch's mouth was moving, but at that distance, and against the noise of the band, Walter could not hear the words. Faye patted Bunch on the back, affectionate, maternal, and helped him into the old Ford. Walter was relieved to see that she was driving his car.

"There he goes," someone said. "Roy Bunch, attorney at law. My sister had him for a divorce years ago. She said that Bunch was a real trip." It had to be Star.

"Having a good time?" she asked. She smoked a very long cigarette. It could have been mistaken for a wand.

"I was just leaving." He did not, however, take a single step toward The Old Home Place.

"Not yet. I've been meaning to talk to you. Alone. You

were with Bunch and he had your full attention. He doesn't
get anyone's full attention as much as he likes." She took his
cup and pumped it full. He nearly bummed a cigarette, finding himself in need of a wand of his own.

"That book of yours—the first one with the stories in it.
I finished it yesterday. I haven't had a chance to read the
next two. This damn party has taken up most of my time."

"I don't remember much about that book, to tell the
truth." And, he thought, you haven't had any time for arias
in the canebrake, either.

"Don't be modest."

She took his hand and led him through the party. He
went without protest. She had two lawn chairs situated on a
small rise to the rear of the hopping, dancing crowd. Did she
arrange it this way? he thought. Her hand was small and
cool, and from the rise the band, dancers, and loiterers
appeared to be at their feet. Like a king and queen, he
thought. Oh, God.

She wanted to tell him things, and there the music was
not so overpowering. Still, she was forced to lean against
him, shouting into his ear.

"Why did you write that story about Paris? The one in
1885, I think you said. The one with that real mean detective who hates the man whose head is a cabbage?"

Dimly, feebly, the story came back to Walter. He had
been twenty-five, twenty-six when he wrote it; a parody, like
all else, intentional or otherwise, that he had ever done. This
one was his version of Poe's Auguste Dupin. My detective,
he recalled, was not a logician, but a badly failed wizard. Or
bullshit to that effect.

"I don't know," he half shouted. "It seemed like a good
idea at the time."

Her face went blank at his words, and, with a surge of
uneasiness, he pictured her singing again. Her proximity, her
breath in his ear, had undone him a little.

"When I wrote it," he said, "I wanted it to be funny. The detective and the man with the cabbage head...interested me."

Inexplicably, this answer satisfied her more than the first—but not enough to keep her from asking more questions.

"What about that other story? The one about the man who built model airplanes all the time. How he's working and working on them. And that was all he did. He didn't have a real job, and his wife was in the next room all the time with that guy named Carl. They were having sex, I guess. You never did say for sure. While the other guy goes on with the airplanes. I didn't understand that one, but I enjoyed reading it."

"Then that was enough," he said in his best writer's conference voice, which he had not thought that he had in him any more. And she had not asked him what the goddamn stories were about. To his relief, she was once again satisfied with his response. She leaned back, her slim legs thrust in front of her. He tried not to stare at them. Inevitably, she started again.

"I guess I liked them all. Even the one about the people at the party trying to kill themselves. I'd never thought of that. Holding bullets in pliers up next to their heads and heating them with cigarette lighters. It was pretty sick, but that's how things can get. I could see it happening."

"It did happen. I got the idea from the newspaper." What was that one's name, he thought. Oh yeah "How Would You Like to Be Him." That was it. I was, amazingly enough, proud of it. I would've been. Back when I was naive enough to believe that words, fictions, could shock or enrage. More foolishness.

"I thought it had," Star shouted over a drunken, incompetent guitar solo. "I liked the part where a bullet went off and broke that man's jaw. That made the rest of them quit—

did they see how stupid and crazy they were? Things like that go on all the time. Do you think that it could happen at this party?"

Her question disturbed Walter. It was not appropriate for a woman who would sing naked in the woods.

"I don't...I don't know. You probably understand your friends better than I do."

"Friends. That's a good one. Look at them."

A fat man, shirtless and fearfully drunk, sang along with the band; a discordant, slurred version of George Jones' "He Stopped Loving Her Today." The tricky, bizarrely maudlin lyrics filtered through a sheet of slobber and beer that hung and shimmied from the man's mouth. His torso, dominated by a belly that should have been supported by a harness, was powerful—lard and muscle and hair. Ricky came out of the crowd and joined the fat man and the band. He held aloft a lighted Roman candle as he transformed the performance into a duet. Ricky did not know the lyrics, so he hummed with the fat man who began to cry as he reached the middle of the song. The Roman candle disgorged its red and green balls almost in time with the music.

"Life could imitate art," Walter said.

"Yeah. Nothing would surprise me. You don't know him, the guy singing, do you?"

"I don't know anyone."

"His name's Skipper Talley. Ricky and Edgar loved him. Ricky still does. I don't know why. He's an old drunk, that's all. He tried to court Beatrice years ago, they say. Before Ricky was born. She wouldn't get near him. He used to hunt with Ricky and Edgar, but he's too stove up for that now. Can barely walk. He sings every year."

"Roy Bunch told me that Ronald Reagan came here once. And senators and famous people."

"Bunch said that? Edgar talked about those days. How honored he was. He would say 'I've been among the greats.'"

Since I've been out here, I haven't seen anybody that great. Richard Petty was supposed to be here one time, but that was nothing but a rumor. What I've been wanting to ask you about is some more stories. I know lots of them about all kinds of people around here. What if I told you and you wrote them down?"

"I don't know. I haven't given much thought to fiction in...some time."

She patted his arm as if he was afflicted.

Skipper Talley was led away and the band went on without him. The crowd sprawled across the backyard and into the meadow, half drained by its revels. A few couples danced on and Ricky came up to the rise. His chest was streaked with soot and grease and his eyes had a faraway, traumatized sheen to them. He embraced Star, who kissed him chastely on the cheek. When he embraced Walter, he slipped and the two of them nearly tipped over.

"Brother man! Where the fuck you been?"

"Here," Walter said with some alarm. "At your party."

"A hell of a thing it is. But no, where have you been the last two weeks? You didn't say nothing about where you were going."

"Charleston. Columbia. A few other places."

Ricky squatted beside him, hunkered low, like an aborigine.

"Tell me about it. Who'd you stay with?"

"No one."

"Man," Ricky said. "I couldn't do that."

"He might've wanted it that way," Star said, a trace of irritation in her voice.

"I ain't disputing that." Ricky, unlike Walter, could not hear how Star sounded.

"A short trip. That's all," Walter said.

"Whatever. You heard about the fireworks show? The biggest that's ever been seen. An old friend of mine sold me

131

some *professional* displays. We got a shitload of Roman can-
dles and sky rockets, but we got more powerful stuff too.
Yes sir."

"That's wonderful," Walter said.

"Sit back and relax. It's about to start." Ricky trotted off
into the darkness.

"He can hardly wait," Star said. "Been planning it...well
since not long after Edgar died."

"And Obie too? He told me about the show."

"He's the one that sets the things off. They're big, too.
Mortars, they're called. It used to be whatever they could
pick up down in South Carolina. Ricky wanted it to be
extral special this time. And Ricky...you'll just have to see
what he does. It's kinda pretty, in a tacky way." She pointed
toward the meadow and the barn. "It's gonna be over that
way."

They shifted their chairs around for a better view, as the
guests below spread their blankets or reclined on the
ground—like small-town Americans in a Norman Rockwell
version of Independence Day. Heat and insects aside, Walter
had to admit that he was impressed with the setting. There
were few lights to mar the full effect of whatever grandiosi-
ty Ricky and Obie could attain. And does Star sing as part
of the show? Walter thought. That's not an image to dwell
upon.

"There he comes," someone yelled.

Ricky, attired in chaps, buckskin vest, and Stetson, galloped out of the dark. He was mounted on Hickory, and
nearly rode into the guests before he halted. Those closest to
the edge of the meadow scrambled backwards amid shouts
and good-natured catcalls.

"Ladies and gentlemen!" Ricky cried, waving his hat like
an outer-space version of Buffalo Bill Cody. "Welcome to the
thirtieth annual Loomis fireworks presentation."

"Your Daddy made up those words," Star said. "Ricky

and Beatrice spent a lot of last night trying to remember them. Ricky wrote down what he guessed was right."

"...the greatest nation in the history of everything that's been. We got a lot to be grateful for, and it'll keep on that way as long as we don't forget what matters, or let our guard down or act like we don't have any sense—and all those things can be problems, which ain't exactly news..."

"That's *not* how Edgar put it," Star said. "It's the best Ricky can do, though."

Hickory pranced and whinnied and Ricky tightened the reins before going on. Walter was positive that he had never seen or heard anything like it.

"...back then when our forefathers WHIPPED THE ASS OFF THE BRITISH we set aside this day. To make ourselves understand...ASS-WHIPPING." The crowd clapped and cheered each time the word ass came up in the speech.

"...and we been WHIPPING ASS ever since. But we ain't mean people. Oh, hell no. We're peaceful and good and smart and that's how come we're here tonight."

Reverently, Ricky dropped his delivery into a lower register. His words were, however, sharp and clear.

"...and tonight we gonna pay tribute to my Daddy, Mr. Edgar Loomis. He's gone, but we gonna keep right on rocking. We'll never be able to replace him, but we're gonna go on and on..." A plaintive throb welled up in Ricky's throat. Don't cry, Walter thought. Say it all.

"...and while we're going on, we gonna think about America and my Daddy and all we got and that we're gonna get. So help us God. Amen."

There was silence as Ricky and Hickory wheeled off through the meadow. Applause followed. Walter clapped loud and long, stopping only when he realized that Star was eyeing him. She had not clapped at all.

"What's next?" Walter asked. Before Star could reply, a single rocket climbed high, then blossomed over the barn. As

133

its last embers fell and died, an entire barrage of larger, more powerful rockets zoomed off from their unseen launching point. There had been fireworks on the Battery in Charleston when Walter was a boy, but Ricky and Obie's production was at alarmingly close range. Walter jerked slightly with each new explosion, as if the rockets were aimed right at him.

One round followed another, the rockets joined by the mortars, which discharged what resembled flaming basketballs. The whole end of the farm—meadow, barn, ranch house, and trees—was illuminated in green, gold, red, blue, silver, and white, all in burning metallic. The explosions echoed off of each other, combining into one continuous blast. Everyone ooohed and aaahed at the appropriate time. Neither Walter nor Star spoke. It was far too loud.

Ricky was in the meadow, bathed in the colors, racing Hickory up and down, thudding to sudden stops, causing the horse to rear up on its hind legs. Walter could not take his eyes off of him. Ricky had attained a pure, transcendent senselessness; incoherent speeches, shining bombs, wild horses and all. He is sanctified, Walter thought. The laughter came then, and Walter shook with it amid the detonations.

"What's funny?" Star yelled.

Ricky was still at it, putting himself and Hickory through the loopy, half-burlesque, half-serious routine. There was more applause, but it was faint in the crash of bombs and rockets. And then there was a thing altogether unexpected. A column of colors mushroomed upward, creating a greater light than had yet been seen. Ricky pulled up, gaping toward the barn, and the shock wave followed, bending man and horse as if in a high wind. The wave hit the rise; then, a half a second later, the assembled guests were immersed in it. Walter and Star went over, rolling down the slight incline. The light did not diminish and new waves came on, along with more fireballs, slashing and dancing everywhere at once. Pieces of things filled the air.

Walter ended up on his back, the fireballs racing over him like cartoon shooting stars. He got to his feet, stumbling and crouching. Star was nowhere in sight, but he did not think of her. There was a single necessity; escape the light and fire.

As he slithered away, he found himself in a tangle of the cursing, the gasping, the weeping, and the drunk. Some of them, their faces bent in ways that Walter had never before seen, smoldered and glowed, having been struck high and low. The ground glowed too, and the skinny tree that Walter and Bunch had sat under ignited all at once. A sign, Walter somehow managed to think, as the embers and branches swam above his head. A bad sign. Directions were clear, however; the far side of the ranch house, the gnome and deer garden of Beatrice. This much was clear to Walter and those who retained enough consciousness to wriggle toward shelter.

Skipper Talley wallowed along on all fours. Walter thudded into him, but kept his feet. Remaining even partially upright was both a necessity and a victory. This was as much as Walter knew; Skipper Talley may still have been singing. As Walter got closer to the house, he gained a sidelong awareness of other crawling figures, too hurt to go upright. They did not have faces as far as Walter could tell. The race, with the fireballs and flames at their backs, seemed endless. There were screams and howls as the projectiles struck home. But the cursing and yapping had ceased—and there was almost no sense of movement. The house, so close before, could have been miles off.

Walter, his throat dried to cracking, crazily brushing embers from his head and arms, finally rounded the corner

135

of the ranch house and found Beatrice. The explosions had had an electrical effect; her hair stood straight up.

"What...what happened?" she asked, the pair of them pressed against a brick wall, huddled behind the azaleas. Walter, his head clearing slightly, saw that the fireballs were still raining down, but had lessened in frequency. Whatever lay beyond the meadow was playing itself out.

"What happened?" she asked again. Walter shook his head.

"An...event." He was startled by the even, matter-of-fact, absurd description. She nodded as if he had given the correct answer.

Many had dropped, panting and moaning, to the ground. A blue fireball struck the roof and showered sparks and embers. Most did not move, but some raced in circles before falling again, covering their heads with their hands. Some made for the cars, trying to take their leave to the whine of grinding gears, metal on metal, smashed fenders and bumpers. A green fireball bounced off the roof of a Z-28 and its flash revealed two of the muscle buddies from the volleyball net. They fled from the cars, sprinting up the road toward the highway. Whoever drove the Z-28 backed into a ditch; the headlights pointed straight up, as if proclaiming the premiere of some unimaginable film.

"It's never been like this before," Beatrice said. "Not when Edgar ran things. It was beautiful then. Who are you?" Her tone was polite, distracted, and she was more dazed than Walter first thought. He told her his name.

"Oh yes. Well..." She was out of words, for the time being, and Walter took the opportunity to get away from her.

Someone had turned on a garden hose and was sluicing down those who smoldered. Walter stepped into the spray and was soon dripping with blessed coolness. The light had receded further, and the blasts were fainter, without their earlier power. Walter's ears hurt, and he had a few slight burns, but after checking himself, he found no other injuries.

Star manned the hose. At first, Walter had not realized who was wetting him down, and he asked if he could help. She told him to call the fire department, the hospital, and anyone else he could think of. She was efficient and detached, as if she was a veteran of such debacles.

The interior of the ranch house, packed with the accumulated possessions of Beatrice and Ricky, was, at first, unfamiliar. This was because the furniture, the shoes, and the rest of it, had shifted and tumbled. Beatrice's friends, including the soldierly man in the bolo tie, who appeared to be in the throes of a stroke, wailed and keened. Walter got to the telephone and called 911. Just to be safe, he called the hospital and fire department separately. The dispatcher at the local volunteer company said that trucks, from all over, were on the way, that some had started before the calls came in because the first explosions were visible from miles off. As Walter hung up, faint sirens reached him. From the kitchen window, he could see the cheerful blaze of the barn. Other fires were dotted in a half moon configuration around the meadow and among the closest stands of pine. With surprising objectivity, he considered the possibility of the fire reaching the deeper woods and The Old Home Place. It *is* an event, he thought.

He directed the paramedics to the soldierly man, who quaked and rolled his eyes on the living room floor. Outside, Star had turned the hose on Skipper Talley, who remained on all fours, emitting sharp, doggish barks of near-erotic relief. There were no more fireballs—just the flames, floodlights, and the assorted lights from fire trucks, ambulances, and police cars.

"What happened?" Ricky asked. He was singed red and black, the hair gone from one side of his head. And he was unhorsed. Beatrice had asked the same question, Walter recalled. None of us, he thought, truly wish to review the evidence.

"Where's Hickory?" Star asked, still hosing down Skipper Talley.

"Threw me. That's never happened before. Hell, I was the only one who could handle him. Goddamn horse. Threw me and ran for the fire."

"Where's Obie?" Star asked.

"He was in the middle of it. It got...all wrong. We had it set up just the way Daddy used to do it. Only...I don't know."

"That's *not* the way Edgar did it." Beatrice had emerged from the azaleas and her expression, the rigidity of her stance, made Walter uneasy. There are those here, he thought, who may wish to ascribe blame.

"Edgar had the right touch. You *never* have," Beatrice hissed.

"Momma." Ricky went no further. He dropped his hands to his sides and stared at the ground.

"Never have, never will. Goddamn you!" She went at him, slapping him hard across the face, first with one hand, and then with the other. Ricky stood and took it, as if it were only justice. Some of the remaining guests gathered, watching—like this was the last act of the evening's entertainment. It went on until two of Ricky's buddies stepped in and grabbed Beatrice, forcing her back. Wordlessly, Ricky marched back toward the flames, out of the floodlights and the clusters of the injured. Walter was curious as to where he was going, but it wasn't in him to follow.

9

There were repercussions, and they began at once. The barn burned down to the foundation; nothing of it stood in the hot, Sunday dawn. Walter, Star, Beatrice, and Skipper Talley, who was oddly sober, tramped around the ruins, inhaling the fumes from incinerated horse flesh. Every animal, all twelve of them, and Hickory besides, had been consumed. Their bones and skulls protruded from their hides—white, black-streaked, dull red—their teeth set in permanent grins.

"A hell of a thing," Skipper Talley kept saying—until Beatrice, her hair still on end asked him to please shut up.

"Yes, ma'am," he burped. "I'll do that." He looked off in the direction of the firemen. They came from nine separate companies and several had sworn to Walter that the Event was the worst call that they had ever answered.

Walter had not slept. There was too much motion, too much to attend to. Sixteen revelers—muscle boys, Beatrice's friends, those unfortunate enough to have attended Ricky Loomis' Fourth of July Gala, were in the hospital—mostly for burns and broken bones inflicted in fleeing from the fireballs. The soldierly man in the bolo tie had indeed had a stroke, but he lived. One had died.

Paula, Obie's cowgirl sweetheart, had told her story. Her costume had been reduced to smudged rags, and her ankles were badly sprained—blue, purple, and swollen into lumps.

139

But hers was a story that she had to tell, seated in the candle-lit ranch house kitchen, to the proper authorities, who, as Sheriff Peavey put it, "deemed an investigation to be necessary." Walter, propped against a counter, had been in the audience. He found Paula's tale as terrible as that instant when the fireballs rained upon his head.

There was, Paula said in her tiny, weepy voice, a great big pile of mortars and rockets right in the middle of the barn, in the space where the rows of stalls faced each other. And there were more out in the tack room. Obie had told her that Ricky had paid over fifteen thousand for the fireworks, including special types designed for the show. There was one that was extra special—it was supposed to spell out Mr. Edgar's name in the sky. They were saving it for the very end. There were so many that she and Obie had to keep hauling them out and lining them up where they were to be fired—to a point about thirty yards from the barn. Ricky had ridden up right before they were to start and told them to use every last mortar and rocket. Paula said that Ricky could have been drunk. He was nice, like usual, but he was real excited too. Obie said that he needed help, but Ricky kept going on about how he had to ride and about how Obie understood the plan. Obie asked what plan was that? Ricky laughed and Obie said that he would do his best, that being what Obie said a lot of the time.

"I loved him, you know," Paula sniffed. "He was a fine man."

Paula was not quite sure how it happened. After Ricky galloped off, and the show was going good, Obie went back to the barn, holding one of the emergency flares that he used to set off what he called the displays. "He musta forgot," Paula choked. "He was enjoying himself—like a kid. The last I seen of him, he was laughing."

Obie had told her about the flares. There was a box of them in the barn. The man that Ricky had gotten all those bombs from said that flares burned for a long time and that they were best for producing "a continuous fusillade." Obie had gotten a kick out of "continuous fusillade." Every time he set off another mortar, he would say it.

"Like…'there goes another continuous fusillade.' Oh Lord, he was having such a good time."

Obie had told her that he had not used flares in the past. Plain old matches had been fine, but Ricky wanted this show to be professional. So Obie went back to the barn. There must have been forty or fifty mortars there then, the biggest and best—the ones Ricky wanted saved for the last.

"They was the ones that did it," Paula said as she began to cry in full force. Sheriff Peavey handed her a handkerchief. He was tall, and amorphous, with a bulldog face. He patted her on the shoulder until she could resume her story, a story Walter bet would be the only one she would know for as long as she lived. Beatrice, who had been listening closely, handed her a glass of water. Some, there were a number of others beside the family and the law considering Paula's story, had questions as to the whereabouts of that damn Ricky. Beatrice, grim-faced, asked the same question. Walter caught Star's eye and she looked away. He better be far away, Walter had thought then.

Paula had ignited a few of the mortars herself—Obie had showed her how—and was about to set off a few more before helping Obie drag the big ones out to the firing line. She was having a real good time, she said—once she got used to the booms. And it was all so pretty. She had wished she had a videotape of that night—until it all changed. She had her back to the barn, admiring how well Ricky handled Hickory, who was one beautiful, but mean horse, when it got as light as day time and hotter than she had ever known. And she was picked up and thrown—like a great big hand had tossed her. When she came down, she was halfway into the meadow—with fire racing all around her.

141

"Some was above me. Some cut along the ground. They was like...the Devil's eyeballs."

The image sums it all up pretty well, Walter thought.

She lay there a minute, but had to get up and run. The heat was awful. It mighta started in the barn, she said, and it ate up all the air there was. When she stood, she found out that her ankles were torn up pretty bad. She ran and ran anyway, the fireballs slapping into her, she said. She was out near the highway before she understood that her back was burning some and that she ought to get some help. From that distance, she had a good view of the bursting, blazing barn.

"I seen then that there wasn't no chance for Obie."

At that point, Paula's story could go no further. She wept in one sustained gush, the tears cutting canals in her puffy, sooty cheeks. Star led her to a bedroom and made her lie down. Her keening, however, was quite audible in the kitchen. Peavey's chief deputy, trim and athletic, with a two-dimensional face, said that Paula told one hell of a story. Peavey said that that was all for now, but there were other witnesses to be interviewed. He would, he drawled, be back later. As he departed, his phalanx of deputies before him, he also said that he very much wanted a word with Ricky Loomis.

"There's been somebody like Peavey wanting to discuss things with Ricky for always," Beatrice said after the sheriff and his boys had clanked away. Walter had started to ask her why, but it had not seemed like the best time.

A boot was all that could be discovered of Obie. The heel was torn off, but the rest was amazingly intact. A fireman told Walter that there was a foot, a sock, and part of an ankle inside, but there was no good reason to see it—unless you have an interest in that kind of thing. Walter identified the boot—a snakeskin model—before the fireman stowed it in a plastic bag.

The boot had been found not far from the crater, which was about twenty feet across and seven feet deep, gouged out of the concrete foundation, chunks of which, mingled with timbers, shingles, boarding, stable equipment and portions of horse, lay all over. Some of it had been hurled into the ranch house itself—blown through windows, or bored through the roof and walls. Walter hoped, even offered up a short prayer, that Obie had not had an inkling of what was to come.

"He dropped the flare. Just like Paula told it. It fits," Star said, peering into the crater. She had barely spoken to Walter since soliciting him about her literary ambitions. "And before he had a chance to pick it up, it happened," she concluded, like a television detective wrapping up a case before the final commercial.

"Poor old Obie," Skipper Talley said, having returned from watching the firemen roll up their hoses. "He sure ain't going squirrel hunting with me in the fall."

"Fool," Beatrice said. "Fools all around here." She stomped away.

"What'd I say?" Skipper Tally thoughtfully rubbed his white and red mottled gut.

"Forget it," Star said. "Go on home."

"Poor old Obie. There wasn't nobody else like him. I'm gonna go find out if my truck will run." Talking to himself, he waddled across the smoking meadow grass, stepping around the jagged lumps of barn, toward the scarred ranch house. There was not a single intact window on the side facing the barn.

"God, this place stinks," Star said.

"Star, where's Ricky? Did he..."

"Get himself killed too? Not him. He comes through every time."

"Why isn't he here?"

"That's his way. He'll show up, though. Not for awhile, maybe. But he'll be back. He doesn't know anywhere else to go."

"This is a disaster."

"Is that what it is? A mess, anyhow. We'll be cleaning up for a long time. If anybody can figure out how to get it done."

"Will you miss Obie?"

Star smiled at Walter's question. "Like Skipper will? Oh, yeah. Obie was real unique. You ever see where he lived? Where the tack room used to be. Pink and teal and lace curtains."

One of the first days I was here, Walter thought. Right now, it feels like I've never been anywhere else.

The Old Home Place, that sturdy stockade of Loomis power, tradition, and endurance, had come through remarkably well. Walter plugged the few broken window panes with cardboard torn from boxes. He even had electricity—unlike the ranch house. Some books and plates had been toppled from their shelves, but all else seemed to be in order. If it's not, he thought as he showered, I'll find out later. He was as exhausted as he had ever been. There was a task, however, that he forced himself to complete. In the journal he wrote: "Ricky's special celebration—an event that will live forever. I put down these lines without the slightest trace of irony. More on this later." He closed the journal and was out before his head settled on the pillow.

They slowly infiltrated his sleep—creakings, rustlings, and feathery, careful footsteps. He resisted awakening, the discovery of more of the unexpected. The fear descended upon him when his name was whispered. He catapulted straight up, standing erect beside the bed before he was fully awake, naked in the moonlight that washed into the room. A shape filled the doorway, summoning him—croaking, broken.

"Walt, man." The shape was Ricky. He inched into the room, heralded by the smell—pork, sweat, and smoke. Walter, for a revulsion-filled, semiconscious second, thought that Ricky might embrace him, as he had done at the party, before the Event, and that they would reel back into the bed—a single shape.

"Yes." Walter forced himself to say, as if Ricky's arrival was perfectly normal. "You're here. Go to the kitchen."

After dressing, he found Ricky hunched over the kitchen sink, drinking directly from the faucet. Under the light, Ricky's appearance was slightly more ghastly than the last time Walter had glimpsed him; dirtier, with mud caked over his shoes, smeared up his shanks and thighs, blotting his torso.

Ricky satisfied his thirst, yanked a pack of sliced ham from the refrigerator, and ate noisily. It was past ten by the clock on the stove and time, Walter thought, for a beer.

"Tired, huh?" Ricky asked between mouthfuls.

"From the Event."

"The what?"

"The Event. The explosion."

Ricky sighed. "Yeah. I really knew that." He sat down across the table from Walter and rubbed his face, kneading the flesh—which appeared devoid of elasticity. Abruptly, he ceased his rubbings.

"I'm dirty, Walt. Dirty as shit."

"You can shower if you want."

"That might be what I need. Give me a new outlook. You been wondering where I was?"

"It's been the subject of some talk."

Ricky demanded the names of those who had done this talking, and Walter told him all of it—about Paula, Beatrice, the survivors of the Event and the firemen. About how Sheriff Peavey would be paying future visits. About the discovery of what remained of Obie. When Walter concluded his recitation, Ricky began to rub again.

"It wasn't supposed to be that way. I swear it. I wanted...the best Fourth of July ever. One that wouldn't be forgotten..."

Walter was kind enough not to remind him that this particular Fourth would be discussed for some time to come.

"...that's bad about Obie," Ricky said. "God, I loved that little dude. When it hit, when Hickory throwed me, the barn roof went right up. A wall just...disappeared in front of me. I tried to get to Obie...that fire. I think that's when I lost my hair." He gently rubbed the battered, scalped-looking portion of his head. To Walter, Ricky's new hairdo was particularly hideous, giving him a skinned, raw chicken-like aspect.

"Ricky, where have you been?"

"Oh." Ricky looked hurt, as if it was beneath Walter to ask such a question at such a time. Walter did not press him, but Ricky went on. He never fails to explain, Walter thought.

"You know how I am. Took to the woods. Whenever things been bad, that's where I go. The woods got a quality we'll never have—human beings that is. Daddy said it was peace and grace. He taught me that. To tell the truth, I was at his resting place. I went there naturally, by instinct you could say. I talked to him, too. Don't think that I'm crazy or nothing. I talk to him a lot. Even if he ain't here in body. It's his spirit. And he'll talk back—I wouldn't call it a conversation though—I feel his words coming into me. What about that? You believe me?" Ricky begged with his dark feverish eyes. Walter was awake enough now to be properly diplomatic.

"That's not for me to say. If it happened, it happened." The answer pleased Ricky.

"You understand. That's from the blood we got between

146

us. If you got in trouble, you'd go down to his resting place, wouldn't you? I ain't saying you'd *talk* to him, but being there would make you feel better, I bet."

"Perhaps." Could Ricky appreciate my flight from Edgar's memorial? he thought.

"It was weird, Walt. Truly strange. When I got there, I was hurting all over—especially where my hair got burned off. I couldn't figure out what to do next. When Momma come at me that way—you were there—it tore me up. Having my Momma do like that on account of what happened. Which was beyond my control. Totally. Which don't mean that I won't take some responsibility. I accept that. I understand. And I'm sorry about it. I wanted what was best, and it didn't work out..."

Walter considered Ricky's words, trying to determine where he had heard them, or similar words, before. As Ricky droned on, developing his arguments for responsibility and forgiveness, Walter discerned a pattern; talk show guests—the ones who married thirteen-year-old girls, or practiced Satanism, or murdered their parents because they had been denied a new car. They all wanted understanding and forgiveness regardless of the stupid enormity of their deeds. Ricky is certainly up-to-date, he thought. A completely modern man.

"...I can make amends. I'm not like some people. I can say that I'm sorry. That's no problem for me. Daddy understood this. As the night went on, I walked up the hill so I could get a better view—to check out the fire. It had died down. The smoke, that smell, they weren't as strong. It ended. It couldn't last forever. I went back to Daddy and it come to me: all of us can start over, start fresh. I felt, and felt real hard, that Daddy was closer to me than ever before. Since he died that is. Telling me all that stuff, that good stuff, he used to say about never giving in, standing up for yourself and all. About being a man. Not that macho bullshit.

Oh no. Being a man through and through without acting or showing off. I got to concentrate on that part, and all the rest of it too. Do you think I was showing off when...things got out of hand?"

The moon had risen to its apogee, bright and hard beyond the walls of The Old Home Place. Nightbirds sang. The outside is wet—hot, Walter thought, and it stinks. Or it could be Ricky I smell. He shook his head in response to the sad, absurd question.

"Thanks for supporting me on this," Ricky said. "Daddy agreed with me, too. There's that blood again. I also accept the fact that I'm gonna have a whole lot of explaining to do. But if you and Daddy don't condemn me, I'll be fine. And Momma's gonna understand too—some day."

Ricky, mutilated, deluded, was too intense. A twitch of genuine pity coursed through Walter. Why? he thought. Because I've also counted myself among the fugitives?

"A lot of people besides Momma are mad at me? How about Star?"

"Star wasn't...mad. We all had a lot on our minds. And she worked hard to relieve the suffering." And how would I characterize Star's response? Strangely objective? Disconnected?

Reluctantly, Ricky inquired into the nature and extent of this suffering. Walter recounted all of it—the injuries, the damages. He tried not to make it sound worse than it was, but it was plenty bad enough. Ricky fidgeted, gnawing at his lips, cleaning them, making his mouth unnaturally red against the smoky blackness of his face.

"...and so," Walter concluded "the firemen got it under control about two in the morning. They stayed around until after sun-up, putting the smaller fires out and, as they said, assessing damage. As bad as it was, one of them told me that it could've been worse." This was a lie, but Walter felt obligated to provide small comfort. Ricky brightened up, latching on to this saving, absolving point.

"It coulda. The whole place coulda burned. Think about that!"

"Or the whole world."

"Right. The whole world. We should be...thankful that we're alive. Thankful."

"No one would disagree with that."

"Sure. More people, beside Obie, coulda been *killed*. It might be some kinda *miracle*. Like I said, Walt, to get back to what else is on my mind, I'm willing, exactly like I said, to take full responsibility. On the other hand, not all of this was my fault. Anybody who studies what happened, will see that this friend of mine, Donnie Hodge is his name, the guy who designed the special mortars, shoulda been there to help us. He's got to take some responsibility—even if he was over in Charlotte helping to put on the big downtown fireworks show. He had a contract—he says. At least he shoulda warned me. How about that?"

Ricky did not slow down for a reply. Going on, ferreting out the guilty parties, was uppermost to him.

"How about Obie? As much as I loved him, didn't that girlfriend of his say that he took a live flare into the barn? Goddamn! How dangerous can you get?"

Walter grew weary. Ricky had demonstrated that he could go on all night. On and on, Walter thought—exploring the full range of blame and responsibility.

"...and I never held with the laws they got on fireworks. Hell no! How can the state say that a man can't do what he wants on his own land? It's *our* land, Walt! Yours and mine. The government don't have the right..."

Without warning, Ricky dropped his head flat on the table and descended instantly into a profound, drooling sleep. Walter was relieved that he was wrong about Ricky going on all night. Even the most frantic energy must be replenished, he thought. For a few minutes, Walter let him stay where he fell, his head resting beside the package of ham, his moist, red lips parted. This is the slumber of a child, Walter thought, all guilt and innocence. As Ricky began to snore, Walter gently shook him awake and guided him upstairs to Edgar's old room, which was as musty and dead as the one and only time Walter had bothered to enter there. I must clean all of this out soon, Walter thought. I'd forgotten that this will complete the cleansing of The Old Home Place. Funny, if it wasn't for Ricky, I'd let this last, final bit of Edgar remain here.

Ricky smiled and rubbed his eyes, thanking Walter for his help before curling into a ball squarely in the middle of the mattress—and then dropping back into his necessary oblivion. Walter pulled a bedspread over him and quietly closed the door. He remained awake for another half an hour—time enough to commit Ricky's visit to the journal.

In the morning, Ricky took Walter up on his offer of a shower. "Damn," he said, staring at his reflection in the bathroom mirror as Walter handed him a towel and a wash cloth. "I sure am nasty." He asked Walter for scissors and the use of the electric razor that rested on the shelf next to the sink. "Time to get myself prettied up," he said tonelessly.

Walter prepared eggs, toast, and coffee and waited for Ricky to come to the table. The food was turning cold, so Walter ate his portion and put Ricky's into the oven to warm. Ricky emerged. As Walter expected, he had shaved away his remaining hair, exposing a mass of bumps and small cuts. In the too-large shirt and jeans that Walter had laid out for him, he took on a gaunt, plucked appearance— like a Holocaust survivor, or a skinhead attired in his father's garments. Barefooted and wordless, he ate his breakfast, his glumness thick, palpable—as if he had talked himself out during the night. An unlikely possibility, Walter thought—or else he is actually sizing up his situation. Walter poured more coffee and Ricky grunted his thanks.

Ricky was in the middle of his third cup when the telephone rang. Walter heard an official male voice ask for Ricky Loomis. As Walter handed over the receiver, Ricky began to once more gnaw at his lips. He listened more than he spoke, confining his answers to a yes or a no. After he hung up, he drank his coffee, reporting nothing of the call. Walter cleaned up, stifling his curiosity.

"Man, I hate my hair this way," Ricky said. "My lack of hair that is. Makes me come across like some kind of damn freak."

"In certain quarters that style is all the rage," Walter said, flipping on the dishwasher.

"It ain't my style. I want a good head of hair."

Ricky went on gnawing at his lips and maintained his silence. Walter supposed that he was mulling over his lack of a good head of hair. Or the phone call. Then Ricky asked a question.

"Can you give me a ride to Helmsville?"

Walter said that he would. Ricky required all the help that he could get.

"I don't want to stop by Momma's either. Take me straight to town."

"Where in town?"

Ricky tried to come across as casual, but failed.

"The courthouse. My...old friend Sheriff Peavey wants to discuss a coupla things. About the night of..." Ricky could not say the word.

"The Event?"

"That's it. And after you drop me off, could you go find Roy Bunch for me? I think I want him to be there too."

"It might not be as bad as it seems."

"I don't know yet. And don't say nothing to Momma or Star. Shoot, it could be I get the whole business straightened out in ten minutes."

"Could be." The sympathy twitched through Walter once more. It must be his poor, nobby head, he thought. Could it be duty?

They passed the ruins of the barn and the charred pines that marked the progress of the Event. Ricky gave no sign, no reaction to the scene. He sat straight up, apparently concentrating only on what lay straight ahead. For a worried moment, Walter thought that he had lapsed into a catatonic state. Then, when the truck came abreast of the ranch house, which now had plastic sheeting over the ruined windows and the holes in the roof, Ricky ducked into the floorboards. Once they were on the highway, Ricky resumed his stiff, inert posture until they pulled into the courthouse parking lot.

Ricky thanked Walter as he alighted from the truck. "You've been real understanding about all this," he said. Walter nodded. I've been nodding since before last midnight. Is there another possible response?

"Tell Bunch that I won't say nothing important until he gets here. If Bunch ain't in his office, wait for him."

He watched Ricky cross the asphalt, making for the rear of the courthouse and a door beneath a sign that proclaimed the location of the Darden County Sheriff's Department. Ricky held his pants up, the loose, voluminous T-shirt billowing about him. He was still barefoot. He had also assumed a new, disconcerting manner of walking—herky-jerky, automaton-like. Walter sucked in his breath as he watched Ricky go, his own sensation of dread descending, commingling with the sympathy. This cannot turn out well, he thought. Not at all.

Bunch's secretary peered at Walter over her glasses. She was small and neat, like an aging wren or thrush.

"And what might I do for you today?" she inquired brightly. Walter told her and she chirped that Mr. Bunch was with a client, but would be available shortly.

"Have a seat," she said. "Read a magazine."

Walter did as he was told, thumbing through a two-year old copy of *Time*. The office, not surprisingly to Walter, was shabby—a manifestation of at least part of Bunch's sensibility. The gray-brown carpet was spongy, marked by large stains, and the yellow paint, mixed with plaster, flaked perceptibly from the walls. The furniture, a couch and a pair of chairs, had a decrepit, 1960s motel air about them. Clearly, Walter thought, putting up a pleasing front is not an item on Bunch's personal agenda.

The secretary pecked at the keyboard, concentrating upon the word processor's screen. She jumped slightly as the door to the inner office banged open and a skinny, morose young man in a Mega Death T-shirt swayed out. Bunch followed, and he smiled when he saw Walter.

"I can get it for you next week," the morose young man said.

"By Monday. I'd hate for you to go to court by yourself." Bunch lit a Winston. "Two-fifty up front."

"That's more than last time."

"You got bigger trouble than last time." Bunch exhaled loudly as the young man drifted from the office.

"Mr...Loomis," the secretary said, reddening slightly. "I nearly forgot his name. Mr. Loomis needs to see..."

"And so he does, Alda," Bunch interrupted. "A distinct pleasure. As usual."

"This is about Ricky," Walter said. "He's at the sheriff's office and he wants..."

"Me," Bunch said. "Today I'm good at completing other people's statements. Must be ESP. Or just practice."

Bunch had, like most interested parties around Helmsville, taken ample note of the Great Fourth of July

Explosion. There had been television news reports and stories in the Helmsville and Charlotte papers. Walter was ignorant of this public interest, although, as he listened to the summary of what Bunch called bad press, it seemed logical that the Event should be covered by the media. Walter had not given his attention to the media for some time—at least since coming to the farm. Bunch pulled on a jacket, straightened his tie, and said that he had expected to hear from Ricky at some point.

"Yes, indeed," Bunch said, hoisting a briefcase form the anarchic, paper-clotted desk in his private office. "Ricky has sent out the call once more. And I, as his personal counselor, must reply."

"Once more?" Bunch's eyebrows shot up. His expression, part amazement and part irony, made Walter feel a bit baffled, a bit witless.

"Am I betraying a trust? We should talk about that—later." Bunch thrust himself out of the office. Walter stood helplessly in the middle of the waiting room.

"Are you related to Ricky Loomis?" Alda asked. "I couldn't help but hear."

"We're half-brothers. I take it that you know Ricky."

"He's visited Mr. Bunch...a few times." With that, Alda resumed her contemplation of the screen. Walter wanted to find out more, but Alda had thrown up an instant, impregnable wall of professional absorption.

"Tell Mr. Bunch that I'll be back. Ricky will need a ride home—if he's available."

The mysteries of family blood, he thought. About now, Sheriff Peavey must be evaluating the strength and depth of Ricky's powers of apology. God help him—Ricky that is.

Walter rode the elevator down to the same dead lobby that he had discovered during his first search for Bunch. That too had been months ago, the night he got drunk and toured Helmsville. Which, he thought as he stepped into the sunshine of the near-deserted streets, may be the same as touring the world. In an aesthetic and philosophical sense, that is. I desired knowledge of my kinsman. Soon I will have it—but the desire has waned somewhat.

He had time to kill. An art, he thought, that I've grown adept in since becoming co-squire of the Loomis Estate. And I find myself in a necropolis once more. But change goes on even among the dead. The hair and fingernails keep on growing, the programs encoded despite the closing down of the brain and its incessant communiques. I've never had true awareness of these slow changes, these decompositions. For me, it must come like an anvil from the sky—dropping right on top of my head. You pay for your willed obliviousness— and the debt is often considerable.

He walked without regard for direction or destination. There have been many anvils lately. Edgar and his legacy. His memorial. Star and her song. Ricky. The Event. And what was it that I tricked myself with when the money dropped around me? The dream of the safe haven? Some horseshit like that. How uncharacteristically romantic. Like that gothic foolishness—the fear of Edgar's study. There was nothing there, although a void is to be feared—unless it can be transformed into a womb. The safest haven of all. A Freudian cliché, but, nevertheless, the one perfect dream. And a dream it is, for one and all. Me. Ricky.

The weather had broken in the last couple of days, although the heat was powerful. Walter was sweating after a couple of blocks. He rounded a corner and the courthouse rose up before him, the Confederate soldier on sentry duty into eternity or demolition. Vagrants festooned the court-house steps, baking away on the white granite, fettered to the dead world. Walter retraced his steps, scuttling back from the scene of Ricky's private performance. Ricky has his pride, he thought. He wouldn't want me to intrude. What was it like to live under Edgar's nose for all those years?

How could he perform the role of the good son? Could Edgar possibly have been pleased? Better him than me. The poor bastard.

Walter crossed a four-lane boulevard, stepping, by accident, into Helmsville's gentrified district—Victorian mansions and the slightly-newer Arts and Crafts bungalows from after the turn of the century. The streets were shady, much cooler. He realized that this was his grandparents' old neighborhood—the last he had ever anticipated of Helmsville until his anointing with Edgar's money. The houses were neat and well-maintained; some had been converted to business use. He passed law offices—Bunch's more successful competitors—he thought, clinics of various medical specialists, and the headquarters of the local United Way. Other houses had remained in the hands of families—up-scale and fashionable, yet highly-visibly icons of an older order—the yards complete with bicycles, gym sets, and all the litter of children's play. Helmsville's own safe haven, he thought. I should consider taking up residence here. Give up The Old Home Place and settle in town as a lovable, wealthy eccentric. Charity donations and civic affairs, perhaps.

He ascended a steep hill, his spirits buoyed slightly by the serenity of the neighborhood. He had not taken a walk since his investigations in Charleston, and he had been driven from the woods by the summer and Star's song. She could be out there today, he thought, lifting her sublime aria to the sky. Let me not dwell upon such a thing, he thought. It is like my kinship with Ricky—mysterious Ricky. It can lead to chaos, which lurks beyond the boundaries and the light of all safe havens.

The hill afforded an upper-middle-class, appropriately sweeping vista: there were the mansions below, the seats of family and commerce. Most of the downtown was discreetly concealed by foliage. The Neo-Greek dome of the courthouse floated amid the green of the trees. Ricky and Bunch are enveloped there, he thought—explaining, withholding, grappling with the machinery of the courthouse and its engineers. In any case, Ricky is enveloped. Could Star be right? Could he come out of this no matter what?

He halted before an ornate example of the Victorian. This one was neither business nor home, however, but the local museum—named, he guessed for some long-dead philanthropist: Noble Gant III. This name was inscribed upon the tarnished brass plaque that was bolted to the locked door. No hours were posted; Walter was disappointed. He peered through a couple of windows. Dark, plum-colored draperies obscured the interior. A pity, he thought. I could come back some time. The history of Helmsville would be most intriguing. Is there an exhibit devoted to my paternal grandfather? The gambling man with the suite in the North State Hotel? Edgar could have an exhibit too. I'd put up the money, but what could be found of him? He had the knack of leaving enough of a trail to tantalize, but not enough solid evidence to truly apprehend him.

Walter lingered on the museum porch, vainly trying to summon up the exact location of his grandparents' and Margaret's old home. Too many years, he thought. The flavor of the family seat hovers about me, however—familiar and foreign at once. An outpost of gentility among the barbarians of the cotton mills—and now most of the mills are gone and the outpost thrives under new ownership. Paradox abounds. Did Margaret's father recoil in horror at her marriage to Edgar Loomis, the inheritor of ill-gotten riches? If blood tells all, I should recoil in horror myself. And is Ricky the truest inheritor of all?

He halfway loped down the hill, giving himself up to gravity. It did not matter to him now that he could not locate another of his ancestral homes. One was more than enough. And he had to go back to Bunch's office.

"Chaos," he said to the traffic. "I thought I believed in

it. How little I knew."

Alda was gone and Bunch yelled for him to come in. A bottle of Old Crow sat on a stack of files. Bunch was smoking another Winston, and Ricky was across the desk from his personal counselor. He was frozen in that same stiff posture. His hands were folded in his lap and his bare feet were pressed together.

"There's another seat over there," Bunch said, pointing to a plastic dinette chair in the corner of the office. The chair held more files. "Put that shit on the floor and rest yourself," Bunch said. "You want a drink?"

Walter declined the invitation as Bunch poured an inch of Old Crow into a styrofoam cup. He did not offer a drink to Ricky. Walter greeted Ricky, who emitted what may have been a hello.

"How did it go?" Walter asked. Ricky wagged his head and made half-stifled growling sounds.

"Not so great," Bunch said. "Then again, it could've been worse, like too many things are. At least we made bail."

"Oh," Walter said.

"Twenty-five thousand. Ricky here is a man of means, so that wasn't a problem." Bunch tilted the cup to his face before going on. "The District Attorney hereabouts is an asshole, but I got it reduced from forty-two. Judge Synder can be reasonable if he's had a good lunch."

"All those...mother fuckers hate me," Ricky said. Walter had never before heard words forced out of anyone with such pressure.

"Ricky's taking all of this pretty personally. You want to know what our boy is charged with? Involuntary manslaughter, arson, criminal negligence, and violation of the fireworks statutes. The arson and fireworks bullshit are a joke. The D.A. tossed those in for effect. Hell, I got a good chance of getting those dismissed before—or if—we go to trial."

"What you mean—if?" Ricky said. "I'm gonna have my day in court—unless you can get all of it dismissed. Is that what you're saying?"

"That's not it at all. The manslaughter doesn't look promising. Neither does the negligence—for right now."

"Obie was like a brother to me. Goddamn it, he was!"

"Brother or not, he was blown to pieces. What was left of him? A boot?"

"And...a couple of other things," Walter said.

"This is what they call...a vendetta. That's the word. I'm gonna sue all of them for false arrest."

Bunch stood and leaned across the desk. His voice was reasonable, matter-of-fact.

"You can keep that species of shit to yourself if you want me to represent you. Outside of public defender, nobody else would have the job. And I don't want you running off your mouth about this. Understand? You told that moron Peavey way too much before I got to you. Him and the D.A. Hunsucker! What a fucking snake! He sure hated to see me show up."

Bunch turned to Walter and chuckled ruefully.

"Ricky here was blabbing about how sorry he was. I got Peavey to show me his notes. Lucky for us they read like a composition by a high-grade ape. But I could see old Ricky here had come way too close to some rather damning admissions. Hunsucker wouldn't let me see *his* notes. He's smarter, so there's no telling what he's got that can hurt us."

"Fuck you, Bunch," Ricky said, the pressure building back up to what Walter viewed as an alarming level. "I was trying to explain. The truth is..."

"You're really gonna have to shut it up," Bunch said. "The truth could send you to Raleigh. Anyway, the sort of truth you were bleating out would. We'll come up with our own version of the truth. So help us God."

"I don't like being talked to like that," Ricky said.

"Then don't give me cause. Walter, if you're so inclined you can take Ricky home. If you have any sort of influence, make him stay out there. And Ricky, if you keep on, there won't be a thing I can do for you. In fact, Clarence Darrow and Jesus of Nazareth wouldn't make any difference."

"I'll try to help," Walter said.

"Fine." Bunch smacked his lips over another jolt of Old Crow. "And remind him that this whole sorry deal is just getting started."

Ricky stared out the window all the way back, growling and grunting from time to time. He did not actually speak, though, and Walter was glad to finally reach the ranch house. Beatrice, attired in a large straw hat, halter and shorts, was among the shrubbery, trying to prune it into some sort of shape. She paused, clippers in mid-air, when the truck stopped at the end of the driveway.

The yard was a mess, with most of the Mexicans and ornamental animals knocked on their sides. A few had lost limbs and heads. Hundreds of black circles marked the fire-balls' impact points and the scent of charred flesh and vegetation hung over all. Beatrice remained suspended, except for the turning of her head as she watched Ricky come down the driveway. He went directly into the house without speaking to her. Star, as if by magic, materialized in the front door and waved to Walter. He pressed the accelerator too quickly and too hard and the truck spun and fishtailed up the road to The Old Home Place.

10

"The problem may be that of—how did old Walt Whitman put it—original energy unchecked? Words to that effect."

Bunch was on his second Old Crow and water—liquor and water as he called it. Walter nursed a beer. They had met in the topless bar where Walter had conducted a portion of his monumental, spring-time drunk. He had requested the meeting and left it to Bunch to choose the site. It was no coincidence that Bunch had picked this bar. Recently, Walter had discerned patterns—alarming patterns—that strengthened his convictions concerning the pervasiveness of chaos. Chaos has its own channels, wide and amply-marked, he had written in his journal.

"You should be familiar with the line," Bunch said. "A former laborer in the academic business, wrestling with the themes and nuances of the literary classics, forging future classics in your own hand. How about it?"

"Whitman. Reeks of messianic assertiveness. And you should appreciate the fact that in the future there will be no literary classics of any sort. Only information will exist." Bunch was in his irritating mode, Walter thought. Ricky was the announced subject of the meeting. Which meant that the line from Whitman was apt. Ricky exuded original energy and it was entirely unchecked. Bunch, in his bantering, vaguely needling fashion, had talked around the subject for the better part of an hour. It was also true, however, that subjects of equal importance had recently been introduced. There were, for example, the lawsuits; fourteen civil actions in the name of horse owners and the injured. Altogether, the aggrieved parties were asking around a million, and the insurance company had raised strenuous objections to paying any of it—given the sources of The Event and the criminal charges against Ricky.

Walter's guts had twisted, coil-like, at this most recent news. All had been revealed in another, earlier meeting called by Star. She had been most formal that day in Bunch's office. Equipped with a briefcase of rich, dark leather, she laid out the insurance company's position, having been in futile negotiations for the previous two days. Bunch had, in a somewhat more rambling manner, discussed the complaints from those who had suffered as a result of The Event while Walter, Beatrice, and Ricky had listened. After these presentations, and as Walter struggled to absorb their implications, Beatrice had asked what all of this was really supposed to mean. Star, as polished as a first-rate certified public accountant, had stated that they stood to lose the farm—and all else that they owned. Beatrice had shouted, not actual words, but a guttural, near-mechanical groan that was aimed at Ricky, who growled and grunted as he had on the day he was charged. Bunch had told them to shut up, to stop behaving like Goddamn idiots. As for Walter, he had gulped like a trout on a stream bank. It had taken Star ten minutes to regain full control.

When the meeting ended, Beatrice fled, Ricky in her wake. Star had marched out soon afterwards, in her shorts and tank top, briefcase in hand. That had been three weeks ago. Bunch had filed answers to the suits and Star, according to Bunch, was making a detailed evaluation of their finances. Walter's accounts had been examined, and whatever he and Ricky had in the bank was all the capital they could count on—unless they wished to sell any, or all, of the

land. Naturally, there would be no income from the stable—
and the logging and farming revenues, as Star had informed
Walter over the telephone, would not bring a profit until
next spring—if they were able to get contracts. Mysteriously,
she added that she "was working on something special that
could solve their problems." We're all accomplices now,
Walter had thought numerous times since the meeting. He
had, with this in mind, stayed away from the ranch house.
Each time he drove by—to fetch groceries or to motor aim-
lessly up and down the back roads, stewing and obsessed
with possible losses—he had seen them trying to repair the
damage from The Event. Skipper Talley was there, working
with Ricky, balanced uneasily on the roof, the pair of them
gingerly pulling at damaged shingles. Star would wave, but
nothing could have persuaded Walter to stop.

"I'm trying to make it easier for you," Bunch said.
"Light chit-chat can help."

Walter watched a dancer who shuffled about the small
stage. "I'm not in the mood," he eventually said. "You
haven't been exactly forthcoming about Ricky."

"There is a question of attorney-client privilege. To be
honest, though, much of Ricky's past is part of the public
record."

"I've had intimations. I was too oblivious, stupid, or lazy
to check into them."

"Ricky generates a load of intimations."

"I'm...entangled with him."

Bunch appeared to take an interest in the newest dancer;
they shuffled on and off the stage at regular intervals. Walter
recognized her; the small girl who had hustled him for a
drink. He doubted that she would remember him. That was
a number of drinks ago, he thought.

"Do you like her?" he asked.

Bunch laughed, phlegm-rich. "In theory I like them all."

"What's your lady friend up to? I met her...that night.

Very nice."

"Faye is *nice*. And I have no idea what she's up to. But we were, as you wished, speaking of Ricky. And entanglements."

"A multi-faceted subject?" The dancer had not improved since Walter's encounter with her. Graceless and awkward, she paced robotically in pasties, G-string, and cowboy hat. Traditional, Walter thought. The cowboy hat brought Paula to mind. She was one of the plaintiffs. She only wants that which is due her, he thought. Indemnification and so on.

"It was, oh, fifteen years ago—back in my public defender days—when I myself became entangled with Ricky," Bunch began. "And I was truthful about not meeting your father until a few months before he died. We did talk on the phone a few times. He had an impressive voice—like Walter Cronkite, with a hint of Rhett Butler."

Like the voice of God, Walter thought.

"Why did Ricky need a public defender?"

"You've never heard this? What passes for conversation out there on the Loomis barony? Weather and crops?"

"Ricky is also somewhat less than forthcoming on some subjects."

"True enough." Bunch lit a Winston and signalled the bartender for another drink. The small girl's number ended and a very tall, heavily built black woman took the stage.

"Breaking and entering," Bunch said, after sampling the new drink. "He was a senior in high school, and a good football player. Tailback. Lots of yards, lots of touchdowns. Fast and shifty. Inborn quality perhaps? Anyway, he was scouted by swarms of coaches. Scholarship material—without a criminal record. Poor Ricky was born too soon. Today, crimes don't create such problems. I heard too that there were insufficiencies—like his SAT scores being in the dull normal range. Now, that wouldn't hold him back either."

"Ricky proceeds from induction—not deduction. He is

capable of a wide range of mental activities that wouldn't show up on standardized tests."

"Well said. He induced two other scholar athletes to help him knock over their biggest rival's gym—the week of the final game of the season, playoffs not included. They fueled up on headache-weed grass and beer and broke in around four in the morning. They had a lot of fun. First, they carted off a number of helmets and jerseys, as many as they could cram into Ricky's car. Then they trashed the locker room, extensive water damage there, and the coach's office. And they busted out all the windows they could. I employed the school-boy prank defense, coupled with diminished intent due to inebriation. The court, in its wisdom, bought it—and Ricky got probation. Naturally, he surrendered his role as a Helmsville Fighting Stallion. What he became next was a United States Marine."

Walter could conceive of this: wild oats, fun and games, helling around. The Marine Corps was a natural progression. Utilize that original energy. Pride and discipline. What would suit young Ricky more?

"What's next?"

"Pay close attention. I've seldom provided a narrative of my client's fascinating career."

"Ricky probably liked the Marines. It's an organization that appeals to lusty young fellows."

Bunch snorted, then smiled.

"From what he told me, your father said enlist or never come home. A clear cut choice. Ricky didn't even finish his senior year. Packed right off to Parris Island."

The dancer took a break as Walter eased into his second beer. Another pattern, he thought: vandalism, theft, the Marines, and Edgar's Jehovah-like wrath. It's all of a piece.

"So he joined up, thus securing his redemption and return."

"Not quite. He lasted about a year, which, if you think

165

about it, is pretty good for Ricky. His Marine record—I've got copies and they're strictly confidential—say that he was 'discharged for the good of the service.' He was in California when he was drummed out. Stayed out there for three more years. I'm assuming that your father wouldn't let him come home. Further disgrace and all that. I don't know what he did with himself. He claims he went to college, but he couldn't name the school. And he hinted a couple of times that he was involved with shady, high-powered types. Who knows? Was he actually in California? He could've been anywhere."

"But he did return. Star said that he couldn't stay away, so…"

"He earned your father's blessing? Did Beatrice smooth it over? Did hearts soften? You got me. How about Star? She's an original. Damned if she isn't starting to come across as the mistress of Loomis-Land."

"How'd Ricky meet her?"

"Don't know. Fate, most likely. I'm acquainted with her family…"

Star said that Bunch was once her sister's lawyer, Walter thought. I encounter a minor, yet enticing element in the pattern.

"…and they're what used to be called southern white trash. I'm not familiar with the current term. Probably average American. At any rate, she has Ricky, and Ricky has her. Her folks are dead and her horde of siblings have moved, or died. I can say that she and Ricky hooked up right after he was sprung from prison."

The small girl was back, sliding the cowboy hat none too deftly back and forth in front of her crotch. No one in the audience paid much attention. She concentrated hard on the task at hand, though. She's really giving it her all, Walter thought. Ricky in prison. It was bound to be.

"What do you have to say about that?" Bunch demanded. "Are you stunned by this shocking revelation?"

"Not exactly. I don't condemn him either."

"That's big of you. I served as his personal counselor on that little deal too. And I did right by him. This was in '86, when the nation recoiled in disgust and proclaimed that dope, in Ricky's situation smoking-type dope, was a monstrous affront to our values. We get like that every ten years or so."

"He sold marijuana. Go on."

"Not just sold it. Grew it. He'd been living with Beatrice, not working, and was, I take it, at loose ends. He and three similarly-minded friends—Ricky has never been without a full complement of such pals. They went in for agriculture and venture capitalism. The planted big patches down in some secluded bottom lands on your father's place. They were about to harvest—it was high-grade sinsemilla—when they got busted. It was, for Darden County, an elaborate operation: helicopters, deputies in flak jackets toting M-16s. Ricky and his associates were on the premises when the law dropped in, tilling the soil like honest husbandmen. Ricky might've made it out. He was in the woods for two days—him and his shotgun—then he surrendered."

"Like he did after the Fourth of July?"

"Not quite. He was persuaded by your father. He went straight to the hiding place, and convinced Ricky to give himself up."

"Was my father aware of what...Ricky was growing?"

Bunch did not answer. The bartender yawned and a red-headed dancer punched up "Achy-Breaky Heart" on the jukebox.

"Edgar was said to know everything that went on out there," Walter said. "That's according to Ricky."

"We're getting into suppositions here," Bunch said carefully. "I've entertained a few suppositions myself, but didn't reach any conclusions. There are doubts."

"What sort of doubts?"

"I wouldn't speculate." Bunch smiled. "I've been talking a little shit here. Forgive me."

Walter did not press him. Bunch, for whatever reason, won't say, he thought.

"What was the disposition of Ricky's case?" Walter quietly asked. Obviously relieved at the change of subject, Bunch resumed his lawyerly facade.

"Like I said, I did the best I could. Ricky talked..."

"He has a tendency toward explanation."

"Oh, yes. He talked until the authorities begged him to shut up. The disposition itself was in the nature of a compromise. Turning state's evidence is the layman's term. Ricky's partners got fifteen years each. Ricky got four at a minimum security pen in the mountains outside Asheville—it's like a summer camp for wayward youth. The partners are doing their time in Raleigh. Your traditional prison experience, you might say: maximum security, gangsters of all varieties, homemade knives, and sodomy. Ricky probably wasn't aware of his status as a snitch. He would've lasted maybe a month in the big-league slammer."

"Ricky must've been grateful for your efforts."

"Shit. When the sentence was pronounced, he went crazy. Screaming and thrashing around. Crying. It took three deputies to haul him off. He had dreamed, he told me this later, that he would get probation. At his sentencing he called me a few choice names—I'm used to that, dealing with the public as I do—but after he got control of himself he wrote this letter. He apologized to me, then said that his daddy had promised him probation. Whether this was part of a dream or drawn from objective reality I don't know. He said too that your father had power, that he was pals with some of the most important people in the world. Your father was punishing him—like when he forced Ricky to enlist. Ricky was to take this punishment like a man. Once he was in prison, he actually enjoyed it. Weight-lifting, sunshine, plenty of exercise, and a routine laid down from above. He accepted your father's judgement. He wrote me three, four times a year. The last letter came just before his release. Daddy had forgiven him for getting caught and would allow him to come home and live with Beatrice. This was in late '90, if I remember right."

The small girl with the cowboy hat was no more alluring the second time around. Walter's beer was warm and he ordered a fresh one. Bunch smoked and swirled the ice around in his drink. There must be, Walter thought, further questions. The accumulation of evidence.

"Do you have those letters?"

"Confidential. They're not what I'd call masterpieces of chiseled English prose. And there's not much to them—except what I've told you. Look, I've spilled too much as it is…"

"I didn't ask to see them."

"That's right. And you can't. I will say that all of this is the absolute truth—the limits of available information, to coin a phrase. Do you believe me?"

"It's all very believable. And I'm in your debt."

"Skip that shit. You have a right."

"Forgiveness for being caught. That's what Ricky said?"

"That's the one line that led me to further…"

"Suppositions?"

"Which I don't intend to examine further. What you do is your own affair. And consider, too, Ricky's grasp of fact."

"His fantasy life is rich and full. And it may, or may not, be my affair."

The small girl, the cowboy hat now pulled down close to her ears, slew-footed up to Walter.

"Hey," she called out.

"A smooth come-on," Bunch said into his drink.

"You're the guy I met in here one time," she said. "Give me a nice tip."

Walter handed her a twenty. She smiled with healthy white teeth.

"You wanna get me a drink?" she asked.

"That won't be necessary. The money's all yours. For old time's sake."

She left, fingering the bill.

"I didn't realized that you had established a relationship with Helmsville's show business community," Bunch said.

"A festive evening—some time ago."

"That twenty's got to be her record tip—for not doing anything extra, that is."

"I'm not in the market for basics or extras."

"I'm going to ask you a personal question. Are you ready?"

Walter shrugged. Why not? He had pried into Ricky's buried life. Patterns had emerged. There had been significant glimpses into the entanglements.

"O.K." Bunch said, swiveling on his barstool to face Walter. "Why do you keep hanging around? You got the money, the big score. What could've brought you to get mixed up with Ricky and the rest of this shit? You could've sold your share of the farm—there was another fine wad of cash to be had there—and been six months already in the south of France. Or wherever you would want to go. You could've been an absentee landlord—there would've been distance. Troubles are less like troubles at a distance. And why don't you leave now? To the extent of getting off that damn farm."

Walter stared into Bunch's wide, impassive face.

"Sorry," Bunch said. "Forgive the curiosity."

"I'm...I'm not sure why. I've asked myself the same questions. Put it down to...to what? Deracination? Stasis? Entropy?" And there's fear too, he thought. And the illusion of the safe haven.

"If you say so," Bunch muttered after considering

Walter's words. "Only I would've been out of there the day I met Ricky. That's all the cheap advice I'll give you tonight."

Bunch paid their tab. In the parking lot, moths circled and crackled against the neon.

"It's not too late," Bunch said. "I'll keep you informed about those chicken-shit lawsuits—wherever you might be. You could lose the land, like Star said, but it could be that your money won't get touched. Land's a curse. I apologize. That's a second piece of cheap advice."

"It's the place...I've come to. As for the rest of it, I don't know what I'll do."

"Deracination. Entrophy. A hell of an answer to a simple question."

Walter laughed. In that second he perceived an unwelcome image: himself and Bunch perched teetering above a shady brink.

"It was my best answer," Walter said.

Solemnly, Bunch shook his hand. Walter had never pictured Bunch capable of assuming a formal, dignified gravity. But he had achieved that state.

"Watch out for yourself," Bunch said. "Seriously."

"And be careful?"

"That too."

At The Old Home Place, he labored over the journal until his eyes were leaden, burning.

He had reasons to recall Bunch's admonitions. In the middle of August, a portion of the ranch house roof fell in, plummeting Skipper Talley into Beatrice's bedroom. Besides the damage inflicted by The Event, the contractor who was hired to make repairs discovered water damage brought on by faulty gutters and clogged downspouts. The moisture had backed up, spreading to the roof's center pole, the wood rotting beneath the shingles. It was so bad that a number of the rafters were like mush, the contractor noted. The whole roof would have to come out.

Skipper Talley's weight had been the direct cause, plunging him, in a shower of splinters, sheetrock, and insulation, into the middle of Beatrice's almost new, designer brass bed, which, naturally enough, collapsed into the floor. As for the damage to Skipper Talley, he sustained two broken legs and a badly slashed posterior. Star persuaded him not to sue, in exchange for payment of his medical bills and a small amount of cash. Beatrice, weeping and shouting—which had become her major forms of communication—had proclaimed that her endurance was at an end. She packed and moved to a condo in Helmsville. Star had seen to the arrangements, also guaranteeing Beatrice a healthy monthly allowance. The condo, Star said, was perfect for Beatrice, although there was no space for the lawn figures—which remained broken and forlorn on the ranch house lawn.

"She'll be happier there," Star said. She was across the kitchen table from Walter, smoking and drinking lemonade. She had called before paying her visit, and, for once, Walter was spared the panic that accompanied the arrival of a guest. "And she'll be out of the way. God, she can drive you fucking crazy."

Walter nodded. Cigarette smoke wafted in artificial cloud banks through the sunlight. I'm forever holding conferences in this kitchen, he thought. The nerve center for The Old Home Place.

"Do you think she'll move back after the repairs are finished?" he asked. Star's legs, as always, were beautifully tanned, thrust out before her as she leaned back in her chair. Tanned like the rest of her, Walter thought.

"She's satisfied in town. Close to her old friends and the mall. She says that she can't live with Ricky. Ruined her life, she says. And the repairs. It could take three months—if they can get done at all. Cale Dimmer, he's the contractor, told me yesterday that the house is built as sorry as he's ever seen. I never woulda thought so."

"How's Ricky?" Walter had not seen him for weeks, although Ricky had been on his mind. Ricky and Edgar had been the main topics in his journal ever since his meeting with Bunch. The speculations are potentially endless, he had written. Futile, but fascinating.

"The hair's growing back." Star did not appear willing to go any further, and Walter, edgy as he usually was in her presence, did not push her.

"Were you there when Skipper had his accident?"

"I was in my room—at the computer going over these real important figures. It was like a serious interruption."

It's so absurd, so improbable and violent, Walter thought. A Three Stooges scene—routine catastrophe.

"To...ah...change the subject," Star said, her breasts straining and expanding the visage of Axel Rose on her tank top. "I didn't come here to catch up on Ricky and Beatrice. I'm sure if you were *that* interested you would've dropped by."

Walter's palms were sweating and he wiped them against his pants legs.

"I've got a business proposition. I've worked it out real good. Ricky's signed and I wanted to see if you would too."

"What kind of proposition?" Caution and dread caused Walter's voice to catch. Star smiled.

"Take it easy. I'm on your side. The deal's like this. We're gonna get killed on the lawsuits. Bunch says that if we're smart, we'll settle out of court. Ricky's worthless friends, Beatrice's old fartbags, they want money fast. We can get off, I figure, with close to half of what they're suing for. Does that sound good, or what? It would be a ton of money from you and Ricky, and Ricky's not gonna need much of an income for a few years anyway. If you understand what I'm saying. Bunch told me yesterday that it doesn't look promising—those are Bunch's words—to keep Ricky outta jail. But there would be plenty for when he's released or paroled. Whatever."

"What does Ricky say?"

"I don't tell him this kinda stuff. You understand? Don't want him to get upset. But to get back to the deal. You've already heard about the monthly income, the stable's gone, and if we built another one, our reputation isn't real hot. I wouldn't count on any horses getting boarded here. And I got the feeling that we won't rent out any acreage for soybeans and corn either. The growers call in July. And it's August now. So the main question is whether you want to hold on to as much as you can, which is a lot. A lot more than Ricky. He'd gone through plenty—him and Beatrice—before this happened. And you wanta hold on to the land, too. Edgar used to say that the land is the most important thing. 'The basis of wealth,' he said. There won't be more land.'"

As she spoke, her blue, virginal eyes tunnelled into him. He could not avoid them.

"Here's how it is," she went on, logically, practically. "I've been talking to Weyerhauser's office outta Charlotte. You know, they take a little wood outta here already. They cut selectively on about fifteen acres. That's how Edgar wanted it. He was always going on about preserving the land and all that. Which is great—if you don't have explosions and get sued by fourteen assholes. Well, the deal I got worked out will let them cut more."

"How much more?" Walter, despite the smoke, had a whiff of her smell. Clean, he thought. And wild.

"Enough so that we can settle all this legal stuff. What about it? I told them I'd give them the word tomorrow."

"It...could be for the best."

She smiled again, her tongue darting over her lips. She did that deliberately, Walter thought.

He signed after a cursory look at the contract. It was a solid, imposing document, and Star's scheme appeared to be sensible. He might have signed if it had not. For her to leave was his single goal. Besides, he thought, what's a few more trees? Her deal can provide me with some safety. Money safety.

"That was easy," she said. "You're a reasonable guy. The cutting starts in September. Hey, you haven't asked how much you and Ricky stand to get."

"I haven't? I must be relieved that you negotiated such a fine contract."

"That's it? You weren't having yourself deep thoughts about art and such?"

She laughed. Laugh at me, he thought. Now get out.

"It's a million two," she said. "Ricky, from what I could tell, was pretty pleased."

"They must be going to cut an awful lot of trees."

"That's right, but they'll replant late in the fall."

"What would Edgar's judgement be?"

"Pissed off. But he's dead."

Are you aware that Ricky converses with him on a daily basis? Walter thought. Would he tell her? She would put it down to...what? Have I ever heard her utter anything of consequence about him?

"I admire you for working this out. I couldn't have done it. And Ricky's troubles have probably kept him from tending to business."

"So that's your angle on Ricky."

"O.K. My angle's defective. Sorry."

"You're mighty understanding."

"Thanks."

"I read the rest of your books. You're not so understanding there. Do you remember my idea about the stories? It was right before..."

"The Event. Perhaps after things aren't in such a state of

175

flux..."

"What did you call it? 'The Event?' I like that. That's the other you—the one in your books."

"A split personality."

She smiled and touched his arm, leaving her hand there. He eased away and she nodded slowly, almost imperceptibly.

"You're funny. Not like anybody else."

"Is that a compliment?"

"Can't you tell? You don't mind compliments, do you?"

"No one does."

"If the compliment is sincere. I'm real sincere, Walter."

His palms were close to dripping. She gave no indication that she was ready to leave, and in his agitated condition, he could not think of a lie that was believable enough to get rid of her. He went for fresh lemonade, feeling blank, paralyzed. It doesn't have to be a good lie, he thought. What will it be? Groceries. Yes. To Helmsville for groceries. That's not bad. As soon as I chug down this lemonade. When he turned from the refrigerator, a glass in each hand, she was lighting a joint. He cried out in alarm—like a heroine in an old-time melodrama—and a glass fell from his hand.

"It's celebration time," she chuckled. "The deal to save the land is finalized, and I've told you how great you are. But first, you gotta mop up some."

He was bolted to the floor, the lemonade spreading about his feet. A tableau vivant, he thought. The woodland singer's celebration, the dumb-struck squire of The Old Home Place, and the smoke.

He had not indulged in marijuana since his graduate school days—mostly because it terrified him once he was in its grasp. This time, at Star's slightly contemptuous urging, and in the maw of a larger terror, he sucked the dope in until it permeated and electrified every particle of his being. As the first joint was consumed, she produced a second from the briefcase—which, to Walter in his near-helpless condition, had been transformed into a kind of magician's prop. Star, who showed no obvious effects of the dope, said that Ricky was never without a steady supply. That since his arrest he had been blowing dope around the clock—a joint in one hand and the television remote in the other. Beatrice, right up until the day she moved out, had bitched and sworn at him over this habit. What a bore. These were the only comments about Ricky she offered during the celebration.

Inevitably, there were further tableaux vivants—interspersed with scurrying, furtive movement. He hardly spoke, and she continued to laugh—as when he insisted on locking the doors after she removed her tank top. He tried to avoid her breasts, but she seized him—her strength was remarkable—and homed in his face with her tongue. He gasped and lunged back. I have just the place, she said, pushing him upstairs. They careened into Edgar's bed—the exact spot where Ricky had curled into his fetal ball.

She was kind—extraordinarily so, he thought, as she coaxed him along. Whatever was natural in him had been buried for some time, however. He apologized as her fingers played across his bare, white shoulder. It's all right, she said. Nerves. It could be nerves. They lay side by side, and he wished he could ask about her song, to interrogate her on all manner of subjects. He could not find the words, however. Later, she again attempted to arouse him, and, more or less united, they achieved an adequate, quivering degree of success. This pleased her, and she kissed him deeply. He was too numb from the dope and everything else that had transpired, to make her stop.

Fully dressed, he asked why she had initiated the celebration.

"I've planned it for months. Maybe since the night I met you. I'd never run across a guy like you. And your books turned me on. The long one..."

"*Dancing at the Abattoir,*" Walter said in a faraway voice. "A repellant vision of human carnality" was the verdict of *The New York Times*, expressed in a short, decidedly mixed review that praised the author for his skill while chiding him for his "chilly objectivity in depicting human relationships." It was the most prominent review any of his books ever received—not that it helped to sell many copies.

"My books, my merely...arriving here, brought on...all of this?"

"Why not? And you're being Ricky's brother and Edgar's son."

"Will you tell Ricky?"

"I'm not a moron. Are you gonna tell him?"

Walter laughed—a cackle rising to the level of low-grade hysteria.

"Better not," Star said. "It'd get him pretty sad. Worse than he is already."

"Would he shoot me?" This notion caused Walter to cackle harder.

"No! And that's not what I call funny. How could you think that? He loves you. 'Walt's the greatest.' He says that all the time."

"And you planned this. You did tell me that, didn't you?"

"I plan everything."

He locked the door behind her, and went immediately to his journal—desperate to believe that recording the events of that morning would slacken their hold upon him. He described it all without comment, jamming the words across the page. He read over the entry and added a final line: This prose has the touch of a transcendental pornographer.

Writing did not help, and as the marijuana wore off the terror lingered. I have, he thought, fucked my half-brother's woman, to put it in the most primitive and appropriate terms. In truth, she fucked me—in a manner of speaking. He showered, uselessly trying to wash away her wild, clean smell.

I've got to do something, he thought as he stood on the front porch, expecting Ricky to roar up—growling, grunting, foaming to get at him. Will there be a measure of relief in purposeful motion?

In Edgar's room, her smell, and the smell of her calculated lust, were jarringly strong. He heaved open a window, and the damp, fetid moisture of the August noon-time heightened the intensity of the other odors. Goddamn, he thought. I'll never get rid of it. He measured his options. Purgation was the logical choice.

He backed the truck to the front steps, and, despite laboring against the deep afterglow of the dope and the limp, feebleness of his legs and loins, he succeeded in lugging Edgar's bedding down the stairs, crashing the boxsprings heavily into the pick-up. In full motion now, he bumped and slid the chest of drawers, nightstand, and lamp down and out of The Old Home Place. With part of the job completed, he felt a bit less terror-bound. Well, he thought, I've been meaning to toss this junk since I came here. Destroy the evidence of Edgar and, now, of Star's celebration. She's given me the impetus. I ought to thank her.

He stuffed Edgar's suits, shoes, and the rest of his clothes into the heavy black lawn bags he had bought at the Carolina Home Improvement World when he had believed that he possessed the energy and drive to recreate The Old Home Place in his own image. The bags finally came in handy, he thought. I'm getting good at dumping. My own sorry, moth-eaten possessions should be next. For instance, what am I doing with all those books? I haven't opened a quarter of them in years—haven't taken one from the shelf since I fled here. Ha. The last, the final place for me.

The purgation completed, he conducted a final survey of

Edgar's room. The bareness was satisfying and the smell's power considerably reduced. Emptying out is a fine sensation, he thought as he flung back the closet door for a final check. But something remained.

How could I have overlooked this? he thought. In a corner, in the dimness, was a cardboard storage file—of the type Walter had once stored manuscripts in. He brought it into the center of the room and, after hesitating, lifted the lid.

There were three bound folio volumes. *My History*, read the title, *The Journals of Edgar Dawes Loomis: A Chronicle of His Times.*

11

My father, Stamey Carothers Loomis, was formidable and obvious. He was reticent, and intimidating—prized traits in the semi-civilized, frontier-bent South he was born into. He retained these characteristics throughout his life, among both the high and low that he dealt with. Presidents, bankers, sharecroppers and pool hall touts were all of the same stuff where he was concerned. His aspirations and appetites were bold—though hidden beneath the dour, laconic exterior of a country undertaker, a trade he briefly practiced in his youth. The handling and presentation of the dead may well have shaped his shrewd and unerring judgement of his fellow beings.

Walter copied this passage of the *History* into his journal. The apartment, part of a complex of one hundred identical units, was located "less than a mile from Charlotte's most prestigious mall," as it was advertised in the local newspaper. The ad was the first that Walter read after he arrived in Charlotte—late in the afternoon on the day of Star's Celebration. He spent the night in a motel, and the next morning signed a lease on the apartment, paying a deposit and two months' rent in advance with cash. Next, he rented furniture and linens. Only the basics, he told the agent over the apartment manager's telephone: bed, two chairs, two lamps, and a sturdy table. The table is most important, he said. I need it as soon as possible.

I made no attempt to "understand" father. He projected himself as a permanent feature of the landscape. He simply was—like a mountain or a river. My mother, Helena Oceania Truelove Loomis, was his fit companion. Her strength was in wordless affection and selfless acts. She suffered, but she also tempered Father's more extreme inclinations. She died when I was nineteen. Sudden pneumonia. I was at the university and drove across the state in a steady winter rain to her funeral. I did not truly know her well. This was my loss. My memories of her are bound by love.

Walter's latest flight was not quite panic-stricken. Purpose, of a pressing variety, provided motivation. He had not plunged immediately into Edgar's *History*. To undertake such an activity at The Old Home Place would have been as dangerous as coupling with Star. Exercising admirable control, he dumped Edgar's belongings at the landfill, pushing his truck as fast as he could past the crumbling and apparently deserted ranch house. When he packed, he had taken the crucial documents and a few other essentials. Passing through Helmsville, he withdrew ten thousand dollars from his checking account. The figure was weighty and substantial; it would suffice for his task, for the work ahead.

Charlotte was large enough and characterless—a tangle of suburbs and malls—perfect for concealment. Concealment was a requirement, and the apartment and its location fit his specifications—a solid vista of asphalt, stucco, poured concrete, and glass. Anywhere USA, he thought, Southern Division. A supermarket was close by: the part of Charlotte he had escaped to had a market and a strip mall at every intersection. He stocked the kitchen with frozen and canned foods, as well as three cases of beer. My version of the scholar/monk's cell, he thought, as he hastily established his latest safe haven.

He could not examine Edgar's *History* until the setting

was right. His first night in Charlotte, he locked the three volumes in the truck and left his keys with the desk clerk. He did not dare to bring the *History* into his room; perfect conditions were demanded. He evaluated the potential for foolishness. If not for Star, he might never have found the *History*. And because of her, his disappearance might still have been called for. She swore that she would never talk, but, as had been the case throughout his life, Walter put no faith in such promises. Vows of trust were subject to instant and arbitrary revision. Another possibility presented itself: that Edgar's *History* contained nothing of worth. It may well be as barren as the paltry scraps discovered in the study— the surfaces of a life. Then again, he thought, it could be an extended version of the carvings on the monument—boastings, rationalizations, and the like.

These anxieties proved unfounded as he launched his explorations. The apartment in order, he slowly and deliberately opened the first volume. The table was laid out with pens, legal pads, and Walter's own journals. He had, in keeping with his strategy, determined to proceed chronologically, resisting the temptation to skip ahead. I am a scholar, he wrote, and I must live up to that title throughout the course of this project.

The first volume had apparently been composed when Edgar was in his fifties—vigorous and confident in all that he was, had been, and would be. Volume One, Edgar announced in a short preface, would provide a narrative of his life up to his first marriage. The subsequent two volumes were edited versions of his journal, begun in 1941 *when the second major phase of my time commenced.* The persona that strode forth from these words was the Edgar of Walter's childhood—that unnaturally erect, commanding figure. How Ricky must have trembled, Walter wrote. So many years of daddy's proclamations. And what would Roy Bunch say of this lately-discovered evidence?

Bunch, however, like Star and Ricky, Beatrice, The Event, the lawsuits, and the rest of it, was far away. It was only Walter and Edgar. Alone together at last. The prose was serviceable—the plain style, once prized among scholars—animated here and there with florid, slightly old-fashioned flourishes, like a bad imitation of a late Victorian novel. Despite the flaws, Walter grudgingly admitted that Edgar's prose was readable, regardless—and perhaps because of—its occasional bombast.

After characterizing his parents, Edgar had summarized the family history, most of which coincided with those brief remarks of Ricky's about the Loomis heritage. Unlike Ricky, however, Walter did not resort to nostalgia in dealing with his materials. The Loomis tribe originated in the hills far to the west of Helmsville—some from East Tennessee. The rest were not positive of a specific, geographical position. Where they came from did not have a name. They were from the mountains, but not of the mountains—bad farmers, moonshiners, with a half-educated lawyer and a preacher in one generation. The men avoided the Confederate press gangs by hiding deep in the Appalachians. *They emerged,* Edgar wrote, *only when they learned that Lee had surrendered and the imbecility of combat had ceased.* The cotton mills of Helmsville had lured Edgar's grandfather and two of his brothers. They soon understood that the mills were a losing proposition—unless you happened to own one—and they set themselves up in other lines; a hardware clerk, a policeman. Stamey's father, Horace, traveled for the National Shoe Company. Stamey plotted his own course when he was a boy: gambler and land speculator.

My only uncle, Randall Loomis, vanished when Father was twenty-five. Some said that he was killed in France during the First World War; or that he remained there after he was discharged from the service. I find this latter bit of con-

jecture rather doubtful. From Father's sparse account of Uncle Randall, he probably died in some trench or shell hole. He was large and good-natured, and, I would imagine, none too careful. The war was his escape—the first Loomis to partake of such an adventure. He was a romantic. Uncle Randall ran away when Father won Mother from him. It was a fair fight, and Father emerged victorious. The Trueloves, foot-washing Baptists as they were, favored Uncle Randall, who lacked the drive and sense of self-preservation to avoid being crushed in this twilight contest we call existence. He had, before the fortunate arrival of the war, been content to make freight deliveries for the Piedmont & Northern Railroad and play the trumpet in the Helmsville town band—hardly a calling, in Father's estimation, for a brother of his own blood. Uncle Randall loafed and performed in Sunday afternoon concerts and on Confederate Memorial Day. Father said that Randall was a dreamer, and Mother had initially found this characteristic to be quite charming. Father, however, had already acquired considerable land and money. On April 5, 1917, my parents were married at the Weeping Mary Baptist Church. Father donated two thousand dollars to the church building fund, the gift mollifying his in-laws and putting the stiff-necked preacher and deacons in his debt. He liked to relate how his wedding day was the first and last time he set foot in that church. Mother would smile sadly at this. She was a regular and devout Baptist, but Father forbade her from coercing me into her faith. It will make him into a hypocrite and a sniveling Sunday School brat, he said. I would pat Mother's poor, frail shoulder, secretly relieved by Father's edict. He saw no inconsistency, however, in continuing his donations over the years. By his standards, generosity was to be regular and consistent, or those who benefit from your largesse would turn upon you. I have followed Father's example, and can attest to its correctness.

The development of lasting traditions, Walter wrote. Stamey had avoided the draft by claiming that the farm produced food for the war effort. This excuse placated the local draft board, three of whose five members, all prominent citizens, regularly took their seats in Stamey's poker game at the North State Hotel. In truth, the only crops grown on the farm consisted of Helena's large vegetable garden and a few acres of corn. At that point, Stamey let most of his holdings lie fallow. It was enough to own, not develop. Stamey's exemption was not tampered with, and he was known in Helmsville as a great buyer of Liberty Bonds. Edgar was born, as was graven on the monument, on November 10, 1920. The farm, The Old Home Place that Stamey had built for his bride, was "a boy's paradise."

From the time I was six or seven, the land was my personal domain, a playground of mystical proportion. When not imprisoned in the enforced tedium of school, I was free to step out the door on any morning and not return until dinner time, or supper as we called it in those days. Mother occasionally chided me for not attending to chores; Father, never less than direct and forceful, led her to understanding. The boy will learn from his time alone on the land, he said. Edgar will learn in as many ways as there are. Mother accepted Father's position. As the chores were minimal, I took care to complete them prior to my rambles and excursions. This pleased Mother.

When Edgar was ten a black family named Nichols moved to the farm and took up residence in a four-room shanty Stamey had had built for them. The Nicholses were to provide the muscle for "improving the place." Improvements consisted of timber cutting, the clearing of plots for more corn, and "beautification"—there were to be fences and pastures for both "practical and aesthetic reasons." Reading between the lines, Walter deduced that Stamey did not go in for agriculture with much enthusiasm. He had set himself up as a gentleman farmer. His real business was cards and accumulation.

The Nicholses had a son, Oscar, and a daughter named Grace. Oscar was Edgar's age. Grace was two years older and helped her mother tend to The Old Home Place. The boys tramped the woods and fields, constructed tree houses and forts, and swam in the Reedy River and its tributaries. Perfection, Walter thought. No wonder Edgar was assured that the world should perform for him.

Oscar, some nine weeks my senior, was my constant companion. He was well-made, strong, and intelligent. No mean outdoorsman, he taught me the arts of fishing and small game hunting, which he had learned from Henry, his father. Ruth, Oscar's mother, was as fine a cook as ever existed. The catfish and perch she prepared were unrivaled by the most renowned and costly cuisine I later sampled abroad and in the great cities of this nation. I will never forget those meals, Oscar and I devouring the hot, crispy fish and fresh cornbread as Ruth beamed down upon us. Henry Nichols, as Father said many times, was a first class worker, and carried out his instructions perfectly—before going on to develop new improvements of his own. Naturally, Henry performed the actual labor, as Father's affairs kept him in Helmsville, or traveling throughout the south—and the rest of the country as well. It was expected that Oscar and I lend a hand in helping Henry and his crew of three or four day laborers, which we gladly did since Henry had the knack of transforming hard work into play. I learned much in those days that would see me in good stead in the future. Henry was a patient and excellent teacher—far superior to those school marms and eunuchs who presided over the Helmsville public schools. Henry gave me a practical educa-

tion in the enlightened stewardship of the earth.

Walter popped a beer. In the hermetically-sealed apartment, there was not a hint of the traffic from Charlotte's perpetually-congested streets. What is most unreal? he thought. This apartment, or those words I've been hunched over? It could be fiction that I've been sucked into, the story of how Edgar wished his life to have been.

Walter resumed his work, absorbing, cautiously drawing conclusions. Edgar's early youth had been idyllic, or else recreated as such. School was both a triumph and a bore. His classmates, the offspring of mill workers, storekeepers, and farmers, were dull, opinionated, and ignorant. He won all of the academic prizes, and excelled in football and baseball. His father's profession denied him admission to Ramseur Institute, the local prep school whose graduates regularly trooped off to lofty universities. Rejection of this nature cultivated toughness. At a tenth grade social he *broke the nose and cheekbone of a Ramseur dandy for slandering Father. Father paid the medical bills and congratulated me for my spunk. I never lost a fight during my years at school—or later, for that matter.* There were incidents with larger implication than youthful fistfights.

The Nicholses departed from us. One evening they were there, and the next morning they were gone. The shanty was left neat and tidy. They did not take any of the clothes, furniture, or household items that we had bestowed as gifts— gifts given with the greatest good will. Father could not understand. They left without saying good-bye. This rupture with my second family could have been my fault. I am thankful that my parents never learned the facts of the situation. Now I must set them down.

A regret, Walter wrote. Nearly sixty years later. He

turned the page.

Grace was eighteen. In time's passage, she had developed well. She was, like her family, light-skinned. Her carriage and demeanor were exquisite to behold. Since the earliest days of the Nicholses' residence, we had been easy with each other—joking, laughing, and playing like brother and sister. For some time prior to the unfortunate occurrence, I had conceived of another sort of relation with her. When I compared her to the pasty-faced virgins in their saddle shoes and cheerleader's costumes, those peroxided children who allowed me to be their escort to dances, who favored me by letting me buy dinner and flowers for them, Grace was a vision of dignified, yet sensual bliss.

It was not hard for Walter to conjure up the scene. The river was close by; they may have been near the monument's site. *She ranged freely through my thoughts. Dusky and lovely. Nothing like my stupid schoolmate's conception of the promiscuous Negro female. She hid her sexual self beneath a demure primness. I sought her out.*

She was picking blackberries for one of her mother's pies. Horrible, Walter wrote. His mouth was dry and he sucked in beer. Horror is predictable.

Henry and Oscar, who was out of school and working with his father, were a mile or two off, attending to improvements. Grace resisted, at first, treating it as a prank. Edgar pleaded. When the pleas had no effect, he demanded. *Once we were as brother and sister. I, in my boyish ardor, which was both natural and unfortunate, forever altered that connection.*

When it was over, he tried to make amends. He spoke of love (the oldest lie of all, Walter thought). He did not return the blows that she rained upon his face. When he offered her money, she laughed—then spit on him. He knocked her to

189

the ground and left here there. He feared the rage of his
father, but the Nicholses' departure had spared him. The
Nicholses' replacements, a large brood with six strapping
sons, and no daughters, arrived a month later.

An old, old story, Walter wrote. Intolerably depressing.
Love, he called it. Rape as love. Perfectly natural. Betrayal
as the commonest of human impulses. But am I one to take
on the colorations of the moralist?

Troops of women followed Grace. The prostitutes at the
North State Hotel were soon on speaking terms with Edgar.
If Stamey disapproved it was not recorded in the *History*. He
may have viewed Edgar's trysts as another method of edu-
cation, Walter wrote.

*A whore is a fine thing. They are among the most
intriguing women that one is likely to meet. Whenever I
have ventured in my travels, I have engaged them, and not
simply for their physical expertise. Their stories, whether in
Helmsville, or London, or Havana, are fascinating. I have
paid for the stories alone; simple narratives that serve as
learned commentaries on fundamental rituals. Sex, like
other aspects of life, requires ritual in order for us to com-
prehend truth and confirm meaning. The most significant
rituals, those that mean the most, are of your own creation.*

Edgar could be speaking theoretically, Walter thought.
Perhaps not. There was the funeral. Ricky and The Event.
Edgar doesn't seem one for theory—and his rituals would
require others, as performers, as props. He marked his place
in the *History*, raised the blinds, and stared out on the parking lot.

Edgar had arrived in Chapel Hill in the fall of 1937. He
had graduated a year early from Helmsville High, impatient
for the larger world of the state university. There was no further mention of Grace Nichols in the *History*. Stamey and

Helena were proud of him; the first Loomis to attend college, and an altogether polished and aggressive young man. Stamey afforded Edgar a comfortable campus life, being the only man of consequence in the region of Helmsville who had prospered through the Great Depression. The Loomis tribe was fully immune, Walter wrote. Breadlines? Strikes? Starvation? Edgar owned a new Packard and had an allowance of one hundred and fifty dollars a month. His senior year, a history major, a member of Phi Beta Kappa, the amount had risen to two hundred and fifty.

I must say that I led a privileged life when I attended the university—where money and comfort were concerned, that is. Many men in my class were compelled into the usual menial campus jobs: waiting tables, stoking furnaces, and shelving library books. I befriended a few of them, the boys who, like myself, lacked the proper background for social distinction. I was blackballed two years running during fraternity rush. The single rationale was Father's business—as if those high-nosed aristocrats from east of Raleigh did not come from families far more ruthless than Father was ever capable of being: corrupt judges, corpulent landowners, and old money that was gotten through one transparent swindle or another. My days at Chapel Hill were solitary—and also my most democratic. A brilliant young New York Jew, an outcast as I was, came close to convincing me to leave for Madrid, to enlist in the International Brigade. This was in late 1938 when the Spanish War was winding down, the Loyalists clearly defeated. What would have been the course of my career if I had fought for socialism? In America, radicalism leads to dead ends.

Youthful idealism, Walter thought. An intoxicating brand of role-playing. I never had that itch, lacking the courageous, romantic sense of self—a quality not in short supply in young Edgar's character. Do I envy him? He had no fear of action, of large gestures, no matter how crude or contradictory. A life rich with incident—rape, fist fights, whoring, socialism. History was an immense playground, a larger version of The Old Home Place.

The war made me—as it did my generation. What would have been my fate had there been peace? What would I have become? A comfortable citizen, a life of static banality, all sense of possibility thwarted. I graduated in June of 1941. Father, already taken by the stomach cancer that would kill him in two years, argued for law school. I hesitated. The secure indolence of college had passed. Rejection aside, it had been great fun, but it was properly part of what was no more. The war was coming. David Karpinsky, my Jewish friend, graduated a year ahead of me and joined the Royal Air Force. We corresponded regularly. "I have my own Spitfire," he wrote. "And I am finally putting my beliefs into action. Principles present their own moral dilemmas. Yesterday I shot down a Heinkel. It blew up right over the Channel. Before it did, the engines aflame, the rear gunner waved to me. Then he was obliterated. This gave me the shakes." That was from his last letter. Such qualms may have killed him, although I have yet to learn what became of David. Qualms or not, his end was preferable to the safe, slow death of ordinary life. There was drama then. I followed the war carefully in the months after college—the back and forth slaughter between Rommel and the British in the western desert, the Panzers overrunning half of Russia. I went to the movies for the newsreels, all that terrific footage from the various fronts. It was at the movies that I met Margaret Henderson—my first love, my first wife.

Walter pushed away from the table as the *History* reached out, encircling him. It *has* to be like a damned movie, he thought. And more unnerving than Edgar's favorite newsreels of the Nazi legions beneath the Arc de Triomphe. The plot, like all plots, is stale. Despite the repetition, the inevitability. You must watch, futilely calling to the actors to stop before it is too late. But I must go on. That much is required.

She was like those girls who attended the dances at Chapel Hill in their evening gowns, alighting from the cars in front of the fraternity houses—brainless, tuxedoed dates on their arms. Once I drifted past with David Karpinsky. We had had a few beers, arguing good-naturedly at a bar over books and politics. Karpinsky could tell that I was quite taken by the scene. "Loomis," he said in his thick Brooklyn accent, "You're a sucker for the trappings of the leisure class. Which, in my estimation, are so much bullshit."

How could Edgar not fall spell to the glittering there? Margaret was that kind of girl—a Sweet Briar graduate. She had done her dancing at the University of Virginia, which was more snobbish than Chapel Hill.

I'll never forget how she looked that night. Her friend, a girl from high school, a girl whose name I have forgotten, introduced us in front of the Darden Theater. Mrs. Miniver was playing. We sat together and I sniffed her perfume and the smooth, high-toned flesh. She said that Mrs. Miniver was wonderful. It was ridiculous, but I agreed with her. So true to life, I said. Or some nonsense along those lines—a standard lie by an instantly-smitten young man. I called her later that night. The next evening we sat through Mrs. Miniver again. I held her hand—a greater conquest than all the whores and professional virgins I had taken to that point.

They began with books and movies. Edgar was enthusiastic over the modern classics: Conrad, Lawrence, Joyce. Margaret must have wrinkled her nose at Joyce, Walter

thought. She liked Margaret Mitchell and Thomas Wolfe—
and any film that played in Helmsville. Edgar took care not
to dispute her aesthetic preferences. They kept company,
swam in the country club pool, and necked on couches, in
the theater balcony, in cars, and anywhere else they could
find. She confessed that she had promised her mother to
keep her virginity intact until marriage. Choking and crying
on his shoulder, she said that she was "afraid of sex. Really."
He held her and soothed her, feeling noble, biding his time.
Virginity, he wrote *is a state of mind. "You won't force me
to do—anything," she said. "Hush, Margaret," I replied.
"Lie still awhile."*

He gloated over their outings to the country club, where,
after tennis and swimming, he would charm her parents over
dinner with his excellent manners and expensive clothes. He
later learned that his charm had a limited reach. The name
of Loomis was an impediment to full approval from
Helmsville's ruling class. Stamey, now a widower, in pain
and sustaining himself on milk and custard, would listen
intently as Edgar recounted the decorous aura of the
Henderson household and the solid connections he was
making at the club. It's all to the good, Stamey said. You're
consolidating. That's the ticket. Edgar had typed this quota-
tion from his father in capital letters.

The fall of 1941 came on. Two German armies bashed at
Moscow and the British dug in for a stand at Tobruk.
Margaret paid occasional visits to The Old Home Place.
Edgar was putting his own mark on the farm, picking up
where Henry Nichols had left off as he directed the six black
boys who had grown into men. They cleared woods for pasture land, dug drainage ditches, and built fences. Overseeing
these projects, including the construction of the now-demol-
ished stable, was satisfying. *It was my intention to make the
land pay. I had boundless endurance and energy in those
days. Father had been content with a yearly crop of corn and*

little else—leaving supervision to a string of incompetent managers. I fired the last one and took over. This soon paid off. Once the stable was complete, and the riding trails cut, the stalls filled with boarded horses. The income was steady and the overhead at a minimum.

The men who worked under him followed orders well, and he labored beside them. *They loved me. And I loved them. We were elemental, basic, and in a few months I had progressed some distance from the intellectual diversions of campus bull sessions. I had dug down to the primitive core: the day came when Margaret followed me there.*

No one, Walter wrote, would have accused my mother of primitiveness. She would have been insulted. Edgar was already adept at presenting various faces. Did she see him with the blacks, a vision of the founding of the South's first plantation? Forging mere dirt into a dream of money and harmony.

One day in mid-September, Margaret drove out to see me. She arrived earlier than expected for our late afternoon walk, and I did not have the opportunity to bathe and change from my work clothes. It was Indian Summer and she encountered me and my negroes at the edge of the road. She was lovely, dressed in slacks like Marlene Dietrich. There was nothing of the purely Teutonic in her, however. She was pure in another sense—a Southern Anglo-Saxon beauty—slim, tanned, her brown hair lightened by a summer of poolside indolence. She giggled at my appearance, eyeing me with a degree of carnal curiosity I had never before witnessed in her. I must say, my heart beat faster. I apologized for how I looked and asked her to wait at the house while I cleaned up. "Don't do that," she said. "I'm sorry that I came early. I had to get out of the house. And I wanted to see you." I was smeared with red mud and swelled like any male who has joyously employed his body. We set out through the pines, the needles swishing softly at our feet. I had not the slightest inkling of what would occur.

Walter could guess, which did not lessen the queasy expectation.

The sun's descent had just commenced as we seated our-selves on a rocky promontory that jutted out over the river. We chatted amiably over small things and she smoked. Then she said that she had never fully envisioned me as a man of the soil. I took this in jest and laughed. She frowned. "I'm serious," she said. And in what other ways have you envi-sioned me, I asked. "I'm not sure," she said. I kissed her and she pressed herself against me, enfolding, straining, offering all. She said that she loved me and I said that I loved her as well. I believe that I did—then. And later too—for a period of years.

If it had ended there, Walter would have been relieved.

As I have noted before in this rather fragmentary account of my life, sex is a ritual. I had performed it as such since my disastrous incident with Grace. With Margaret, this now willing partner, this perfect child of my region's elite, I orchestrated our love making with deliberate intensi-ty. I do not know where my sense of direction, my innate grasp of where the rightness of all we did originated. Now I believe that it was derived in part from my affinity for the land, the earth that Father had gained by the turning of cards and through the accurate reading of other men's faces. Unlike Father, the farm meant more to me than mere acreage. I had released within myself an omnipotent sim-plicity—that atavistic quality that I had found through working with negroes. Margaret, the Margaret of that

*time—she was to change, to deny those days we had—
stepped into this simplicity with me.*

*We went naked—nudity being at the heart of the ritual—
the only attire possible in our Eden. I pursued her, the pair
of us as gleeful as nymphs and shepherds in an Elizabethan
sonnet. If I had played the pipes, those scenes would have
corresponded in every respect, an elegant enrapturing poetry. I can summon her up yet, more than thirty years later, her
paleness flashing among the trees, teasing, calling out to me.
The breezes played over our flesh as she drew me onward—
into her. I deliberately held back from catching her, extend-
ing the chase as much as we could bear it—until I fell upon
her. She never failed to choose the exact, perfect moment—
when the desire for my quarry had reached an absolute
zenith, my erect penis, my spear she called it, straining ever
forward as I came after her, crouching low, snarling—like
the first man responding to the most basic impulse.*

*There was one special day. The chase had extended a
mile or more, up and down hill. We had not performed the
ritual for more than a week as she had gone to Asheville
with her parents. The weather was cooler, and there would
not be many days left for our hunts. This made me nearly
insane with wanting her. I had given barely enough attention
to my various projects. Trasker, the oldest and most percep-
tive of the negroes, had inquired as to whether or not my
sweetheart was to visit after work. She must, I said. Trasker
smiled. On the intuitive level, where he and his brothers
dwelled, there was a profound appreciation for the inter-
twining of the spirit and the flesh. After all, those negroes,
fine men with fine women of their own, had retained the
juices that are required to animate life—unlike the
comatose, death-in-life existence of most of the whites I
lived among. In later years, I revelled in finding others who
were suffused with this proud nectar.*

Margaret led me to a field that my crew and I had

*cleared the previous months. Her back was to me, her mus-
cles perfectly synchronized beneath her perfect skin. The distance shortened between us. Abruptly, she whirled and faced
about—a gesture of surrender that maddened me with mind-
emptying, beautiful lust. I took her three times in rapid suc-
cession, on all fours in the stubble, our bodies slick with the
divine secretions of our animal selves. Spent, we lay side by
side beneath the healing, consuming sun. There was no need
for words. Absently, we stroked each other, smearing the
juices about, rubbing them on our faces and mouths. I had
absolutely no sense of anything beyond the field. Then she
began to sing, sitting up, her legs bent beneath her. It was
more like a chant than a song—holy and unadorned.
Somewhat like the glorias in her family's High Church
Episcopal services—only without reference to the God of
heaven or the sacrifice of Christ. The song took hold of me,
pouring into my being. I wept. At the sight of my tears, she
ceased her song. Go on, I said. You must never stop.*

It was midday, very hot, and none of Walter's neighbors
were in sight. If anyone had glimpsed Walter, there might
have been cause for alarm. He walked with a painful, psychotic stride as if against a stiff headwind. After two cir-
cumnavigations of the apartment complex, he rested on a
bench outside the manager's office.

How many women sang for Edgar? he thought. What
had Obie said? Obie, in whose coffin rested a shin and a
foot. Women came to The Old Home Place. First Margaret,
then the rich women from New York, the daughters of
South American aristocrats. And Beatrice. The strains of
Beatrice's song! Surely not a High Church Gloria. Did an
aged, patriarchal Edgar command a song from Star? Rituals
must be conducted on a regular basis if they are to endure.
And they must be introduced to new devotees. Did Edgar
initiate Ricky into the most profound mystery of the

woods—the ground where the dope grew tall? He did so with The Event—the Fourth of July extravaganza. Did Star sing for Ricky? Or someone else? There is only one other.

He had to return to the *History*, but was clamped down to the bench. The apartment complex had the air of a deserted fortress. Everyone else, he thought, is about their business, attending to their personal ordinariness. Ordinary. What a blessing that would be. What if I burned the *History?* What would be lost? It would be further confirmation of my cowardice, a betrayal of the scholar's quest. When I have completed my studies, I will be cleansed. This, at least, is my prayer.

As the autumn of 1941 wore on, the rituals had moved indoors. Edgar rented his own suite at the North State Hotel—a floor above his father's. There, after Edgar completed his Herculean tasks with his crew of wise, happy negroes, and after Margaret had whiled away the day as an indolent southern maiden, they made love with the same savage, wordless frankness as in the fields. She sang, even when she had no wish to. There were clinical descriptions of the rituals' refinements—which gradually had less to do with sex than with Edgar's blossoming sense of omnipotence and control. *I understood fully the gifts that have been bestowed upon me, and some of what I had gained was a result of my estrangement and alienation from so-called decent society.* Loomis as superman, Walter wrote without smiling.

We understood that the realm of experience was far larger than we cared to admit. For example, once the rituals began, I ignored all else, except for my work at the farm. I stopped following the war, even as it drew closer to me. The realm that we dwelled in had narrowed to the earth, our bodies, and the hotel suite. I loved her because she had been

199

unafraid to take the rituals as far as we could. That was my belief at the time. Actually, however, she was unafraid by virtue of her illusions: that the rituals were a transitory whim on my part. Some day, she thought, I would be transformed into the perfect personification of her romantic ideals—as virile, exciting, and paradoxically tame as the lacquered film stars who she mooned over at the theater. Margaret fancied the rituals as a fleshy, temporary amusement, while I had instantly conceived of them as life-long essentials. Late in the year, she began to draw away from me. We met each night, but she began to ask questions: "Why must I sing? Don't you think it's silly? Why do you make me bathe you and wash your hair? And I'm tired of dressing up like a slut for you." Initially, I brushed aside her objections. Later, when her questions and objections did not stop, I'm afraid I forced her into silence and utter, abject submission. This, in turn, caused a re-emergence of my adolescent guilt over Grace. Guilt is a tiresome, middle-class emotion that I have since succeeded in eradicating. In those days, however, I was young and green. I comforted Margaret, promised to moderate my actions, lying all the while. I could no more cease the rituals than I could voluntarily cease breathing. The future between us appeared to be settled. I would eventually extricate myself from her, love or no love. She would be fine. No doubt she would have married one of those safe, respectable boys who were born to run mills and play golf at the country club. She might have been better off if she had. I did not count on the impact of December 7, 1941. Roosevelt called it a day that would live in infamy. Infamy indeed. It was the dawn of a life that I could only have evoked in fantasy.

He spent the night at the hotel—after driving home a weeping Margaret. She said that he had hurt her, but he was not specific as to the nature of the injury. He apologized, and she said that her mother disapproved of how much time she spent with him, even if he was head and shoulders above his origins. He had seen her to the front door, but she would not let him in, nor would she let him kiss her good night. *I could clearly see where we were heading—an end. I was both saddened and relieved. The night was unseasonably warm, with clouds tumbling westward in the wind, under a moon-bright sky. I drove around for awhile, bought a pint of whiskey from a bell hop, and dropped in on Father's poker game.*

This scene comes back to me because it occurred on the night before the world's possibilities were laid at my feet. The players were well-dressed, except for Father, who affected a deliberate seediness to draw in those men shallow enough to be impressed by clothes. The mayor, a staunch Presbyterian and expert railer against liquor, was sitting in on the game, along with two of John Henderson's (my future father-in-law) cronies from the American-Taylor mills and the Darden Country Club. There was also a man named Walsh who I had seen at other games over the previous month or two. He was soberly dressed: dark suit, expensive, understated tie, and a starched white shirt. The other men, except for Father and Walsh, had removed their jackets, and had the careless, rumpled air of those who had been at their cards for some time. The mayor and John Henderson's cronies had full tumblers of whiskey next to their stack of chips. Father drank milk. Even before the onset of his cancer, he rarely drank—and never while at work. Walsh drank coffee. He and Father each had accumulated a large mass of chips.

Father looked very bad. He had lost a great deal of weight during the summer, being eaten, as he was, by cancer. That night, it was like seeing him for the first and last time. Death was on him. The skin was stretched tightly over his skull and his movements were painfully slow and deliberate. Dealing cards was close to the limits of his endurance.

201

Neither of us had directly confronted what was happening to him. Father would not have permitted it. He had an iron strength. When Mother died, he had borne the loss well. Her death had not been the same for me, the same as that curious clarity I had that night as I witnessed Father's death-in-life. Mother had been suddenly carried off. When I went to college, she was fit and smiling. I returned to find her in a coffin. But Father was visibly wilting before my eyes—and yet he struggled on. He died in October 1943, when I was in London having a splendid time. I patted the pint of bourbon that rested in my inside jacket pocket. I too seldom drank, but after the scenes with Margaret I craved the spreading warmth of alcohol. I had consumed quite a bit between the lobby and Father's suite, where it blended with the resignation and tranquility that I felt on that special, final night before things would never be as they had been before.

Father did not offer me a place at the table; the game was not for purposes of amusement. I would have declined if he had. I was not sure why I had come to his suite. It could have been that I required company, and in the darkened, deserted streets of my town there was no other company to be had. Margaret, with her inbred, illogical qualms, had drained me—a sensation that I have loathed and resisted all of my life. I value my vitality and my own blunt appetites. I secretly reject decorum, while maintaining a mask appropriate to that particular trait.

The cards fell with equal favor between Father and Walsh, as the other men cursed, joked, and drank. Both were careful players—unlike their partners, who tricked themselves into believing that the game was all in fun. Fun: what a low, despicable thing. The inclination toward fun in my own character once chagrined and maddened me. A man must make himself an instrument of his own policy. Fun is a hindrance to that creation. And yet I loved Margaret, and this love ran contrary to my truest version of myself. I was stranded, drifting.

Father laid a king-high straight on the green felt of the table and raked the chips toward him. Walsh, who had folded early in the hand, congratulated Father with a slight smile. Father did not respond. He had suspected that Walsh, too, was a professional gambler, despite expertly keeping to his businessman-from-Spartanburg routine. Father was a gifted man, both simple and complex. His rituals, those of money and acquisition, had been handed down to me through heredity and by example. In his limited way, he too was a creation of his own policy. I shall forever retain the image of his pale, long-fingered hands drawing the tinkling, brightly-colored chips to him.

Walsh excused himself from the next round. I am sure that he was aware that I had been watching him, sizing up his slow, murderous power. Walsh had a well-developed front, but Father was right about him. He was a professional, but I had learned to penetrate surfaces early on. For some reason, I thought of David Karpinsky and his Spitfire, the two of them commingled, no doubt, in an English field or flattened against the bed of the North Sea. David, intelligence and passion aside, was a primary text, like most of the men and women that I would compete against and seduce. They were easy, easier than I could ever have guessed. Seduction, in whatever form it takes, is the closest that I come to fun.

Walsh lit a cigar, after first offering one to me. He inquired as to whether I had completed my schooling. He was quite adept at small talk. He possessed one of those cultured, Lowcountry accents that was incongruous for a back country gambler. The Gentleman Sharper, I remember thinking. A traditional American figure, like Melville's Confidence Man. Half-drunk as I was, I came close to blurting out the allusion. Walsh, whose real name might well have been of the old, aristocratic South Carolina stock— Ravenel or Coker—could have appreciated the reference.

He went on in that voice, describing in a general way his own days at the Citadel, which confirmed my romantic impression of him. Who knows if he ever went to college at all? But as I listened, I was drawn closer to him. What rituals, beside the game, did he ascribe to? What secret gestures and motions were his, and his alone?

He smoked, drank his coffee, and talked. I paid heed to the sound more than the words themselves. It soothed and comforted me. I was on the point of going upstairs, draining off the rest of the bourbon and either going to sleep or calling Audrey, the most refined and proper whore in residence at the North State Hotel. I could violate her refinement, pretending that she was Margaret, whose timid propriety could never be destroyed. I excused myself. Father merely nodded. He was immersed in the current round of five card stud.

I thanked Walsh for the conversation, and that is when he did a strange thing. He grasped my arm and compelled me to gaze into his eyes. They were dark and astonishingly vivid—the eyes of an unhealthily knowing child—set there in the face of a substantial businessman.

And young Mister Loomis, he said, opportunity arises from those we are forced to live with. Those who fail to pay attention, they convince themselves that they are safe, and that they deserve their safety.

He smiled sweetly. He was as seductive as anyone I have ever encountered—including double-agents, assassins, high-ranking military officers, and statesmen.

In my suite, I wrote of my encounter with Walsh. I never saw him again, and I never had the chance to ask Father what had become of him. Walsh's words were not particularly original; this I found from my wartime reading of Nietzsche: "The meek shall inherit the earth? Very good. We shall take it from them" and so on. I suppose it must have

been the moment, the fortunate juxtaposition of time, ener-
gy, and my personal travails. I carried those notes for
years—put down on the cheap stationery from the North
State Hotel. I have now transcribed them into this volume.
Odd to think that I might not have begun without Walsh.

On the last night of things as they were, I wrote and
drank, filling all the pages in the room, and calling the front
desk for more bourbon and stationery. I went at it furious-
ly, setting down, in rather incoherent fashion, an account of
the woodland rituals, my theories pertaining to the basic
urges of men, and ending with Walsh at the card game. In
the hour before dawn, as the air crews of the Imperial
Japanese Navy readied for their wondrously irrevocable act,
I summoned Audrey from her bed to mine. I paid her triple
the going rate, and she willingly submitted to all I
required—including my nude reading of my midnight com-
position. "That's some stuff," she yawned, cat-like and
compliant. "There's not another sport in the county who
could dream that up. It's a cinch I couldn't." She left me as
the sunlight filtered through the thin white curtains. Several
hours later, I was awakened by Margaret chattering inco-
herently into the telephone. Pearl Harbor, she said. It was
like a prophecy designed with me in mind.

Monstrous, Walter wrote. Redolent with the monstrous-
ness of the secret life. And he was, and is, my father. I am,
to use the biblical phrase, spawned from his loins.

He paused; submerged in the old, familiar uneasiness.
He had not desired a father, but was pinioned to one
nonetheless. He had never wanted a mother either. The
newly unearthed Margaret generated further uneasiness.
Ricky had said that her picture was next to Edgar's heart; a
gesture of love, past and present.

He scratched at the expanse of blank yellow paper. There
are images to reckon with. Margaret "hurt" in the North

State Hotel, a whore named Audrey as a suitable surrogate for Edgar's rituals. There was a naked, running Margaret who could not be reconciled with the professionally genteel Charleston matron. This is much less plausible than Edgar— Phi Beta Kappa, CIA operative, and wealthy landowner— fucking, drinking, and formulating his crude philosophy in the dark, windy hours before Pearl Harbor. He embraced the war with the greatest enthusiasm possible, as if it was staged for him. The creation of new rituals—costume dramas, complete with blood and fire, that were beyond his wildest projections.

I am squirming now, and it has to do with the flesh: my linkage to him, to Margaret, to Ricky. He tried to will himself blank. Soon, with a tic in his left eye, he grasped that blankness was forever ruled out as an option. He dropped the pen, then slowly and deliberately took it up again.

If I had such authority, there would not have been a single connection to anyone. People have forever assailed me; frightening, demanding, ludicrous wraiths.

He went on, working up a slight momentum; a pale imitation of Edgar at the North State Hotel.

All that I have endeavored to reject is unavoidable. I *am* connected, like it or not. And I am my father's boy in that I stand apart. Was his escape a success? He utilized his brains and appetites to create a myth of supremacy. I employed writing and furtiveness as a disguise. It was a bad disguise. Margaret absorbed gestures and adorned herself with the trappings of ready-made roles to make sense where no sense existed—to push the inexplicable behind her. Ricky's aping of Edgar resolves itself through innocence and ignorance into catastrophe.

THIS IS A FAMILY, he wrote in huge capitals that sloped at a steep angle across a fresh page. The line complete, he studied it for a moment, then threw the pen against the wall. The point dug a tiny black hole into the sky blue paint.

Fully clothed, tucked into a ball, a resisting Walter succumbed to dreams animated and staged by his father. Edgar's face was young—the one that he owned when he left Walter for the last time. The voice was old, however, and it framed questions. Were not my words written for you, boy? Are you not cursed with the duty of a final accounting? The words were not spoken harshly, but instead unfolded in a reasonable, matter-of-fact tone. Edgar's face went away, to be followed by a shrill, semi-musical clangor and blinding halos of light.

12

Following Pearl Harbor, the detailed narratives of ritual and philosophic insights were replaced by communiques that revealed less of Edgar's state of mind. Form follows content, Walter wrote. The art of omission supersedes that of inclusion.

He was near the end of volume one—two weeks of reading, re-reading, and note taking. He had left the apartment once—to reprovision at the supermarket. If he had approached a mirror, he might have been shocked by how dirty and unkempt he was, his time having been taken, both waking and sleeping, by his father.

After working to exhaustion, he would spin into a coma-like sleep. The *History* was draining him dry, as if Edgar's vitality was renewing itself through Walter's labors. Not all of the dreams involved Edgar. Star, Ricky, disapproving department chairmen, his ex-wife, Margaret, glowering tenure committees, Obie on one stark, frightening occasion—all had their allotted time slot in Walter's sleep. And there were pages—flying in hurricane-force winds down gigantic corridors, the words on them pulsing, growing, whipping upwards into an indistinct sky. Later, he was a child again, enclosed in a sterilized container of some sort, hurtling along on a journey without destination. Edgar, however, dominated all of these scenes. He whispered, shrieked, cooed, and demanded. Walter could not make out all of the words, although many of those that he could identify came directly from the *History*. The exhortations concerning blood, rituals, and the will to power bothered Walter less than the concrete, specific demands.

Once, as Walter was rolled into his customary fetal ball, Edgar summoned him from a purple darkness, commanding, stentorian. Timing, boy, is everything, he said. Every other son of a bitch you meet has a ball of copperheads inside their skulls. When are you going to *really* learn that. Oh you can pretend that you know. You've got to start *paying attention*. You can't just *hide*. They'll find you, no matter what.

After this, Walter could not return to the *History* for an entire afternoon. Eventually, he did. I can't go on, he wrote. But I will.

As the nature of the *History* changed, Walter, between nightmare and near-narcolepsy, was left to wrestle with tantalizing conjecture. The last pages of Volume One covered Edgar's wartime experiences.

He had enlisted several days after Roosevelt asked Congress to declare war. Stamey objected strongly, reminding Edgar of his uncle's escape into the First War. Edgar replied that the war was meant for him. After he was commissioned a second lieutenant, and after his acceptance into the O.S.S., he underwent intelligence training in Washington, which he referred to as "the capital of the universe." He was posted to London, where he served as special assistant to a colonel in charge of coordinating operations with the French resistance in the Pas-de-Calais. He pleased his superiors, was promoted to captain, received numerous love letters from Margaret, and consorted with a woman named Florence whose husband was with the Sussex regiment at Monte Cassino and whose father sat in The House of Lords. Great fun, Walter wrote. Until the mission.

It all went wrong; but from Edgar's words, Walter could not be sure how the disaster occurred. Edgar was part of a six-man Anglo-American team that was dropped across the Channel. The idea was to work with the French in setting up clandestine radio transmitters so as to confuse the Germans about the exact location of the D-Day landings. There were obscure, oblique references to the unreliability of their maquis contacts. The team leader, a Major Cromartie, was shot early on. And there was *a big surly Yorkshireman named Tomlinson. In truth, I owe my life to him, although it was most fortunate that he died when he did. In my report, I gave him proper credit. The least I could do.* Edgar was the lone survivor.

Despite the failure of the mission, Edgar became the youngest major in his section when the war ended, earning a personal commendation from the legendary Wild Bill Donovan and a citation from British Intelligence as well. The Old Boy Network, Walter thought. Major Cromartie and the heroic Tomlinson must not have been members in good standing. Yes, my father had a fine time in the war. Edgar summed it up best, however: *The war was invaluable in shaping not only my world view, but also in giving me experiences I could never have gotten elsewhere. I was a part of the large, grinding process of historical inevitability that forged a new Edgar Loomis, a new America, and a new world. Possibility became infinite, drama was heightened to a new level. We live yet in the wake of all that occurred in these years. Thank God. It is a war that will never end.*

On the last page were two short entries:

May 28, 1946: I marry Margaret at St. Albans Episcopal Church, Helmsville, N.C. We honeymoon at Greenbriar and in Washington.

September 5, 1947: I receive notice of my appointment to the Central Intelligence Agency.

The abrupt curtness agitated Walter. Edgar omitted the crucial parts, he thought; the transformation of the atavistic first man into a keeper of secrets. What could he not say? Perhaps the transformation never occurred. And perhaps he was unaware if it did. There is nothing about the first days of his marriage, or about Margaret. What did he and Margaret do while he awaited the day of his anointing by the CIA? Did they perform their rituals, with Margaret singing selections from Fred Astaire and Ginger Rogers musicals?

The second volume offered no firm answers. Edgar had reverted to diary form, while often excluding specific dates. Walter suspected that Edgar had typed out specific passages from a longer original copy, omitting material for his own reasons. Again it could be that he was writing the story of his life as he wished it to be, Walter thought. And who was his intended audience?

There was the time in Teheran, most probably in the early fifties. Edgar was embroiled in a fracas with the third secretary from the American Embassy.

When things got hot, when the Pahlevis really counted on us, Wyman funked it. I told him so at the reception at the Shah's palace. A victory party, really. Quite a place, peacock throne and all. The Shah's people came across like they had pulled the whole thing off themselves, strutting and preening like so many puffed-up little wogs. The agency staff stayed in the background, which was only appropriate. Wyman sulked when I confronted him. Goddamn Princeton boy. The Foreign Service snobs try to make our job impossible. The station chief was secretly delighted when I made my public display, that bit of slapstick I cooked up when I grabbed Wyman by his Brooks Brothers lapels. The chief had to issue an apology, but he told me in private that anything to piss off the diplomats was fine by him.

Other passages were sketchier. *A profitable side trip to*

Baghdad. The British Petroleum representatives were most cordial, most forthcoming. I can bank their promises. Encountered Rostakovich, the KGB's number two in Tehran. Sneaky, as usual, and trying to act like he wasn't in Baghdad on similar business. Claims to know Uncle Joe Stalin. I doubt it.

Margaret met me at the airport last night. The first thing out of her mouth was blather about me getting re-assigned some place where we can live together. Argued all evening. She hid in the bedroom most of the next day. I let her stew. As always, she is selfish in none of the grand ways. Expects me to take her to an exotic locale that is without the potential for strife and conflict. Some mythical backwater where I can count the number of coconuts being loaded on Soviet freighters. How does she expect me to advance?

Edgar was briefly in Rio de Janeiro, then Paraguay. About a third of the way into Volume Two, came the first reference to Walter.

October 10, 1950. On this day my first child, Walter, was born. I don't know why I waited this long to record this fact. He is five now, and I have seen him three times since his birth. Some day we must spend time together. Margaret tells me that he is well-behaved and has taken to kindergarten. Walter, and her complaints, are the main subjects of her letters. She has forgotten her earlier, romantic notions about the Agency, which were nine parts Hollywood and one part Graham Greene. It is a business, like any other, only much more exciting and important. Anyway, Walter's birthday is next week. Must send a gift. Perhaps from Santiago.

He did dispatch gifts, Walter wrote. Strange foreign puzzles and gimcracks. I played with them, and the soldiers, trucks, airplanes, and the electric train—all spread across the Tree of Life rug that Margaret brought from Helmsville. There were only the two of us. Did she have any friends?

Any neighbors who came over in the evening? No. Only the telephone, always long distance, and her letters. She composed at the antique dining room table she discovered in a shop in the Virginia countryside. When she wrote, she wrinkled her forehead, pausing between passages before going on.

Occasionally, Edgar offered judgments of a political and historical nature.

A panel of junketing congressmen is a moveable cancer. I had to entertain four of them last week. Here on a fact-finding mission, as they called it. I was stuck with them as part of my cover as 'special liaison' to the embassy. The Agency is excellent when it comes to euphemism. Truly, there is real pleasure in devising language to confound your enemies and inform your friends. If I did not relish field work so, I would wish for an active position in the language section. At any rate, the congressmen were earnest liberals, northeasterners. In all seriousness one of them solemnly informed me that we must find out what the Mexican people need in formulating our policy toward their government. I held my tongue. What the Mexican people, like all people en masse, are in need of is constant reminding as to who owns them. The whole episode reminded me of Senator McCarthy and the Un-American Activities Committee before him. They were hysterical oafs, but the cultural and international chit-chat with their opponents has convinced me that even the moronic can be right now and then.

From what Walter could piece together, Edgar created himself as a Latin American-Caribbean specialist. His expertise led him to mingle with cabinet members, wealthy landowners, military men, those in the bottom half of the very highest echelons of power—loyal supporters of Somoza, Truijillo, the institutional party in Mexico, and Flugencio Batista. If he had been chummy with the very top dogs,

Walter wrote, it would be in the *History*. Edgar was never one to hide his light under a bushel.

After Mexico, Edgar was in Nicaragua, the Dominican Republic, and Colombia before finding a solid niche for himself in Cuba. There were veiled references to forged documents, large sums of money, the disappearance of enemies, allies, and former allies. Edgar went at it with energy and ingenuity. *I am making myself indispensable,* he crowed. *Station Chief for Havana? That's where the action is in this part of the world.*

Cuba in the good old days, Walter wrote. Before the drab, crushing Castro Revolution. The light, colors, and characters must have thrilled Edgar. The mambo and machine guns. Batista, Meyer Lansky, and Fidel in the hills with his sporting rifle and his murderous slogans. Edgar must not have seen what was coming.

A most interesting evening with Dr. Sanchez from the interior ministry. He also invited Colonel Bustamonte of the state's police. He is a stumpy, dark fellow, at least two-thirds negro—a waterfront thug without nerves or manners. We took an instant liking to one another, self-made man that he is. He was ignorant as to the silverware, so he ate the whole meal with a soup spoon. Dr. Sanchez, with his European medical degree and his pseudo-Spanish charm, pretended not to be offended. The food was French and the servants handsome teenagers. Sanchez hand picks them, I hear. Bustamonte made comic, odious faces at them. After dinner, we spent over two hours discussing monetary and security arrangements. Dr. Sanchez and the Colonel were most cooperative, the latter's advanced state of drunkenness having loosened him up considerably. Later, there was a private exhibition in Dr. Sanchez's courtyard: four boys, three girls, and a Great Dane. As rituals go, it was too lifeless and calculated for my taste. Bustamonte passed out, before the dog took the stage. I was relieved that I had procured his signature immediately after dinner.

Walter's head ached. Business and ritual, he wrote. The ordinary course of affairs. Edgar fancied himself and the games that he played as larger-than-life. And this—despite his sense of irony. Was this what he had pointed himself toward in those mythic days in the woods and the nights at the North State Hotel?

By 1958, Edgar was the Agency's bagman and an acknowledged insider for Cuba, a frequent guest at the casinos and the Presidential Palace. If he heard the rumblings from Castro in the Sierra Madre Orientale he did not write of them, absorbed as he was in his role of big-time operator. *A man could get rich here. There's talk of oil in El Caney Province. Dr. Sanchez passed this tip on to me. He is still useful, although he will not remain so forever. Here, only El Presidente endures.* Then Edgar had to go back to Washington. There was trouble with Margaret. He arrived in time for Christmas. I was nine then, Walter thought: a Christmas of dense silences and prolonged acrimony.

Margaret is impossible. I tried to convince her to move to the farm, where she could see her parents and provide Walter with a wholesome environment—which he badly needs, from the look of him. She would not hear of it. "I hate it here," she said. "And I hate it there too." I could have evoked the woods, but what was the use. "What do you do in Cuba?" she yelled. Her features twist in the most unattractive manner when she yells. "Why don't you answer my letters?" Because they are rot, I said. All you think about is yourself. My calm, my objectivity, enraged her further. She glared at me with pure hatred. I loved her, or had loved her. We did not speak the rest of the day. Walter played with his new toys. So docile, with his sheep's eyes. He never addressed me directly, not even to call me his daddy. I was a stranger there. And then, the very next week, came the terrible news from Havana. I will always regret that I was not there when Castro rolled into the city. I could have, perhaps, saved the day.

Yes, Walter wrote, I remember those days only too well. Even in the same room he was very far away.

When Batista fled with his money and his courtiers, Edgar tried to look on the bright side. *I'm positive that I can do business with the Liberator. Beneath that costume of his, the beard and the fatigues, lives another ruling class Cuban. Business will resume soon enough, all revolutionary rhetoric aside.* History proved Edgar wrong, Walter wrote. This pleases me. That grim, handsome man who stomped and brooded. His sense of who he was must've been damaged.

Naturally, Edgar admitted nothing in print. Cuba dropped from the *History* for a spell. Edgar was posted to Washington and given a series of minor, desk-bound assignments. Apparently, there were authorities outside the Agency who had questions concerning his activities in the last months of the old Regime. And there were those within the Agency who questioned Edgar's lack of precision in predicting events. Edgar stewed. *How could a man of my experience and connections have been wasted in this fashion? I put in requests for any type of foreign assignment, but nothing came open. That was the official line, as it were. By God, I would have taken Belgium, and packed my bitch of a wife and her child off with me. I had, I suppose, accepted being shackled to a desk and to Margaret.*

Things changed. Soon he was in Miami. Later, it was Honduras; training camps in the jungle along the coast, reconnaissance voyages into hostile waters. He was having fun again, Walter wrote. He was needed. He was redeemed.

But history is grief.

We got back to the Keys at first light. My hands shook as I wrote this. The trip was beyond horror. Vasquez and two others died during the crossing. They were badly burned, charred all over. Vasquez, his eyes white and red against the black of his flesh, howled right to his last breath. He asked for a rosary, but of course there was none to be had. I could not look at him. He was young, a rich boy—all cockiness and jokes. His father had to be told, but I could not do it. Staples, who had a terrible compound fracture in his right arm, the bone jutting out whitely, wanted to shoot Vasquez, to put him out of his misery. I had to take the carbine away. Staples, dumb Texan that he is, babbled on about the navy and the marines deserting us. He may have spoken for all of us. The landing ground and the killing zone beyond were lit up. If Staples had not taken the launch at gun point, God knows where we would have ended up. You could see the explosions and fires, hear the battle thirty miles at sea. Arias said that when he left the T-34s were about to break onto the beach. I did not ask why he abandoned his platoon. Such questions were inappropriate at the time. Staples cursed at Arias until he passed out. I think all of us went a bit crazy when the ammunition ships blew up. Our carriers and destroyers must have been just over the horizon. There is a great deal to be answered for.

Disasters, Walter wrote, should be instructive. They seldom are, however. We blunder down the same paths. Edgar, the historian—the lone survivor of the lost Major Cromartie's mission—had learned almost nothing. There is a perpetual replication of frenzied, bloody acts. This, too, is history.

He underlined these last words.

Following the Bay of Pigs, Jack Kennedy was much on Edgar's mind. He employed the standard right-wing vocabulary: gutless, incompetent, prisoner of liberal superstition. Of Edgar's dismissal from the CIA in the general blame-laying after the catastrophe, there was not a word. Walter, however, retained memories: violent truces, Edgar's clinched, dumb-struck confusion. Edgar furiously watched the evening news, muttering when Kennedy, boyish, confident, his famous hair kissed by a gentle breeze, appeared. Then, one morning, Margaret led Walter to the car and their flight. Their departure was omitted from the *History*. Instead, there was a curious passage that Walter copied into his journal.

Human activity follows along lines of energy. The greater the change, which originates from the individual's dynamic formulation of the self, the farther he may project himself. There is no absolute end-only infinity, a motion surpassing the concept of death. The energy consumes its creator. As they meld into a single entity. Such is also the case with nations and civilization itself. It is a truism that decay results when energy ceases to be renewed. An obvious rule in all things, but so quickly forgotten. It could be that we are bent in death's direction, deluded by a false sense of peace and ease. Henry Adams would have us believe that this is the end of all things—a stasis that is death. It is not difficult to see Death's enticements, illusory though they may be. There may even be a grandeur, as with the end of Carthage—or Hitler's Germany. However, the usual line of diminishing energy is marked by a slow decline. It is only toward the absolute end that the particular doom of a nation, or an individual, becomes apparent. Then policy is beside the point. The French and British are coming to understand this. The Soviets will. As for my native land, the possibility of energy renewal is potentially limitless. We know nothing of history, and our ignorance may be our saving grace. We have men who are intelligent enough, ruthless enough to recreate and regenerate themselves. We must talk of democracy and

*republics while taking all that we need to survive and tri-
umph. The yammering of public discourse is a necessary
ruse. It is when we begin to believe the platitudes, when we
wish to be loved, and not feared, that we put ourselves in a
dangerous position; a position that denies all necessary
surges of forceful, creative energy. Energy and Fear; they
keep us vital. As for myself, I will pursue that energy, and,
naturally, the rituals that are required to give it meaning. All
will be on a smaller scale than in the past. I have wasted
many of my talents, thwarted my own vision through weak-
ness—and also through no fault of my own. But times
change, and I will fight my own private war, gathering unto
me what powers I can. This seems the best course of
action—the only available strategy.*

Is it all gibberish? Walter wrote. Why does it give me the
creeps?

Edgar skirted over his involvement with "the consulting
business" that he tried to launch after his disgrace. The
nature and quality of his consultations were not described.
It was part of Edgar's effort to win his way back into a
world that he loved so well. No one, however, wanted his
services; he was, in effect, blacklisted. What acts could he
have committed, Walter wrote, that would bar him from
such a Darwinian arena? I will never know.

Exile and renewal came; the return to The Old Home
Place.

*My land, my freehold. Here I will stay. There is much to
be done. I have lost all that I once held to be permanent and
lasting. This could be a blessing. If I have been cast out, I
will create my own domain. From this day, I so consecrate
myself.*

Sacred words, Walter wrote—without God. What an

enormous conception he had of himself. If the thrust of desire was a virtue unto itself, Edgar would have been counted among the saints—or the demons. Wherever he landed was the most important place on earth.

Edgar, like his father, proved adept at land speculation. He bought and sold large parcels that went for subdivisions, factory sites, interstate highways. He focused tightly on the markets, booming in the south of the early sixties, bringing to his dealings the same quick, merciless intelligence that he once applied to rituals and his career with the CIA. He also worked hard at improving The Old Home Place, enlisting a new crew of black men who made his projects take shape and form. As in the days before the war, he worked beside them, paying far better wages than they could have gotten elsewhere. For this, they loved him—or so he said.

Within three years, after rich crops of soybeans, alfalfa, and corn, he struck his first agreements with the new combines that had begun to dominate agriculture. With a heavy heart, he dismissed his crew and let the professionals take the risks while he accumulated large rental fees. *The money is pouring in. What could be easier? A man with a tenth of my talent could do as well.* And so he went, successful and restless, his kingdom not quite challenging enough, right up to his union with Beatrice.

I have taken a peasant woman—not for love's sake. She fills a need, and is attractive and submissive to a degree that is almost unsettling. She is twenty-seven, healthy and strong, though not from farming stock. I was smitten with her malleability. It is fair to say that she worships me. This I find intoxicating—as any man would. Like all peasants, however, she is without imagination and flair—the qualities that Margaret possessed for such a fleeting time. Few women can measure up to my precepts as to how life is to be lived. This holds true for most men as well. They mistake comfort for power. Yesterday, I tried to introduce Beatrice to the old rituals. She comprehended nothing. She scuffled rather than ran, folding into submission at the first opportunity. Afterwards, I did not bother to request a song. Did I do all right? she asked. I lied and said that she had. That night she prepared a large ham and half a dozen vegetables—for the two of us. I had scant appetite, which disappointed her. There were no further attempts at ritual—with Beatrice.

Beatrice cooked, cleaned, and Edgar soon lost interest. She wept over his other women. Edgar told her of his needs and pitied her. She accepted these needs when Edgar promised not to shame her in public. He practiced considerable discretion and Beatrice came to appreciate his position. *She understands my conception of love, or has grown used to it. "I won't go after another man," she said. "Just as long as you give me some of that love too."* When she became pregnant, Edgar had the Ranch House built for her. *The house made her very happy, and I expect that the child will too. She is a most undemanding creature.*

My new son, Ricky Nelson Loomis, was born last week, April 1, 1964. I allowed Beatrice to choose the name, which may have been a mistake. Lydia, down from New York during Beatrice's confinement, laughed when I told her. She has perfected to an art-form that brittle, sophisticated, sexually-charged veneer that I find enticing in small doses. Following an afternoon in the woods, she had me tell her all about Beatrice. Her amusement eventually irritated me and I asked that she please stop. The boy is healthy and robust—his cry was loud and fully masculine. I hoped then for a proper heir—provided that he owned the necessary wit and strength. At the time, there was much promise.

So I, the vanished son, Walter wrote, end up with a larger share. Later disappointments for Edgar, I suppose.

Another reason why Ricky would want to kill me.

Ricky's childhood lacked the hatred that Walter had, for a time, grown up with. Edgar positively doted on the child. As in Ricky's version of the past, which Walter had not initially believed, father and son shared in all the joys of The Old Home Place. There was fishing, hunting, swimming, and Edgar's monologues on politics, culture, and the sanctity and enduring power of the land.

I admired Ricky's physicality. He was a smiling, quicksilver little fellow who loved me with the same devotion as his mother, who, by the way, was doing an adequate, if stolid job, with her duties. He regarded all of life as a pretext for play, and his energy, that key ingredient, was boundless. Obie, the man I hired to tend the stable, taught him to ride. I showed him a few pointers myself. He was a natural. I was concerned, at times, that his powers of concentration were not what they should be. I did not dream then of the problems that would develop from this defect.

There were excursions to New York, Los Angeles, Washington, New Orleans, and other cities. There were football games in Chapel Hill and treats, gifts, and amusements of every kind. Christmas was a month-long festival each year, and there was no end to the indulgences of fatherly love. If Ricky ever asked why his parents kept separate houses, it was not recorded by Edgar. He must've thought it normal, as he told me, Walter wrote. And where was I in, oh, 1970-1971? Oh, yes. Scuffling along, toiling at my useless Ph.D. in Austin, in flat, featureless Texas. I was never a goddamn "quicksilver little fellow." Just a lump on the carpet, surrounded by my parents' voices.

Walter turned the pen over in his hand, fighting, once again, the desire to throw it against the wall. Instead, he fell into the bed, spiraling down to sleep through the sudden, uncontrolled rush of unscholarly self-pity.

13

When he came to, he ate two portions of frozen macaroni and cheese. He did not risk a glance at the *History*. Self-pity, he thought. And jealousy of Ricky. Foolishness, but it can't be denied. Is this what Edgar would have wanted? Did he come to me in my sleep and croon seductively against Ricky Nelson Loomis? No *History* for awhile. Evacuation is needed. Now.

It was Friday night and the crowd at the mall was large: parents with children made half-demented by the sensory overload; teenagers immersed in social and mating activities; retirees in walking shoes endlessly circling. And what drove me to the haunts of my fellow citizens? Walter thought as he lifted a spoonful of Baskin-Robbins strawberry swirl to his mouth. I may be losing perspective. Self-pity, coupled with hitherto buried sentimentality about a lost childhood. Or too much of Edgar's *History*.

The ice cream's cool sweetness dripped through him. The whole project is insane, he thought, scraping the cup for the last bit of taste. What will I do when it is complete? Write up my findings? Who is my intended audience, as they used to say at writers' conferences? And then there is *Edgar's* intended audience. I doubt that any report I write will begin to match the original document. It's as if *Great Expectations* had been composed by the Marquis De Sade. A good line. I'll put it in the journal. But to return to a fundamental dilemma: Am I holed up here with Edgar, waking and sleeping because I can't bear to return to The Old Home Place? A proposition worth examining.

Without settling anything, he decided to leave. That's when he saw Beatrice.

She was dressed in a billowy, flowered jumpsuit, her hair hidden beneath a hot pink turban. She was on him before he could flee.

"Ah...," she began.

"Walter."

"I don't know why I have such a hard time with your name. What're you doing here?"

"Ice cream." He held up the stained cup for her inspection. "And you?"

"Shopping. This is Tommy."

A man young enough to be Ricky's kid brother stepped up, carefully placed an armload of packages on a table, and shook Walter's hand. He resembled Ricky too, or one of Ricky's buddies from The Event.

"How's it going?" Tommy asked with a disconnected smile. Walter said that things were just fine.

"I like to come over once or twice a month," Beatrice said. "The mall in Helmsville just isn't high class. You're in Charlotte to eat ice cream?"

"Well...not exactly. I've never been here." Does she know how long I've been gone? he thought, calculating the chances as to whether or not Ricky and Star had told her of his disappearance. And she would tell *them* where *he* had been sighted.

"Tomorrow...," he said, not knowing what would come out next. "Tomorrow, or maybe even tonight, I'm driving down to Atlanta. I have some old friends there. Could stay for a couple of weeks. A month. My plans aren't firm yet."

Beatrice stared at him before nodding.

"That'll be real nice. Atlanta's fun. Going to see the Braves play?"

"Yes. That's what...my friends suggested."

"They ain't worth a shit this year," Tommy said.

"I didn't know you liked baseball," Beatrice said. "And Tommy you better watch your mouth. I've told you about bad language." Tommy blushed and said that he was sorry.

"National pastime," Walter said. Even Beatrice, he thought, can probably see through such pathetic falsehoods.

"I hope you have a good time," Beatrice said. "We're moving to Charlotte next month." She gestured at Tommy, who had purchased a cone and was furiously licking. His tongue was too large for his mouth and covered the entire double scoop of chocolate fudge royale. They're a couple, Walter realized. As if I wasn't dazed enough. Edgar, the Edgar of my dreams, has arranged this. It is simply another facet of his powers—over life, over death.

"Get me a hot fudge sundae, Tommy," Beatrice said. "He's the best-natured boy. You sure don't believe in getting dressed up. I like to get all dolled up when I come to Charlotte."

Walter had on his normal outfit for scholarship; a wrinkled tee-shirt, stained shorts, and sneakers. It was poor judgment to have emerged from the cave of the *History*.

"Try to stay comfortable," he said. "The heat."

"Uh-huh." Beatrice stepped closer, inspecting him. "You feeling O.K.?" she asked. "You're kinda pale. And you've lost weight too. But that don't hurt none."

"I'm fine," Walter said. "Fine." This is the most elaborate conversation I've ever had with this woman, he thought. Could she guess that I've been reading about her—the unsatisfactory, submissive peasant, her legs spread. But Beatrice has transcended; now she's perky, out-going, brash—and with Ricky's clone in tow.

"How're Ricky and Star?" Beatrice asked.

Walter sighed, slightly relieved. Perhaps she had not seem them. Could I be so blessed?

"Oh...about the same."

Beatrice frowned. "Star's too good for him, even if he is my son. Did you know that she helped me get started in my new life? I get a nice allowance every two weeks. She sees to that. Took all those old worries off my mind. 'Beatrice,' she said, 'you're wasting yourself out here in this falling-down house. Move to town!' So that's what I did. She introduced me to Tommy too. Thank you honey."

Tommy gave her the sundae and stood to one side—as if in attendance. She took rapid, lady-like bites, talking as she ate.

"Next time you see that Ricky, you tell him that I'm still mad. I appreciate that he's got problems of his own..."

"Any news about...legal matters?" Walter asked. Since the celebration with Star and the unearthing of the *History*, he had given scant thought to the ramifications of The Event.

"You'd know better than me," Beatrice smacked. "Now I appreciate that Ricky's got serious problems, but there's no excuse for what he done. His father would never let things get out of hand."

"Do you really want me to say that?"

"Oh, well. I guess you better not. Any how, I am *happy*. I can't wait to get settled in Charlotte. There's so much to do. We got the prettiest condo."

"Shopping and so forth."

"That's right. Did you say you're leaving for Atlanta tonight? Me and Tommy are staying at the Marriot."

"I may. There are a few errands to attend to."

"Like what?" Tommy asked.

"None of your business," Beatrice said, playfully slapping Tommy's arm. "I'm gonna have to teach you some manners. Ain't that right, honey?"

Tommy blushed again and guffawed.

"Tell me," Walter said. "What was Ricky like as a

child?"

Beatrice sucked at a ball of ice cream and fudge before answering. *Does she sense my tenseness?* Walter thought, alarmed that he had given away too much.

"He was a good child. Yes. Good. All boy, if you know what I mean. I never worried about him. Until he got older."

"All boy," Walter said.

"Un-huh. Into everything. How come you'd ask?" She waited for his answer, slowly stirring the sundae.

"Curiosity. Nothing more," Walter said.

He resolved not to leave the apartment again until his work was ended. *Family History* is the more accurate term, he thought, once more locked into the apartment. As he took up the *History* he came across some of Edgar's world-famous friends who Ricky had counted on during his legal troubles. Dr. Sanchez, the former Minister of the Interior, spent a month at The Old Home Place. He was living in Miami, where he had developed a lucrative medical practice—breast enhancements for topless dancers and reconstructive plastic surgery. He was also the director of an organization called the World-Wide Anti-Communist Congress.

We had very high high level discussions. I hoped that my advice serves to temper the exuberance of Sanchez's associates. They do not yet understand that covert operations must be truly covert. Otherwise, such ill-planned actions are at least an embarrassment. At their worst, they are the basis for a debacle. The Congress is financially strong, however. Donations from all over, and Nixon's tax people granted non-profit status. Excellent potential for a write-off. The time has passed tediously, though. Sanchez's anti-communism is of the tiresome variety, and it's come to be his only subject. He cannot appreciate the fact that everyone is against communism. Besides being a fraud of the religious type, it is bad for business—in a fairly surface respect, how-

ever. If we did not have communism, how could we prosper? What would we struggle against? Without struggle, we grow flabby in body and spirit.

General Sloan came down for a week. Served with Patton. Old Third Army man. Korea of course. Fascinating when on the subject of Vietnam in the early days. Barbarians, he said of the Viet Cong, the NVA. But you have to admire their methods. Sloan is more to my liking than Sanchez; stupid, but bluff, and hearty. A fine deer hunting companion. He is a first-rate shot, although once he barely missed Obie. Blew the bark off a pine right next to Obie's head. We all had a good laugh over that one. Ricky fired at least thirty rounds, and could not hit anything.

I divorced Beatrice after six years of living apart. She cheerfully accepted the settlement, which is generous in the extreme. I told Ricky myself, and the news impressed him not at all. He did not quite grasp my meaning. That could be due to the living arrangements he has grown up with. And he is only nine years old. With the passing of time, I've become afraid that he has inherited his mother's intellect. But he is sturdy and strong enough—which reminds me of myself at his age. Then again, he races without quite knowing where he is going.

About this time, the Fourth of July festivities became an annual extravaganza. As Bunch said, Edgar was able to induce a few celebrities to attend. Ronald Reagan, out of the governor's mansion in Sacramento, and serving his hitch as a traveling spokesman for the conservative ascendancy, spent a few hours at The Old Home Place. *Plain as an old shoe. A good guy in the best American tradition, although I could not determine what he thinks on specific subjects. It could have been that he merely sought relaxation from his schedule, and kept our dialogue light and care-free. Prior to the barbecue and the fireworks display, we took a lively turn around the riding paths. The governor is a fine horseman.*

There was one slightly startling note: he claimed that he was an old cavalryman. General Sloan, who accompanied us, nodded as if this were the truth. They left that night for a Free Enterprise conference in Las Vegas. In America, there is a wonderful blurring of all distinctions between fantasy and reality. In this fashion, heroism is preserved and fear defeated. We must not lose sight of the fact that fear's defeat must always be temporary. Thus we will remain fit and vigilant. Naturally, this is not an observation that I would offer to Governor Reagan.

I have the creeps again, Walter thought. The old time heebie-jeebies. He fortified himself with a beer and three cups of extra-strong instant coffee. I must stay alert—vigilant, as Edgar would put it.

Over time, the world's notables faded away and Edgar was left alone. The lessening of importance was not commented upon, perhaps owing to age, Walter thought. There was a suggestion of turning inward, of channeling his energy for private enjoyment. His investments were secure and he was content to rest upon his entrepreneurial laurels. He embarked on extended visits to Europe with Stephanie, the daughter of a friend, or former friend, from the CIA. Her youth and collegiate hipness appealed to Edgar. *She was not much older than Ricky, but they came from different worlds. I could, I suppose, have provided him with greater guidance. He was Beatrice's child, lacking in sophistication or taste—content to be a flashy running back.*

A few pages later, Walter's name bobbed up from rather standard depictions of Turin and Venice.

Stephanie had been reading a collection of short stories she picked up in New York, and I happened to notice the author's name: Walter Loomis. My son, of all persons. Stephanie thought him "cool," to use her terminology. For all I knew this was the case. I read his stories in an evening. He could write, but he lacked a compelling vision. Instead, he relied on a rather typical contemporary stance; comic violence carefully ladled over junior varsity despair. His jokes were private and not meant to be funny. The author's picture corresponded to his work; a slightly overweight fellow in his late twenties, I'd say; dressed in the proletarian drag of the low level professor. When I thought back on him, I found that I could not imagine him becoming anything. A mere cipher, he was. I decided to keep my eye on his work, and considered contacting him. On that, it was best to wait and see. There could be other, better books in him. His book needed life, some kick in him. He wrote as if we were living in the dying light of creation.

You old bastard, Walter wrote, although without the malice that he felt the first time he laid eyes on Edgar's literary judgments. All the visions were appropriated by the time I arrived. What was left was fragments and slivers. Not much to piece together, Dad. Your kind consumed all the visions. This is what I feared in those days when I stood, like a fool, at the foot of the stairs and dared not enter the study. Yet, I could have a vision after all.

Edgar and Stephanie parted, but she sent him another of Walter's books. *I must say that Walter has some wit, although his talent is ordinary—even for these times—I cannot make up my mind to write him. He is my only connection to Margaret. He is also an unknown part of myself. Would he reject me? He's sure to have his own life, and has never tried to get in touch with me. Both my sons are their mother's boys, although in vastly separate ways. There may only be a secondary, off-handed hatred in Walter for me, a reversed image of Ricky's dog-like love. I must be growing old to care about such matters. Old and soft.*

And what would we have said to each other, Walter thought. Then he remembered something. Again, he stared at the black spot on the wall—the point where he had hurled the pen like a tiny javelin. Bunch told me, he thought. The books, my obscure books, led me here. This is a prank of cosmic profundity. The books were, for Edgar, tangibles. Could he have nurtured the conceit that with his land and money I would develop a goddamn vision? There is another possibility: that what I am writing now, and what I am reading, would propel me to compose the greatest work ever known—a tribute to Edgar Loomis. If he speaks to me in dreams, if he dispenses wisdom to Ricky in the woods, he could have planned all of this; first the inheritance, the discovery of the *History*. He could bring me to him without having to approach me in life. Is this possible? Edgar as emperor and god, he who walked as a deity on his earth.

Walter turned to a clean, bare page, trying to marshal what knowledge and logic were available to him. Rationally, he wrote, none of this is believable. As some would say, all is chance, coincidence. Chaos is my own explanation. Others, fast-talking and impassioned, claim these concepts to be dangerous illusions. There are conspiracies, cabals, oversouls, and minds greater than our own willing us into a lockstep by whim or necessity. Edgar's age, my age, is replete with the manipulation of the hidden hand: war, the CIA, the shooter on the grassy knoll in Dallas (some of Dr. Sanchez's Cuban friends?), hidden political arrangements, secret governments, UFOs, miracles, instant cures—the triumph of the fantastic, the magical over natural law. This is all deluded— which is another way of saying that it is entirely possible.

Edgar's account of Ricky's earliest legal problems ran true to the story that Bunch had told. *His mother says that I am unduly harsh, but I must take a firm hand. He has been pampered and the marines will slap that out of him. When I informed him, he took it well, vowing to straighten out. He must learn to live as a man. Obie and I saw him off at the bus station. Beatrice could not bring herself to come along. Ricky was quite brave.*

The second volume ended with Ricky's exile. He must have been stunned, Walter wrote; stood on end and shaken. Daddy was displeased—far more frightening than boot camp. And did Edgar foresee a part for Ricky in the epic that I was to produce as another monument? He who could not measure up. When Daddy was not there to play with him, he got into mischief. The displeasure of the emperor-god is a terrible thing to behold.

Volume Three was fragmented in a variety of ways. Part of it was typed, part handwritten, and there were notes stuffed randomly between the pages. Walter surmised that Edgar had either grown fatigued with his project, or was diverted by outside forces. The latter, Walter wrote, is most likely. He could never truly tire of writing about himself.

Ricky's drug bust was given an elliptical allusion: *My second son has gotten into a scrape that has the potential for severe repercussions. I took steps to limit the damage.* Bunch's suspicions, which were also Walter's, were neither confirmed nor denied. There was nothing about marijuana, police raids, cajoling Ricky from the woods, or prison. Enigma, Walter wrote; Edgar's best strategy for this episode. I, as the official historian, will select from a menu of potential scenarios. Edgar, the upright law-and-order conservative, willing to surrender his son for just punishment. Edgar, the old-time Havana bagman, who saves himself from a scam gone awry. Ricky may have much in common with Major Cromartie, Tomlinson the heroic Yorkshireman, and Staples, the CIA mercenary. They all suffered for the greater good. Another script might portray Edgar as the patriarch, rescuing the family honor from the blunders of a wayward, prodigal son.

With Ricky's incarceration, the *History's* narrative line receded, replaced by rumination and a fitful kind of obscurity—especially in the yellowed scraps of notes—some contained meaningless columns of numbers, while others alluded to persons and events suspended in lost time.

Simpkins is trying my patience.

Twenty-five years ago I would have handled it with ease. Today, I'm not so sure.

She says that her urine is thick. Why do I listen to such rot?

Taste is vanishing from society. Must I retreat still further?

I heard of a woman in Sicily eating a live bird.

A few broken heads can establish proper order.

Liver spots. That's what Father called them.

There came a lengthier, sustained passage in ink, the penmanship tight and flawless, but with a faint, spidery hint of the accumulation of years. It was dated November 10, 1990. Seventy years old, Walter thought. Not much time for heroism, dreams, or rituals.

I am old. I examined my nakedness in a mirror. At least I am not one of those dottering fools seen on every street corner. Most should have died years ago. No, walking, riding, and the land have allowed me to retain some physical grace. I could pass for a stout fellow of fifty-five or sixty, proud and fierce, attending to my business as I should and leaving my imprint wherever I go. Yet this image does not sustain me. I have turned backwards, as must be inevitable for a man of my years. This morning, I sat in my office, taking the view, overlooking the land where Margaret and I once danced to the music commanded by youth. I relish my needs. To relinquish them is to fall into dust. I have removed most of the furnishings from this house. Clutter offends me. I pare down to essentials. Margaret's face comes back to me. What would be her opinion of the monument I erected? Would she understand it? Ricky and Beatrice merely accept it. Ricky's lady friend, Star is her name, rubbed her hands over the inscriptions—a singularly sexual gesture. She sel-dom speaks. I have not yet conversed with her alone.

Later, there was a shorter, telling passage.

She helps me with the books. She is very quick, with a sharp, native intelligence. And she has taught me the com-puter. Sending her to the local trade school was a proper investment. Sometimes she touches me in a familiar, friend-ly way. Yesterday, I asked her to massage my neck. She gave me an odd, slight smile. Her hands were hard and strong.

An abrupt, uncomfortable sensation passed through Walter. Star's hands are strong, he thought. I have bumbled into something that I should've seen much sooner. Ricky did not teach her to sing in the woods; that was the one ritual that did not pass from father to son. The clues were there all along—a direct line leading from my parents' romps through the Acadian fastness, to my sighting of her from the ridge. To Star. And Edgar. What did she say about Edgar? It was after her celebration, the closing of the timber deal: Edgar, Ricky, and me.

Walter read quickly, anxious for further intimations. A fragment about Cuba. Notes on money and land. The *History* seemed to be winding down to a final nothingness. Edgar's words became fragile-looking, drained of the old force and power.

How many days do I have left? I yearn for victories, even small ones. My new will has been entrusted to a lawyer. Bunch seems to be able to keep his mouth shut. To die; death comes to all, but can it come to me? I have made extensive preparations, but I can never accept what those preparations mean. Some days, after an hour or two of regeneration, I cannot believe that it will happen. An illusion, but also my last, best dream. All of that aside, I have made excellent pro-vision for my son Walter. I have his two latest books, but I have not yet read them. I cannot remain indoors, despite the chill of the season. The sun, the sun of the late fall, draws me forth. Another comes with me, and I saw a new forging of bonds, a bringing together of those that owe much to me, who will commemorate and, at the same time, perpetuate me. My people will, at last, be a family—the greatest and best of my creations.

Walter was sweating. The apartment was chilled to near-refrigerated temperatures. He sweated nevertheless, with a dry mouth and reeking armpits. His hands shook.

"Revelation after revelation!" he cried. "History re-shaped, re-written! All sins forgiven!"

A never-seen next door neighbor pounded the wall. Walter inhaled his odors. "My stench is less significant than the embalmed flesh of the never-rotting dead!" The neighbor pounded again and yelled for Walter to shut up.

"My work!" Walter whispered.

Walter addressed the last pages with the greatest of care, with consideration for their author, the family, and the commonality of the blood.

I am afraid now. At dawn I awakened. He stood at the foot of the bed. He did not speak. I did not move. He was weeping, poor weak thing. What is it? I asked. The will? Two days ago, I told him of my plans for the family's future, of the reunion with his half-brother. Star told me not to, but I wanted to be above board with him. As always, and initially, he took it well, even projecting that directionless enthusiasm he brings to all things. "The Loomis Brothers," he said. "That'll be something, Daddy." This morning there were none of his affirmations, however. He kept standing there, the light coming in behind him. "Are you afraid of my dying?" I asked, as gently as possible. He shook his head, blubbering slightly. How simple he is! "It's none of that,

Daddy," he said. "I been finding out a few things." With
that he left. Star called later. He had seen enough, she said.
It was all by accident. He was exercising his stallion. He
confronted her last night. He wants to assign blame, despite
the fact that no one was harmed. She lied to him, claiming
that she succumbs to my needs to ensure his inheritance—
and their happiness. He is damaged. Is there a way to make
it up to him?

I changed the locks on the doors and gave copies of the
keys to Bunch. He was curious, but like a good lawyer, he
asked no questions. From the study window, I sighted
Ricky, mounted on his fine horse. Since the call, I have not
seen or heard from Star. Perhaps this is for the best.

He has not spoken to me in a week. He is there though.
There was the note this morning, pushed under the door. "I
will never hurt you. I love you," it read. There was no signature. Beatrice called. She wanted money for a new dryer.
She knew nothing. After I hung up, I disconnected the telephone. When I go out, Obie, who also knows nothing,
accompanies me. Safety measures. Witnesses are a necessity.

I cleaned my old forty-five. Had not touched it since the
Bay of Pigs. It is heavy, beautifully blunt. I keep it under my
coat when I leave the house. It does not make me feel safer.

I had to go into Helmsville. Business matters. Ricky
stared hard at me as I passed the stable. As usual, he was
astride his stallion. He cuts quite a figure on horseback,
rather like one of Jeb Stuart's troopers. Violent men. The
new will has a fine symmetry. Little else does. Strange that
in my fear I can think of such things.

A God, even a fearful one, Walter wrote, possesses a
mind wide enough to encompass all. Symmetry and proper
dispensations. All is unfolding like an epic, forgotten film of

the silent era—grainy, lost for generations, but brought to light by a seeker of the truth.

There was snow this morning. I walked out in it. I love the snow—like all southerners. All those years in tropical countries made my love stronger. Pure and crackling, altering the landscape, compelling us to see in a new, however temporary, fashion. I neglected to fetch Obie, excited as I was. On my return, Ricky stepped out of the trees. Son, I asked, what are you after? There was no reply and I drew my forty-five. His expression never changed. He did not move. "Is it the will?" I asked, knowing that this was not why he stalked me. "I love you," he said, then slowly walked back into the trees. He never seemed aware of the pistol. I locked the door behind me. Most of the snow had melted by mid-afternoon. I slept with the forty-five beside me. He is out there. Tomorrow I will take target practices. I want him to hear gunfire.

After a dozen empty pages, came the last line, set dead-center and alone: *We are wounded animals, chewing at our shattered, defiled limbs.*

14

To begin with, there was the rain. At times an insistent mist, it would suddenly come in gouts. It never ceased completely. The Weather Channel commented hourly on the unusual persistence of the pattern. The rain had started in early October, following a great Cape Verde hurricane named Barbara that stomped along the coast from Jacksonville to Norfolk. "Semi-monsoon conditions became the norm," according to the official reports—conditions that that gave the appearance of being permanent. The Carolinas caught the worst of it. Moisture was drawn in from the Gulf, the middle west, the trailing ends of Pacific storms, funneling into the seeping red clay of Darden County.

Walter, attired in a new yellow slicker and rubber boots from K-Mart, had come home. The Loomis Freehold, he thought. That's what Edgar called it when he went into exile. The present version of the rain was of a pelting, needle-nosed consistency that, with the wind, had wrapped his hair into swirls and peaks. At regular intervals he wiped the water from his face. It was hard to see, but a text had been laid open for him. The Old Home Place and the ruins of the ranch house and stable were as he had left them. The natural landscape, however, had been radically altered. Most eloquent, he thought.

The trees were gone—or most of them at any rate. Hundreds had been spirited off to be transformed into toilet paper, toothpicks, the pages of self-help books. The necessities of life, Walter thought. Where the trees once stood, from what he could estimate, was a rolling, featureless bog that surrounded a few islands of upright pines. Laid bare, he marveled. Like a head shaved of all but a few decorative tufts that were left as a joke. There is no ambiguity here, he thought. Visibility was low, but the essential state of things was obvious. It reminded him of a collection of photographs that he had once browsed through in a college library: Flanders in 1918. There was no ambiguity in those vistas either, he thought. All had succumbed to a thorough-going, precisely arranged blight.

He had left Charlotte over a month earlier, two days after completing his examination of the *History*. Flight—aimless and compulsive—had been easy. He carried the *History*, both in its physical form and as a feral, living creature within him, images, words, phrases all revolving like a gigantic celestial wheel. All those scenes, he thought—leading with a cast iron logic to Edgar and Ricky in the snow. If I could purge it from me, and if it were to take corporeal form, it would be a troll, slyly grinning. I don't ride alone.

He had gone as far west as Los Angeles and as far south as Nuevo Laredo, oblivious all the while of Cape Verde hurricanes and monsoon-like patterns. At the Grand Canyon, he mailed a postcard to Valerie, who was, no doubt, issuing her wisdom to a fall semester seminar at Penn. He quoted Edgar's last line, the one about maimed animals, but did not sign his name. She'll know, he thought.

Some nights he slept in the truck, others in the first motel he found. What he liked best was to drive right into the morning. If I can only move, I'll be all right, or as all right as I'm likely to get, he would think. There came those times when his body would not go on, when he had to halt in exhaustion. In spite of the alcohol and over-the-counter sleeping pills, he dreamed those dreams. Then, the *History* took full-throttle, total control. Edgar was both participant and ringmaster, nocturnal, beseeching Walter to take up his pen, brandishing his forty-five. Ricky, vowing his love in mantras was there, Margaret in all of her manifestations, Star in all her glory, along with Cuban politicians and violated English war heroes.

Walter, as had been the case since he took up the *History*, would come to, shivering, the dreams of the *History* hot in his heart as he went back to the road. It was better there, although he was never granted the old blankness that he had once confused with peace. He had once quested after answers—and a part of him still did. His greatest craving now was to be rid of it all. He never reopened the *History* or reviewed his journals. No greater piece of writing would grow from them. Words were an abomination. They sickened him. It had taken all of his strength to write the postcard from the Grand Canyon. I *cannot, will not* write, he whined to a thing very like Edgar. Weakling, the Edgar-thing boomed. My life is great, profane and holy, while your talent is paltry. You failed me. Failure must be my salvation, Walter whimpered.

The flight ended with a curious occurrence. At a Days Inn near Clayton, New Mexico, the dreams ceased. He did not leave his bed for fourteen hours. When he gained his feet, he understood what he had to do. He was to perform a ritual of his own devising. Not exactly sure of the ritual's nature and how it was to be staged, he headed east. Some elements were plain enough: the ritual must involve the *History* and a fitting depository. "The monument and the *History*," he gasped as he crossed the Mississippi at St. Louis. "Edgar might find perfection in that."

He sloshed up to The Old Home Place in the late afternoon. He had been enraptured by his own ritual for eight hundred miles, then stunned by the wreckage that greeted him. It was then that the pictures of Flanders, shell-holes, splintered trees, German corpses, and barbed wire had come back to him. Where my great-uncle Randall careened into his destiny, he thought.

Musty, damp, the house gave no obvious clues of having been disturbed while he was away. Cautiously, he went from room to room, halfway expecting to brush up against Ricky, Star, or even Edgar. Relieved at being alone, he thought that Ricky could be in prison, or that Star might have a condo next door to Beatrice. And Edgar had not troubled him in almost a week. It was true enough that Edgar's spell was there, but it could only hover fitfully in the deep background. He was beginning to feel almost comfortable when he came across the letter. It sat squarely in the middle of the study desk, addressed to him, on that computer paper that he hated so from his teaching days. The identity of the author was plain to him even before he began to read.

Thanks for everything. I've tried to find you. But no luck. We did have some good times together. Despite a few problems. You might not like how things look around here now. I believe it is for the best. Edgar said that the land will last. So that's like it's always been. Except for what you can see yourself. The Weyerhauser people tell me that it will grow back. Things weren't right after Edgar died. Maybe you know that Ricky and I had problems. Maybe you don't. You were kind of hard to figure out. You remind me of Edgar. I'm not sure why. Younger? If you know what I mean. I'm taking your books with me. I hope that's O.K. They made me think. We never did get a chance to write those stories. Too bad. We might have had a Best Seller! The last time I was with Ricky he was the same. That was sad for me. If you can look out for him that would be nice. He never did mean to do all that stuff that got him in trouble. I'm

not sure why he did it. I think you would agree with
that. You are his brother. Kind of. Help him out. He will
need plenty of help. I've got a new life. That's what we
got to spend our time going after. Edgar taught me that.
I miss him. And Ricky. And you too. Beatrice will be fine
for awhile. If you got any legal questions you better talk
to Roy Bunch. He knows some things. Not all. You
could check with the bank too.
Love ya,
Star

"Love ya," Walter said. The rain had picked up, a steady
drone against the roof. He read the letter over. It could be an
appendix to the *History*, he thought.

The trip to Helmsville was an adventure. Three times
Walter detoured around washed-out bridges, and he had to
drive with nerve-wracking deliberateness through miles of
standing water. Helmsville, at nine in the morning, had a
deserted, abandoned feel to it. There were no lights in Mr.
Carl F. Smyre's furniture emporium, and a flapping banner
proclaimed the Carolina Home Improvement World was
going out of business. Downtown, the rain stood straight
up, as if it was gushing from an unseen, heavenly faucet. It's
fitting, Walter thought. The weather has been arranged for
my final homecoming and leave-taking. But first, there is
Roy Bunch.
    "What happened out there?" Walter asked. He had not
removed his dripping slicker, and water puddled beneath his
chair. He held a cup of luke-warm coffee that had been
offered to him by a rather astonished Bunch.
    "A perennial question when it comes to your family."
Bunch lit a Winston. "Do you want to start with the trees?"
    "The lack of trees. And...other things."
    "It's called clear-cutting. Not the accepted procedure.

Weyerhauser was, I'm sure, satisfied. I don't want to come across as stupid, but are the trees a recent revelation for you? You did sign a contract. The one Star negotiated."

"I signed something."

"And the Power of Attorney? You and Ricky both?"

"Power of..."

"Attorney. Star left a copy of that with me too. Not that I've read it or the contract. For safekeeping, is how she put it. She said that you and Ricky might want to review the documents one day. And while we're on the subject, where *is* Star? Ricky? Beatrice? You're the damnedest crowd for simply dropping out of sight."

"What does it mean? The power of attorney gives Star control of...things? Is that it?"

The signing, Walter recalled, had been a hurried occasion, closely linked with Star's celebration. He had not paid much attention. He noticed that Bunch was finding him a diverting spectacle.

"How about a drink? It's early and so on, but a drink can help you gain perspective."

Walter shook his head. He had seen no other person that morning besides Bunch. Bunch could be that last inhabitant of Helmsville, he thought.

"You're sure?" Bunch asked kindly.

"Star took control of my financial affairs. Am I correct?"

Bunch rubbed his chin, watching Walter. He had not shaved that morning and a faint rasping noise issued from his face.

"You and Ricky gave her total control, carte blanche, you might say. You can revoke the power—you and Ricky— but it did give her lots of leverage. She was pretty proud. Getting the settlements taken care of, unencumbering the estate. The improvements that you saw for yourself."

"There were settlements? From The Event...I mean the Fourth of July." The settlements were not mentioned in the letter.

"You bet. Cost you plenty, but less than a jury would've made you fork over. The plaintiffs and their lawyers were reassured by our offers. Profoundly reassured, I'd say. That's the last I saw of Star too. That day in court. Interestingly enough, the copies of the timber contract and the Power of Attorney are postmarked Miami. Is Ricky down there, luxuriating in the sun and gobbling down black beans and rice? Miami could be Ricky's kind of town."

"I don't know where he is." Except that he's not with Star, Walter thought. "When did you get these documents?"

"If I remember right, it was the middle of September. Not a word since. I don't want to pry, but where have you been keeping yourself?"

"Here and there. Extended, working vacation."

Bunch resumed massaging his chin. This is normal for him, Walter thought. He was never one to believe in safe havens.

"A sight, that farm of yours—or whatever it was. I drove out a couple of weeks ago—strictly as part of my duties, you understand."

"Was Ricky there?"

"I'll get to him in a minute. He deserves special consideration. But to return to your estate, there was this convoy of flatbed trailers going in and out. Crews, a hundred, hundred and fifty lumberjack types, busy as could be. In the rain, too, which hadn't paralyzed things as bad as they are now. They were cutting and hacking with a will. Sap was in the air. This foreman asked me what I was doing there. Just to be a smartass, I asked him the same. He said that they were taking out every goddamn tree they could lay metal to. Acres and acres. Prime wood—down to the saplings. Have they stopped until dryer times?"

"It seems like it. They've been pretty successful so far."

Bunch smiled and lit another cigarette.

"You don't mind the woodland carnage? Well, you did sign. The money was some inducement, huh? But yes, those Weyerhauser boys were successful beyond the wildest corporate dreams. They fucking *skinned* the place. In their defense, they claimed to be putting out pine seedlings, which have probably washed away by now. How about this rain? Flood warnings everywhere west of here."

"It's a judgment."

"Biblical. Your bank most likely has all the numbers on your financial coup. And Star's genius has more than made up for what you paid out to those fourteen injured parties."

"The Loomis touch."

"The Star touch, you mean. Only the homestead isn't up to its former aesthetic standards. A crime. It used to be such a show place, as the real estate developers say."

"The landscape corresponds to its owners."

"A brutal judgment."

Bunch has spent years contemplating waste, Walter thought.

"Do you want to hear the rest of it?" Bunch asked.

"I must."

"Not at all. Consider another of those extended, working vacations. And what sort of work did you do?"

"Scholarship. My final, absolute farewell to the profession. I'm permanently cured—I hope. And I do feel another vacation coming on."

"Follow your impulse. Live your dreams. Helmsville could drown at any moment."

"Drowning can take any number of forms."

"What an enigmatic expression! Do you mind if I use it? With proper credit to the source, naturally."

"You were going to tell me the rest of it."

"That I am. The gory details as I know them. We finalized the settlements, I collected my fee, and, with Star's departure, I realized that the Loomis boys, and mothers and girlfriends, were off to parts unknown."

"Beatrice is in Charlotte, where she dwells in true happiness."

Bunch cocked an eyebrow and lit another Winston.

"There's an arresting notion: Charlotte as the land of true happiness. The Loomis clan has a gift for the dramatic and mysterious. How did you determine that Beatrice is happy?"

"I had ice cream with her. She couldn't be better." Walter's laugh was high-pitched. For a second, he fought for control. Bunch went right on smoking, betraying no sign of alarm.

"She must've earned it. She has had her crosses to bear. And did she convey to you information about young Ricky's whereabouts?"

"No. Are you about to address Ricky's situation?"

"The time is at hand. Sheriff Peavey and District Attorney Hunsucker have made inquiries. They were bound to, since Ricky didn't show for any of his court appearances, which gained him a string of contempt citations. And the increased enmity of the superior court. The novel aspect is that after a couple of perfunctory searches the proper authorities haven't tried to locate Ricky."

"Shouldn't he be in jail?"

"You expect him to be?"

What's he getting at? Walter thought. He had considered revealing to Bunch the last days of Edgar, the tale of the reproachful, stalking Ricky, the target practice, the forty-five. The tale had been the basis of many of the old, bad dreams. It's all too mixed up for explanations, he decided.

"What about it?" Bunch asked. "Is your brother a menace to society?"

"That's for society to figure out. I'm fairly ignorant, but if you refuse to come to trial you…"

"Get a shitload of grief. Yeah. Ricky forfeited bail and

all that. The bondsman was pissed. Hunsucker figures that Ricky will show up some day. And Peavey told me that Ricky was so sorry he wasn't worth hunting."

"No word at all?"

"Not even a rumor. I've checked. That's why I went out to your place. No cover. He could be in Beatrice's old house. It's a mess. The rain's ruined what was left of the inside."

"He hasn't been in my house either." And he's not in Miami, Walter thought.

"Not harboring fugitives?"

"It's that I didn't come across him when I got in yesterday."

"If you say so. Another Loomis mystery."

Bunch glanced out the window. The rain had slowed, but seemed as unceasing as ever.

"Eleven inches in two weeks," Bunch said. "No relief in sight."

The bank manager, who had fawned so when Walter claimed his inheritance, was now chilly and nervous. It's true, he said, that a Ms. Star Hollar had taken control of the Loomis accounts. And he had been meaning to speak with Walter and Ricky concerning some rather remarkable irregularities. With that, he left Walter to ponder these as-yet-unstated irregularities. He returned in a few minutes with a file.

"You can see for yourself that the paperwork is in order," the manager said, as he laid out a copy of the Power of Attorney on his desk. "Since Ms. Hollar had assumed her fiduciary role," he went on, "there have been substantial and regular withdrawals. In fact, nearly nine hundred and fifty thousand dollars were transferred to Ms. Hollar's personal account in the Bank of the Bahamas, Nassau." Ms. Hollar had attempted further, similar transactions, but, the manager said, with emphasis, that he had become alarmed.

He had put a hold on all requests from Nassau, while he made every effort to contact Ricky and Walter—which had proven impossible.

"What do we have left?" Walter asked.

The manager punched some computer keys and shook his head at what came up on the screen. Ricky Loomis had six hundred and eighty in an IRA, and a balance of zero in both checking and savings. Walter showed twelve hundred total, which would not begin to cover the penalties for the withdrawals from the CDs and IRAs.

"And," Walter asked carefully, "what has been paid into these accounts?"

After a second consultation with the screen, the manager said that nothing had been deposited since sixty-five hundred in July.

"What about the Weyerhauser fees?" Walter slowly asked.

The manager first toyed with his pen then adjusted his tie. "Mr. Loomis," he said, "we show nothing from Weyerhauser, or anywhere else. Were you expecting something?"

"What does this mean?" Walter asked.

"I'll be frank," the manager said. "Ms. Hollar has taken advantage of you and your brother."

"How?"

"There's your signature, Mr. Loomis," the manager said patiently. "It all seemed in order. Perhaps we could've acted sooner on the withdrawals, although we had no reason to suspect that anything was amiss—until she had gotten nearly all of it."

"Of course," Walter said. "Of course."

He had to talk to someone, and Bunch was the only candidate. He was as Walter had left him, apparently mesmerized by the rain over Helmsville.

"Two existential dialogues on the same day," Bunch said. "Truly, I'm blessed."

Without omitting any of the details, Walter related his financial problems. He wanted to be composed and reasonable as he faintly steamed from the moisture and the heat of the office. Bunch murmured in counterpoint to Walter's speech.

"And so she got close to all of it," Walter said. "Except for the land itself."

"For the time being. Don't forget property taxes, as low as they are in this state. A true bastion of the free market. What do you suppose the land's worth now?"

"Not much?"

"Not shit. You're taking this well."

"Am I?"

"Suppressed trauma?"

Walter laughed. He had laughed all the way back to Bunch, barely managing to compose himself enough to recite his story.

"There are legal remedies," Bunch said. "Despite the Power of Attorney and Star's decamping for a tropical paradise. If she is in the Bahamas for real. You have to give her credit. She understands how it all works. So what about it? You want to track her down?"

"No revenge, please."

"Why not? There are also criminal questions here. She's fucked you—and Ricky—in textbook fashion."

"You could say that," Walter giggled. "She deserves the money, her escape—whatever she's created for herself."

"You're a weird son of a bitch. No offense."

"Heredity!" Walter guffawed.

"The Loomis Curse?" Bunch smiled, full of pity and sadness.

"Don't you see? She understands what money is for. And she carries on the Loomis tradition of ritual and love."

"Ritual? What the hell does that mean?"

"A family...peculiarity."

"Heredity again? I'll leave it at that."

It was about noon, but all was as dim as twilight, the rain slathering across the window. The desk lamp illuminated the lower half of Bunch's puffy face, leaving the rest in shadows, giving him a grim, oracular cast.

"Early on, too soon after I took up this racket, I accepted that we are *limited* in appreciating all that should be important. Things don't make any fucking sense. What's next?"

"Tying up a few loose ends."

"Can I help?"

"Yes," Walter said brightly. "Whatever happened to the North State Hotel?"

"Are you serious? What is this? Therapy through *non sequitur?*"

"It's been on my mind. Do you know?"

Bunch reached into his desk and took a brief nip from a fifth of Old Crow.

"You want one?" he asked.

Walter made bubbles in the heavy, brown liquor. He handed the bottle back to Bunch.

"The North State Hotel is the subject."

"Demolished years ago. When I came to Helmsville, it was a notorious fleabag. Pretty much like the two or three fleabags we still got here. The residents were typical—sociopaths, the lost, winos, canned heat drinkers. I represented a few clients—all guilty—from the North State."

"It was leveled?"

"Right down to the sidewalk. Is there...any other help you want?"

"No. That's fine."

"Then you'd better go. Right now."

The hum of the furnace competed with the downpour as

he rummaged through the cabinets until he found a can of chili and a box of crackers. He was not particularly hungry, but he ate anyway and drank a tall Budweiser—the only item in the refrigerator that had not gone bad.

As he spooned down his dinner, he considered his future. He had almost five thousand left from what he had withdrawn after discovering the *History*. That will do, he thought, to take me far away. I can get a job, one that demands nothing. I will live simply and alone. Which is not unlike the plan I formulated when I came to this damned place. The Loomis Curse extends indefinitely. Being alone is the key. No Edgar, no Ricky, no Star—no one. I've never had a job, other than tricking myself into teaching. What am I qualified for, as the saying goes? My grandfather started out as an undertaker. An honorable, dependable profession— and the market is stable, demand constant. I won't put myself through mortuary science school—learn where to hammer in the pumping needles and how to apply cosmetics to the subjects. I would be satisfied as an assistant, unskilled and invisible. Drive the hearse, handle the dead. The deceased would, I hope, refrain from further demands. Simple respect and consideration is all I want. That's all. There are regrets too. Regrets are perennial. The lost fortune doesn't bother me so much. I was not meant for such magnificence. I never figured out how to spend it well. But a few truths have evaded me. The last ritual will be some compensation. By this time tomorrow, I'll be gone.

The storm had slackened and the low, swollen clouds broke and scudded sluggishly to the east. In the unseen distance, over the mountains, fresh clouds were massing. The portents are temporarily favorable, Walter thought.

The ground was wallow-like and progress was slow, the mud pulling at his boots and splattering his legs. The *History* and the journals were stuffed into a pillow case, the first covering that Walter laid his hands on. The pages would dampen, wrinkling as the words smeared and blotted. I don't mind, he thought. Let the weight increase too. Would that they weighed a ton. The greater the ultimate relief. Over his shoulder, he carried a long-handled shovel, as shiny and unsoiled as the day it was purchased from Carolina Home Improvement World.

The route to the monument, which also led to the river, had indeed been skinned. The clumps of pine were fewer, smaller, giving out less than a mile from The Old Home Place. The crews must've started along here, Walter thought—where the hardwoods were once thickest. Cutting and dragging as Star rented a stylish beach-front bungalow—white sand outside, all the modern luxuries inside. Is Edgar pleased with her? I hope I never find out.

Far off, some real forest remained, revealed now that the spent front had pushed on. When it dries sufficiently, Weyerhauser Corporation will be back, he thought. Get what it bought and paid for.

Where the crews had done their work, the water flowed and pooled along the dips and contours of the surface, forming miniature ponds in too many places to allow Walter easy passage. He had to work around the ponds, tossing the pillow case up the oily, dredged out banks and hoisting himself up after it. After a few such portages, he was filthy, his slicker decorated with gobs of clay, the slimy feel of the earth going right down to his goose-pimpled flesh. Exhausted, he could not go any faster. He examined the sky for signs; he had been out for close to two hours. There was less light than when he started, and the clouds had begun to take on a formidable, phalanx-like configuration. Should I go back? he thought. I can't. I've got to do this. Edgar would appreciate it, if not approve.

With some relief, he came to higher ground; a place where what was left of a road climbed the ridge where he had met the fox and heard Star's song. The slope's run-off had created a stream in his path, and the only way to make time was to avoid the middle of the road and take the high, uneven bank beside it. There were pools, but much less run-off, and he slowed to a shuffle, watching where he stepped. He pulled himself along by planting the shovel and working forward a few feet at a time.

He halted at the crest, wheezing and retching slightly. He had seriously underestimated the requirements of his pilgrimage. Reaching the ridge top was almost worth the pain; however, those other roads ran nowhere, he thought. This one has led me to the first holy terminus. He squinted through the mist and down the steepness of the reverse slope. The monument was not in view. It's close enough, he thought.

What survived of the ridge's oaks were a few gashed stumps, some of which had been yanked out of the ground, their roots protruding upwards at random angles. The fox, he thought, was foxy enough to head out for parts unknown. He sat on an upright stump. This, he thought, must've been one of Edgar's sacred sites. A Stonehenge of self-will. Dashing after Margaret, percolating their juices amid the ancient, majestic trees. Exactly where I now perch among refuse. Star was down there, in that field. Was it a valedictory tune she piped? Just for old time's sake? Was she aware that I, like some voyeur, stood here above? Ricky came here too—where the fox cannot live. A future president may have cantered through on a sixteen-hand high thoroughbred. Grace fled, bearing a heavier load than what's in this pillow case. History. Ritual. The locus of Edgar's dreams. Finally, there is me. The last. And Bunch thought he was kidding about the Loomis Curse.

Regularly-spaced holes, brimming with mud-red broth, held drooping pine seedlings. The holes ran along the river side of the ridge. Garbage—cigarette packs, soft drink, sardine, and vienna sausage cans, a torn work glove—was scattered along the perimeter formed by the holes. Edgar wouldn't like this at all, Walter thought: his creation, raped—vile and poisoned. This trash would grieve him as much as the new, Flanders-style free hold designed by Star and Weyerhauser. I can't conceive of it as justice. Edgar skipped past justice on a regular basis, but trashing is trashing. The earth wasn't his—nor is it mine. I want no part of it.

The full extent of the pillage was redundantly clear. He did not have to fully see to know that it was the same—all blasted, pulverized. The stable too, he thought. Beatrice's dream house. Obie, who once tended Edgar's garden. Flanders? An intellectual conceit. My last, God willing. In Flanders there existed the possibility of pure, dumb courage, right alongside death's fouling. Here there is not that slight, unsatisfactory chance for redemption.

The rain resumed, the new clouds concentrating, taking up attacking positions over the ridge. The mud bubbled, now liquid, racing in rivulets. The field below was, Walter guessed, submerged. With the trees and roots gone, there was nothing to hold things together. There were no checks.

He could not linger. The rain had come sooner than scheduled. For the moment it was sporadic, blown by the wind from the west. Walter did not count on it staying so. He hefted the pillow case. It had the feel of a large rock. It's at hand, he thought. Finish it. Get to the monument and bury Edgar's and my words. Then go. Ricky, wherever, or whatever he is, can have the rest.

It was raining in earnest as he started down. At first, it was not too tricky. With great care, wiping the water from his face, leaning on the shovel, gripping the pillow case, he inched along, the run-off over the toes of his boots. He stumbled twice, almost falling, but the shovel helped him to keep his feet. He was very tired, but the monument could not be far. The rain intensified, blurring everything. Half-blind, he reached the middle of the slope. That's when he heard it, a sustained rush below him that was growing louder. All I have to do is be careful, he told himself, trying to ignore the rushing. And I have to watch my step. Where is the bottom? I can't go back unless I crawl. There is only one direction.

With that, his left foot caught in a hole. What the hell's that doing here? he thought. He raised his leg but the foot was securely lodged, the sludge running over his boot top. He gripped the pillow case tighter and steadied himself with the shovel. I must look like a goddamn idiot, he thought as he jerked and hopped.

His foot, minus the boot, came loose as he lost balance. The shovel flew from his hand, but, in a kind of minor miracle, he grasped the pillowcase to his chest as he commenced a series of mud-spraying somersaults. The slicker flailed about him like useless, rudimentary wings. The pillow case was finally lifted from him, and he had a split-second, upside-down glimpse as it sailed ahead of him, falling in the gray rain.

A lake, he managed to think. There's a lake here. He shot out into and beneath the foam of the rising river. The rushing that he had heard on the slope was immense now—like a locomotive in a nightmare. He landed in the middle, jammed, gap-mouthed to the churning, crushing, newly formed river bed. It was alive—and it craved him. It also tasted of rot, of things long submerged, all boiling up from the engorged, original course of the waters. He had to swim, to resist, but he could not. He was swept away, along with tree limbs, dead animals, refuse without a name, chilled and stinking. He was in it—and it was in him. The *History*, and his journals blended into the flood and disintegrated.

He was hurled along, mostly under water, drawing just breath enough to live. He kicked, grasped futilely, and fought—unable to find anything firm. In those seconds when his head was pushed to the surface, he might have understood that the flood was locked between the ridges, that the latest storm had utterly transformed the old river. It would have been no real understanding, for he was beyond thought. For the time being, his escape was absolute and complete. All rituals were canceled.

As he struggled, his last reserves of strength were consumed. It would have come as a relief to simply surrender, to hug the bottom. No one would find him, and this too had its appeal. Instead of the bliss of annihilation, he collided with something hard, his head driving into it like a torpedo. Instinctively, he wrapped his arms and legs around the thing, scarcely aware of the blow to his head, pulling himself to it like a lover.

It was a pine, overlooked or marked for later consumption by the Weyerhauser Corporation. It stood, despite the torrent, in a tiny bay that had been scooped out of the soft, disintegrating earth. With an effort that he did not think was in him, he gradually lifted himself higher—until he was completely out of the flood.

The other boot had been sucked from his foot and his soiled white socks looked ludicrously obscene. He was terrified of slipping back down, knowing that he could not live in that ferocious rushing. He feebly vomited and a small quantity of water dribbled down his chin and over the punctured, slashed slicker. I have to see where I am, he thought. If I am anywhere.

The pine had marginally improved his condition, although it shook with the river's pounding. He could not stay where he was. The tree was at the base of a small, narrow ridge that ran parallel to the direction he thought he had come—when he could still walk upright. Directions now, from where he teetered and rocked, were inaccurate measures. The flood, the river—they were now the same—swelled and undulated with the storm. It followed the most natural course, rolling all out for the flat, vulnerable stretches beyond the ridges; the roads, the fields, and The Old Home Place on its puny rise. The tree vibrated furiously, bending beneath him.

With considerable squirming and clawing, he maneuvered to the side of the tree closest to the small ridge. After resting briefly, he launched himself backwards. His legs dangled in the flood, which licked avidly at him as, with a cry, he scrambled to higher ground. Eventually, he was able to stand.

The ridge was blade-like, covered with undergrowth: blackberry bushes, naked dogwoods, and vines that he could not name. Once on his feet—he could not feel the thorns that pierced his flesh—he drove himself on. Go higher, he thought. I can't get high enough. He crossed the ridge and fell again. Sitting upright taxed what was left in him. I shouldn't have made it, he thought. I should've gone down with the *History*.

The rain was worse than ever. He did not want to imagine the journey ahead. But it had to be undertaken. He stood. At least there is something beneath me, he thought.

The flood spread below him, eating up the solid world at a slower rate than where he had tumbled down. He could see that, slower or not, it was still inexorable. It would cover where he walked—except for the highest points. His feet accumulated mud. Soon, they were huge, lopsided balls, which actually cushioned and soothed his progress, if making walking that much more difficult. His path, chosen only because it led away from the waters, dipped down to a ravine—which he darted across—and on to still higher ground. The flood, he knew, could arrive there without warning.

He tramped up a gradual incline, constantly renewing the balls of mud. All he knew was that he had to keep on. The incline was without undergrowth. He hoped that it was part of a logging road. Roads can get me out, he thought. He went on, bent low, the rain coming on in drenching gusts. The flood was at his back, and getting louder.

The incline leveled out in a de-nuded plateau and he dared to look back from where he had come. He wished he could spy the monument, to find if it stood impervious and everlasting. There was nothing. I'll bet it's there, he thought, alone and defying the engulfing of the rest of creation. The only landmark upright in the ruins—the erased world. "The scene of my redemption," he snarled. "The final, best joke."

He walked, waded, and swam when he had to. He did not know it, but he was on a tortuous, doglegged trail that would bring him close to The Old Home Place—if the flood did not get there first.

Eventually, he blundered onto a graveled road. The water was perhaps a hundred yards off, advancing steadily. He stopped when he reached the road and watched the flood coming for him. He did not remember a road like this one. He was dizzy and his arms and legs had a loose, rubbery sensation. Why this road? he thought. With gravel. The loggers must've spread it for traction. That's obvious enough.

He stood there for awhile, watching, like a spectator, as the flood lapped up the road. Then, through the rain, he saw a truck, a big diesel model; the kind that transported all those trees, he thought. It was mired to the bumpers in what had once been a cornfield. Walter splashed for it. It has an inside, he thought. I can get out of this.

The door was open and there were no keys—not that the truck was going anywhere. It could take an hour, Walter thought. Then it'll go under too. The cab was relatively dry and there was a can of Beenie-Weenies on the floorboard. He slurped them down. There was a baseball cap too, sporting the logo of the Savage Bass Tackle Shop, Belmont, North Carolina. He clamped the cap down over his head.

It was comforting inside the truck—diesel odor, metal

damp, and all. He did not have to plot a way around the flood. Outside was annihilation. Here, he thought, is a place of rest. As good as any and better than most. He closed his eyes, and his wet, tomato sauce and bean encrusted face took on an oddly angelic quality of repose.

"Do you wanna get outta here?"

Whoever spoke was right beside him, his mouth flush against Walter's ear. Ricky was as muddy as Walter, and shirtless. His breath was pungent and, like his question, it filled the truck cab.

"Walt, if you hang around here, you gonna have problems." With that, Ricky was gone, striding away from the grasp of the flood. Walter had to run, as best he could, to catch him.

15

"Can't say we didn't try. Right Walt?"

Shivering, Walter agreed. There was no electricity, no furnace, no running water. The Old Home Place had flickered out.

Ricky had taken a wingback chair and Walter the couch by the door, establishing a formal distance between them. And the darkness was not so bad, Walter thought. Following the nearly lightless day, night's arrival did not increase his torpid, listless dread. The dread had metastasized, encasing Walter, Ricky, and The Old Home Place. The earlier dread in his life was mere preparation. The new, super dread was embodied in the rain's merry, heartless sizzle, and the flood's rushing. He strained after the rushing, his hearing painfully acute. At times it was far off, but not far enough to promise deliverance. In the next moment it lurked by the door, poised for entry.

"Shoot, we'll be all right. Fucking rain can't last forever."

He heard Ricky without quite seeing him; a shape on the other side of the living room that had gradually grown talkative. After rescuing Walter, Ricky had, through the hallucinatory afternoon, confined himself to terse declarations. The first had come as Walter hobbled into The Old Home Place. Following Ricky was not easy. He had stuck to his own route march pace, fading into the rain, emerging farther

260

ahead, never slowing or checking to see if Walter was on the right path. It was a race that Walter was barely able to complete. At the finish, however, he rejoiced in ignorance. When he crossed the last ankle-deep pasture of muck, and his truck took form, he had wept. The engine confidently purred as Ricky watched Walter prepare for escape.

"Where you going?" Ricky had asked.

"Out of here," Walter had said. "Come on."

"Save your gas." Ricky had reached across Walter and pulled the key.

Once again, Walter had followed him. Down the rise from The Old Home Place, Ricky had waited. There was, Walter had seen, no mistaking Ricky's meaning. The road through the ruins to the highway—which would have taken Walter as far as he could have run—had dropped from sight. Ricky pointed to where it had been—an unnecessary gesture. The facts were plain enough.

The flood had beaten them, thrashing along in its mindless, putrefying grandeur. It looks like it's been here forever, Walter had thought. The ruins were swamped—except for one remaining wall of the ranch house, the single standing landmark. On it came—vaster than when Walter executed his pratfall on the slope above Edgar's monument. It blotted out whatever had existed prior to its creation. Then the cold had clasped itself to Walter and refused to budge.

With none of his old-time yammering fanfare, Ricky put himself and Walter to work. Without a shovel, they had to make do with paint buckets—the remains of Walter's decorating efforts. Ricky said that a ditch and dike would save The Old Home Place. As spent as he was, as broken by the completeness of his imprisonment, Walter had no choice but to help.

Ricky staked out the boundaries with sticks and branches: a square, that if it could have been built, might have delayed the flood. He was positively military in his posture and bearing. Does he know what he is doing? Walter had thought, as he picked up a bucket.

Once the digging commenced, however, Walter comprehended the futility. The buckets, given the soupy texture of the ground, were appropriate tools. They bent and heaved, tossing their loads into mounds. The volume, the endlessness of the storm was against them, however. As fast as they dumped their buckets, they could not match the run-off. The mud dribbled and spewed over their feet and legs. Their ditch was never more than a shallow indentation, full to its brim. The dike shrank as it was constructed, leaving widely-spaced, uneven piles that gradually melted away. Ricky tried to shore up the mounds with two-by-fours, but there were too few. Children at play could've done as well, Walter had thought as they made circuit after pointless circuit around the house. Ricky seldom spoke, or gave any indication that their task was desperate and doomed. He appeared to have withdrawn into himself as he squatted, poured, and lifted. He smiled as he worked, his teeth white against his mud encrusted face—as if the dike had relieved him of other, greater burdens.

The rushing was ever present. Walter paused and listened while Ricky went on like a machine. The flood would scale the rise. The slower, no less implacable waters had inundated the pasture they had crossed in gaining The Old Home Place. The rain directly assaulted their efforts, while these waters gently lapped at and slowly dissolved the mounds. Walter paused often to blow warmth into his stiff, painful hands. Ricky burrowed ahead with muscular efficiency.

With the last of the pale daylight, Walter had collapsed, falling spread eagle across their pathetically low dike. Ricky had repaired the gap and politely suggested the Walter might rest inside. Walter, muddied, stupefied, slack-jawed, barely made the couch.

Ricky had come across a flashlight, a battery-powered radio, canned soup, and warm beer. Walter, aroused by a newscaster describing the "rampaging waters of the Reedy, Broad, and Catawba Rivers," had eaten because Ricky insisted that he keep up his strength. The Reedy had crested that afternoon west of Helmsville "climbing thirty feet over flood stage. It is not possible to accurately gauge the level because of the river's dangerously rapid rise. It has completely covered miles of Darden County. Conditions are expected to worsen overnight." Residents of Darden, Lincoln, Gaston, and Rutherford Counties were to prepare for immediate evacuation.

"That's not for us, is it?" Ricky asked. Do I hear...optimism? Walter thought.

"I said that's not for us."

"No evacuation," Walter said, setting aside the cold, unheated mushroom soup. It tasted of the flood, a taste that he could, he thought, never rid himself of.

"We couldn't evacuate if we wanted to," Ricky laughed. "Man, I'd given a hundred bucks for a picture of you when you seen that road." He's chock-full of good humor yet, Walter thought.

"I'd pay a hundred myself."

"We're not going nowhere, are we?"

"No chance of that."

"We gonna stand and fight."

The radio crackled on about shelters, the National Guard, states of emergency. "The worst flood since 1916," the announcer said. "Although there is no official damage estimate to this point, the unofficial total runs into the hundreds of millions of dollars. The worst is yet to come..." The radio was silenced before the announcer could state what could be worse.

"Worse my ass," Ricky said. "We don't need that kinda

talk. Save the batteries for some music—if I can get any in all this news shit. That's a neat little old radio. Where'd you get it?"

"I can't remember. Probably in Illinois. Why is that important?" He's gearing up, Walter thought. The old Ricky with his original energy.

"Back when you were a teaching."

"Earlier times."

Ricky's smile had taken on a neon quality in the cold darkness.

"Nothing's been the same since you came here."

"I...I don't..." Walter's mouth was dry. In the days before the rushing, he thought, this was the worst situation I had foreseen: alone with Ricky. The smile seemed to draw closer to him.

"I'm not *blaming* you for nothing. You might say that it goes back to Daddy's...dying. His leaving. Your arriving. Pretty close together."

"I don't find any connection. Except for the inheritance."

"None at all? Daddy did want it like that. Me and you sharing all this...goodness."

"Then that's the connection."

"Pure and simple? Think about this a minute. See, there's all kinda other connections between us, me and you—and everybody else. It's come to me—I've been doing heavy thinking lately—that there's no such thing as a accident. How about that?"

The rushing had stabilized, drawing back a degree or two. Is it awaiting a signal? Walter thought. He rinsed his mouth with a warm beer. He was faintly aware that his words and gestures had a tentative, fumbling quality.

"Much of life strikes me as...very accidental."

"Nobody's to blame for accidents? That right?"

"Look, why're you going on like this? They're...larger

issues here. Much larger."

Ricky laughed, the teeth flying up and down.

"I like that. Larger issues. But back to accidents—like we had on the Fourth of July. Which is the opposite, the god-damn opposite, of what people *mean* to do. Later they *claim* they had an accident. Or a mistake. Whatever you wanta call it."

"There is a fine line in many cases." Walter swigged at his beer. Blur the edges, he thought. If I only could.

"Drowning's a large fucking issue."

The cold insinuated itself down into Walter's bones.

"I could've drowned today. We might...drown tonight."

"You scared?"

"Very."

"Me too. Which is why we gonna talk. It helps being scared. I been meaning to have a chat with you, Walt. I've missed you. Years ago, I seen a drowned man. He was puffed up like a circus fat man. Musta had twenty gallons in him. But I'll change the subject. We'll come back to that later. This is a night for large issues. So where you been? I ain't tried to find you. Had to keep a low profile. Understand?"

"A trip. It was dull. Nowhere in particular." I have enough sense remaining not to bring up the *History,* Walter thought. Ricky could not cope with the *History.* Thank God it's lost in the flood.

"Traveling again. I thought so. I'd scratch around this house—mostly at night. Ever tell you about living in California? Damndest place. Plenty to like. Plenty to hate. I don't want to dwell on it. Not now. I might get back into California later. If we got time. There's lots to rap about, but only so much time to do it in. You got things you don't dwell on?"

"Don't we all?" The course of this conversation, Walter thought, is similar to what is outside. Not subject to control.

"Wouldn't be human if we didn't. Guilt, some call it. Daddy didn't hold with guilt. With some of my heavy thinking I've...reconsidered some of Daddy's notions. I've been alone a lot. Most alone I've ever been in my whole life. Didn't think I could stand it, but I did. You the first person I've talked to in...I'm not sure. A long time. So you went on this fine, fine trip. Did you see Star? One day she was there and the next she wasn't. Did you see her?"

Flight was Walter's immediate impulse when Ricky spoke her name, but it was not an option. He had to fall back on words.

"Not for months. I hope she's safe. I don't know why I haven't asked. It must be..."

"It's the fear. Drowning. Yes indeed. That old fear. You didn't run into her in wherever the hell you went? You never did say."

"Nowhere special."

"She thinks a lot of you."

"She's very...nice." Words are no refuge, Walter thought.

"Nice? Is that what she is? She mighta gone to L.A. and you missed her if you went there. She missed you. She'd fit in in L.A. or anywhere. I love her bad, and she run out. I probably had it coming. It wasn't no accident at all. I couldn't straighten out. But if she could see me now, she'd change her mind. You ever been in love?"

"I'm...not positive."

"Goddamn, Walt! If you're in love, you're nothing but positive!"

The rushing had climbed to its earlier level. Walter envisioned it making directly for him. The rushing and Ricky had that much in common. Then, with a dawning sense of wonder, he fell back on a truth—or part of a truth.

"Ricky, I must tell you some unfortunate facts about Star. She could be in the Bahamas."

"Where'd you hear that?"

With deliberate care and whatever haggard gentleness he could summon, he went through the visit to the bank, the power of attorney, and the Weyerhauser contract. He omitted Star's Celebration. His story, given the rushing and their prospects, seemed glaringly out of place. Ricky was absolutely mute and still. "...and I should've told you, but with the flood that was impossible. To be fair, she left a letter requesting me to watch over you, but you've watched over me."

"That's her! That's Star! Smart as can be! I love her smartness! I swear I do!"

Walter blinked and chipped dried mud from his forehead. My conclusions too, he thought. She *does* deserve all that she aimed for. We are in agreement.

"She was extremely thorough, I'll have to admit. Bunch said it was as perfect a fleecing as he'd heard of."

"Bunch don't know the half of it. She could be some kinda genius."

The rushing accelerated. Has it breached our barricade? Walter thought. Ricky's teeth were like beacons.

"When we get outta here," Ricky said, "and get down to the Bahamas, she'll treat us like kings. Once I'm satisfied with that, I'll kill her. I miss her. I love her, but I'm gonna kill her. My love won't stop me. She'd have to accept that. Hey, she might send for us. Wait and see."

"I miss Momma," Ricky said. Once the subject of killing was broached, Walter became too tense for conversation. He roamed from room to room, peering out the windows: blackness, a gnashing void. Ricky was at least a voice. Walter had to return to him.

"She'll be fine. Count on it, Walt. She's kinda high-strung. The next time I see her, I'll bring a present. A kitchen appliance. She really goes for kitchen appliances. I don't want to kill her like I do Star. You can't kill your Momma..."

There's nothing to be gained, Walter thought, in reporting on Beatrice. She's probably with Tommy—snug and comfortable. Back from the mall, mildly interested in the T.V. special reports on the terrible floods in the Helmsville area. She slapped Ricky, both hands across his mouth. Right after The Event. A ritual—like burying the *History*.

"...I don't take killing lightly. There's times when you got to. When you...can't stand whatever it is. I've held off, been forgiving. Star didn't think so. As smart as she is, she can't accept reality. Don't misunderstand me: her feet are on the ground nine times outta ten; but there's things that she can't...leave alone. She's not perfect. Smart, but not perfect..."

Walter's dizziness had returned, but was not so strong as when he found the graveled road or fell through the dike. Killing, he thought. He's going on and on with this killing.

"Do you mean it? Killing?"

Ricky had abruptly shut up. He barely made a sound as he opened the front door, his shape stepping into the greater darkness. Should I follow? Walter thought. Ricky called to him.

Ricky's flashlight roamed over where the dike had stood. There was only the inevitable water, the surface popping with raindrops. The porch steps were covered and the pick-up truck consumed to mid-door. In time, the rushing would link with the slower, seeping part of the flood. They would converge at The Old Home Place.

Back in the living room, there was no reason to speak. Ricky fooled with the radio, picking up a distant station. With the volume at the highest setting, Def Lepard and Megadeath partially obscured the rushing—but not so as to allow Walter to forget it was there. The signal gradually succumbed to static and weakening batteries. Ricky removed the back panel and pointed his flashlight into the radio's innards.

"EverReady's don't last, Walt. Try Duracells next time."

"I'll do that." Killing, Walter thought. There's plenty in the *History*. France, the Bay of Pigs. The slaughter of record. Then there are the last few pages.

"I ain't going back inside," Ricky said. "The last time I could...communicate with Daddy I flashed on that. I told you about my doubts didn't I? It's a shame I can't believe like I used to, to hear him. Not since I went back into the woods. It was never like words. I could appreciate what he was trying to get across without hearing the words. There wasn't nothing you could write down. You have any idea what I'm talking about?"

"Yes." The dreams, Walter thought. Edgar was in everybody's dreams.

"You his son too. You understand."

Walter also knew what Ricky meant about going back inside, but he kept that to himself. Soon enough, Ricky was off and babbling, confessing, explaining.

"I'm gonna be free. That's the law's problem—not mine. I had to take a stand. They had no right to fuck with me like that. Manslaughter! Arson! I said to myself: who they messing with? Ricky, the walls ain't for you. Yeah. I done time. Don't think bad of me, Walt. It was over nothing. I'm not getting into that shit. What's past is gone. Can't let it jam you in. I sorta did it for Daddy, and that's all I'm saying on that. He gave me plenty and I helped him out. Least I could do. Don't disgrace us, he said. You gotta sacrifice. He did a lot for you too. I want to tell you that I'm honored to have you for a brother. When I seen you today, it made me happy. You wanted to bring me in, to help me to learn to accept my punishment. Don't say you didn't. You was doing right by your standards. I accept that. I got standards too. I swore to be free, and I've been pretty goddamn successful. Old Peavey couldn't find me in a year. When those bastards come to cut wood, I had to push farther and farther into the land. I'd been out there right now if it wasn't for this flood. Had three camps, good camps, with tunnels and booby-traps. They was washed out. This flood did one thing: slowed down the cutting. Too bad we can't get to what's left of the timber. That would be some real living—me and you. I engaged in guerilla warfare. I'd come out after the cutters quit for the day. Deflated tires. Threw equipment in the river. That truck you was in, I ruined the engine. Those dumbasses. I watched them—they never suspected I was there. They couldn't figure what the fuck was wrong. This was right when the rains was picking up. Daddy woulda been proud. He admired initiative. He'd been proud of what Star done too. That's why I signed—and you probably signed for the same reason. We couldn't know that...so much of the land, what Daddy loved, would be eaten up. He wouldn't want me to kill Star. I'll get these...contradictions squared away in my mind. He had a lot of...respect for Star. Said she was like a daughter. I'm trying to square away that too..."

A faint trickling. Walter stirred himself and put his hand to the floor. A regular puddle was creeping beneath the front door.

"Ricky?"

"...I'm all for money, but it don't seem right to sell the trees and lose the money too. The woods was mine, along with the houses and fields and Hickory. And Star. Daddy comes to me, outta the blue, says I got to share with my half-brother. That's you, Walt. He said that by sharing we'd be whole and complete. That's a...quotation. Whole and complete. We would rule over all that he'd created and that this farm, our earth he called it, would grow richer and greater. I tried to get my mind clear on sharing. Daddy said that you was neglected. Surely that wasn't his fault. You had your own Momma. She was pretty. Her picture is with him. He took the best care of all of us…"

"It's inside. It's with us."

Walter waited. The puddle increased in size, snaking under the furniture and toward the hall. Ricky would not stop, or slow down.

"…do you understand about Daddy? He was generous. Generous to a fault some might say. He wanted us to be as one, to share. We coulda had a lot more fun than we did. We was always going in opposite directions, you and me. We might have big times ahead. Lots of laughs. I get back with Star, you get you a woman. Get a good woman. How about me tagging along on one of those trips of yours? First we gotta get to the Bahamas. I've wanted to visit there. This is a chance to mix business with pleasure. I'll fix things up with Star. Then I'll kill her. You don't have to help me with that. Asking too much—even for a brother that you are whole and complete with. We accepted each other's differences. You're a smart guy! A professor *and* a writer! Damn! Star's read your books. She wouldn't tell me what was in them. I asked her a million times. Well, here we are. Together at last!"

Having temporarily run down, Ricky paused, drawing in deep, hoarse breaths. Walter had heard bits and pieces— enough to fuel his dread. He was on his hands and knees, the icy water running around him, packing sheets and towels at the bottom of the door.

"That won't do no good," Ricky said.

Ricky was right, but Walter had to act, no matter how useless that act would be. It's like the dike, he thought—a band aid for an amputation. Lines from Ricky's monologue flew in and out of the dread. At one time—a week, a month earlier—the lines would have paralyzed him as fully as had the *History;* in the days prior to the flood and the rushing.

When Walter admitted defeat, the living room floor was

completely covered. The leakage was stronger at the back door, which he had not checked earlier. As if it would have done any good, he thought as he retreated through the kitchen. Here and there, the hall was dry, but it, along with the rest of the first floor, would not remain so for long. This is from the slow rising alone, he thought. The full power has not yet presented itself. He listened once again. It called to him from the lip of the rise, demanding its due. Ricky was in the wing back chair, the water over his feet.

"We might be better off upstairs," Walter said.

"Walt, I'm cold. Could I borrow some clothes?"

"The bedroom closet. Take what you want."

"Thanks. One time, I wanted to kill you. Just for a few minutes. Don't know why I'm telling you now. Could be because of this sit-down talk of ours. Bringing things out."

"But you...don't want to...kill me now?"

Ricky laughed with eerie joy.

"Man, we in this together. Have been all along!"

They changed into whatever they could find in the shaky, fluttering beams from the flashlights. Walter donned jeans and an Altgeld College sweatshirt, Ricky a sweater and corduroy suit from Walter's brief period of dressing academically. The suit was a size too large and the jacket draped across Ricky's shoulder like a cloak. In the study, the rain's drumfire muted the rushing to a degree. Below, The Old Home Place was filling. Walter had gathered the last of the canned food and three beers. They lay on the study floor, preserving whatever was in them for what was ahead. This is it, Walter thought. The final stop. Together—as Ricky said. Stamey's palace, Edgar's refuge. The tricklings have grown to torrents.

Ricky was on his back, arms at his sides, legs pressed against each other. Is he asleep? Walter thought. But the words rolled on again.

"I apologize. Sincerely. About killing you. Put your mind at rest. Nothing but jealousy. Daddy said that jealousy was...an unfit emotion. See, I never expected that I'd get to know you. I was sorta obsessed. I covered it up by being extra friendly. Friendlier than you was to me. I didn't understand you. A lot's come down since then. I was taking Hickory for a run one day—not long after you come in and...took over this house. And I seen your Volkswagen. You were smart to trade it. A pick-up's the right vehicle for country living. But I seen that you was at home, where I used to stay with Daddy and play when I was a kid. And I was gonna get a hammer and beat your fucking brains out. It was nothing personal. It goes back to that sharing, which I hadn't gotten right in my mind. I gotta work to get things right in my mind. I was greedy—that's another unfit emotion. Besides, there were these other...problems. Not that coming here wasn't your right. I hadn't...accepted Daddy's plans for the future. I gotta tell you that I'm ashamed as can be of those negative feelings. I went to Daddy's grave and he made me see how wrong I was..."

"It's O.K. Perfectly O.K." He has a right to beat out my brains, Walter thought.

"It wasn't O.K. I got over being...all negative. That's in the past. I believe that we'll be working together. Once this flood's gone we'll put the farm back in shape. It'll be hard, but with your brains and my muscles there ain't nothing we can't do. What'd you say? You listening?"

"Yes. A bright future."

"You said it! A new age for the Loomis brothers! It don't have to be a farm. Do you realize that the land's cleared—and at no cost? What all could we build here? Malls. There's room for two giant malls. With a whole city around them. Or one mall and throw in a theme park—like Six Flags Over Georgia, or even Disney World! There's millions in theme parks. You might be saying to yourself: what's a theme park got to do with Daddy's spiritual ideas on nature? Keep this in mind: Daddy had nothing against money..."

"Which is why he wouldn't disapprove of what Star did."

"Exactly right! That's my point. You gotta be far-sighted. Daddy said that plenty. He wasn't no air-headed environmentalist! Hell no! *Develop* what you're given. Make it bloom and prosper. I can't remember how many times he said them very words."

The rain dripped through the roof, striking them at slow, measured intervals. It's all the rain that's ever fallen, Walter thought. Oceans were drained that they might hurtle downwards upon our heads. The ocean at the end. The end.

Something in Walter shriveled.

"Ricky," he said. Ricky had lapsed into something approximating contemplation. He did not reply. Walter waited. There isn't much time, Walter thought. But it is only right to wait.

"What is it?" Ricky said. His voice was loud and abrupt. "Are you worse afraid? I don't want to kill you. Is it worse?"

"The same. We're not going to get out of here, are we?"

"What can I say? We did what we could. You gotta be positive. I've seen worse fixes. There was this one time..."

"There are no other times. This is it."

Ricky went to the head of the stairs. The beam from his flashlight was thin and ghostly, providing no comfort.

"Damn. We need us a pump," Ricky said. Walter pulled himself up, resting his back against the rain-streaked wall.

"It's on the stairs, isn't it?"

"It'll never get this high. Besides, this house is mighty sturdy. It'll stand when nothing else can."

"How did Edgar die?" The question vomited out of Walter, involuntarily and unpremeditated. The light swung around, blinding him.

"Why'd you ask that?"

"Could you take the light…"

"In a minute. Sure. You're serious, ain't you?"

"Right now, I couldn't be anything but serious. But if you don't want to talk about it, I understand…"

"I'll talk. You got a point." The light clicked out. White dots danced in front of Walter's eyes. Ricky squatted against the opposite wall.

"Now that I think on it," Ricky said, "I ain't never been in so tight a spot. I can't maneuver. These four little rooms is it. I had fun in this house when I was a kid. You gotta feel sorry for children these days. No country for them to run in. Houses like boxes. I have to have plenty of space—like when I was growing up. Which is why I ain't going back to prison. Can't stand being hemmed in. What about you?"

"I spent most of my life indoors. When I was a boy, there were sailboat voyages along the coast. I was afraid of falling overboard…"

"Sinking like a goddamn rock. Like now," Ricky laughed. His flashlight played across the room and into Walter's eyes.

"Please…"

"Hurts?"

"It's not…necessary. Could you…"

"What could we tell each other about getting hurt? I broke my arm playing ball. A goddamn mare stepped on my foot. Obie had to lift her hoof off me. Stupid horse. Obie's dead. That hurt. Star hurt me. You *aware* of that? Not when she cheated and robbed us. That didn't hurt at all."

"I'm sorry." If only there was no light, Walter thought. The dark was a balm. The rushing sought him out, but he cared nothing now for the exact moment of its arrival.

"Thank you, Walt. I'm sorry for whatever hurt you too. We're *supposed* to be hurt. I figured that out—just that minute."

"An inescapable conclusion."

"Still the professor, ain't you? Inescapable conclusion. Star believed that you being a professor made you special. Naw, I said to her. Walt don't flaunt it. He's plain folks. You wish you'd gone on with your teaching up there, where you come from?"

"Now I do." The light vanished.

Ricky laughed—far too loudly considering the joke. He slapped the floor.

"That's a good one. We're getting off the subject, ain't we. It was your subject, too. You might be gonna die, but I'm not counting on that for me. But if I did croak, where's better than The Old Home Place—where the Loomis family was born?"

"We don't have to discuss Edgar. Or dying. Discussions aren't necessary—unless you want them."

Ricky's light hurtled into him. Walter shielded his face with his hands. The final element of Edgar's vision, he thought. The end as farce. Serves his boys right for being such fools.

"If I want to?" Ricky asked. "Thanks, brother. It wasn't dying as dying you had to discuss. It was Daddy: a real specific dying. I told you the story, but I'll tell it again. There's nothing like a story—especially a family story."

When the flashlight was extinguished, Walt kept his hands over his face, his own warm, foul breath in his nostrils. The last, best story, he thought.

At first, Ricky did not deviate from the tale told on a backyard spring evening: the son in search of the father, riding forth like a young knight. As the story developed, the text was transformed. The words jetted out of Ricky.

"...And I seen him. He didn't see me. Not that he wasn't on the lookout, he was anxious—mighta never had a reason to be anxious in his life—until then. He mighta been heading for town. He never said. He'd sent Obie to Helmsville that morning for horse feed, and he gave Momma money for shopping. She shopped and shopped. I learned all this later. Star...she was in her room. She'd taken the extra bedroom. Locked herself in. Wouldn't say why. Didn't come out unless Momma was home. I'd get by her door, trying to catch any sound from her I could. Couldn't hear a thing, but she was in there. Anyhow, I was on Hickory and looking for Daddy—same as he was for me. We had...problems. I've told you that, haven't I? Remember the problems. This is the occasion for truth. That's what you want?

"I come off this bridal path. It ain't too far from where we sit. You know, I'm glad you asked about Daddy. It's a heavy load, let me tell you. I trotted out as Daddy went by— rode behind his old pick-up. It was a cold day. Snowed that week, a few days before. That ain't important. He seen me in his rearview mirror. And he waved, slow and friendly. Didn't speed up or slow down. He didn't head on over to the Helmsville road neither. Turned onto this dirt track that went to the biggest corn fields. Right close to where I found you today. The track was in fair shape, and he waved to me again—like he wanted me to follow him. That's...that's what he was doing. I see that now. Clear as can be. He was leading me...I wasn't chasing him. Somebody else mighta seen it that way. But, it was just the two of us. Me and Daddy. See, we had this problem...I'll skip that. You don't want me to blab about problems. They in the past. You asked how he died—and I'm gonna tell you.

"He passed the corn fields. He wasn't going fast. Steady—like he knew exactly where he wanted to get to. There's this other field on down the track, which gets narrow there and rutted up. All that's underwater now. Daddy too. Deep, deep down. I stayed back some, hardly breaking Hickory into a canter. I did call to him one time. He shoulda stopped. I was worried he'd get stuck down there by this other field, which wasn't but half-cleared. I can't tell you how worried I was. That problem was hanging over me.

Over us. I'd thought about it. I'd smoke some dope and try to figure out how we got us such a problem. It would be fine if we had some dope right now. So I'd been thinking hard about why Daddy and me, father and son, couldn't sit down, man to man, and discuss...this problem. Sorta like we're doing. I'm relieved to be telling you this story. You're the closest I got to a Daddy, and there's no talking to him ever again. To get back to the story, I was concerned and needed a word with him. No. That's not exactly right. I wanted him to say the *right* words. When all this was happening I was...confused. Didn't know which end was up. You understand how that feels, don't you? I had to get my mind right. He coulda done that for me if he'd wanted to.

"The track was petering out. Narrower and narrower. I coulda reined up, gone home. It never occurred to me. He'd turn around to see if I was still following him. I prayed that he'd pay attention to the track. I think I yelled for him to do just that. He musta figured I was yelling something else. Then he hopped from the track and into that field, right in the middle of these stumps, old rotten stumps, that had been there since before I went to the Marines. You probably did-n't know I was a Marine. Semper Fi. There's lots and lots we got to learn about each other."

Ricky drew in several yawning breaths. For Walter, the rushing could have been a thousand miles away.

"You don't have to..." Walter began.

"I do too. Hear that flood? It's climbing, could climb a mountain if we was that high—Walt, you asked, and I'm gonna say how it was. Daddy weaved around the stumps, then pulled up a pretty good ways from where I stopped. I didn't want him to run into me and Hickory. My head was in some shape right then. Our problems. His crazy-ass dri-ving. It stewed inside me. It hurt. Like it was supposed to..."

"The singing was in there, wasn't it?"

"Lord yes. The singing. How'd you hear about that? I

278

gotta find out what kinda...information you have."

"The singing is with us. Forever." Walter had said it, and while it did nothing to ease his dread, it was the least he owed Ricky.

"Forever? Daddy's tuned in to...? Well, I can't sidetrack myself with problems and singing and what's bullshit and what ain't. The story's mine and Daddy's. The one and only Daddy."

"He got out of the truck?"

"A gun in his hand. Years ago, he'd let me fire it."

"Forty-five caliber service automatic."

"He shared it with you too? When you was a boy? He was leaning forward, aiming with both hands, like you're supposed to, firing as fast as he could pull the trigger. I didn't move an inch. Hickory whinnied and pulled his head around and I had to quiet him, which wasn't easy. We didn't retreat or advance. The firing was pretty wild. A coupla rounds whizzed past my ears. Why you shooting at me? I thought. I love you. You're my Daddy. It didn't make sense. He went through the clip and I guess he didn't have another. He stopped shooting and dropped his forty-five. It was his old army automatic—from the war, from France, he said. He carried it to France on a secret mission. We stood there, stockstill, most of the field between us, staring. I can see him crystal clear. If he'd wanted to hit me, he shoulda drawn me closer, the forty-five being a short-range weapon. That's the first rule he ever told me about that pistol of his.

"He didn't move when I started walking Hickory across the field. It was like...he couldn't believe that I hadn't gone down. I mighta wanted to kill him—like I'm gonna kill Star, like I was gonna kill you. I woulda killed any other man in those...circumstances. It was that stew in my head. It's stewed forever it feels like—including right now. It won't stop neither. It's gone too far. I come on slow. I didn't want him to get excited. I was gonna walk up to him, dismount, and either hug him...or choke him to death. It was a toss-up between the two. I guess it depended on what *he* would do next. Choking woulda been the hardest. I love my Daddy and he was real strong for a man his age. He woulda fought hard, trying to kill me, which he had just tried to do. The closer I come, the clearer it was that he wasn't right. His eyes was...huge, bugging out. Like they coulda popped outta his head. His face was red. On fire... with blood. I'd never seen him look that way. Then he did the damndest thing—and right when I figured I'd hug him, forgive him for our problems and him shooting at me. And we would make promises about how we was gonna act and treat each other. What he done wasn't...what I figured on. He...dove into his truck—I seen then that he'd left the motor running—and come right at me. He floored it, too. With the ground the way it was, his old pick-up went up in the air, the body smashing down on the tires and the suspension. For a second I thought Hickory was gonna throw me right in Daddy's path. But we got around him—I don't know how—and went for the trees where he couldn't chase us. He crashed then, like I told the law and Momma, and Star, who said I was a liar. I lied a little—told everybody that I wasn't there when it happened. And now you know that I was. You and nobody else, except maybe Star.

"He hit one of those old stumps straight on. These hornets, thousands of them, was hibernating there. When Daddy run into their stump, they all came out in a great big flying ball. He fell outta the cab, holding his chest, giving out sounds I'd never heard come out of a human. He was redder than before, the smoke and steam from the busted radiator all around him. He didn't say nothing—no last words. He fell to his knees, then keeled over on his back when the hornets got him. I couldn't get close on account of the hornets. He flopped and kicked—what with his heart blowing up on him. That's what the doctors said: the

heart...exploded. And the stings too. It was like those hornets had been waiting for him.

"They went away, buzzing off in that ball that they come
in. I tethered Hickory and went over to Daddy to watch him
finish dying—which wasn't but about a second by the time I
got to him. He was swollen up something awful. I don't
know if he saw me, but he did raise his hand—like he was
waving good-bye. I thought he understood about me watching him like I did. And I thought he forgave me. Now that I
can't ask him, I ain't positive. Walt, do you think I'm forgiven?"

"Without doubt."

"I don't really want to hear how you found out about
the singing. You don't mind do you?"

"It...it isn't the right time."

"Never will be."

The house had begun to shake, ever so slightly. The rushing pulled at The Old Home Place.

"Do you feel it?" Walter asked.

"Oh yeah," Ricky said. "But I gotta rest. I'm tired as can
be."

"You...deserve a rest."

"Thanks. You too. There's one thing, though. I'm never
gonna kill nobody."

They lay back, side by side. The rushing probed and tore
a path around and through The Old Home Place. The timbers, beams, and walls rocked. Endless grindings rose up to
Walter and Ricky as things broke free from their moorings
and pitched into each other. And now? Walter thought.
Now?

He did not know if he had slept. He was sure, however,
that there were no dreams. Dreamless since the far West, he
thought as he opened his eyes. The study listed at a slight,
strange angle. He became aware of this basic fact when he

stood and had to fight for balance. He steadied himself against a wall and surveyed his surroundings. The sunlight through the draperies had brought him to. The rushing was there, but its full, demonic powers had slackened.

The water had not quite made it into the study, and the stairs were broken off near the top of the landing. It did not register on him that he had been granted a reprieve until he parted the draperies. The flood had not begun to fully recede, but it had taken on a placid, tamer appearance. Its brown, gently rolling surface was all that remained of the world. As he stared out, The Old Home Place settled and murmured. It could topple over yet, he thought. Ricky said that it would survive whatever might come. The flood's smell, the decay that he had been immersed in, suffused each particle of air. It is my own smell, he thought. Mine and Ricky's.

Ricky was not there.

He was not in Edgar's old bedroom either, the site of so many violations and betrayals. In the room of the dead birds, he was met by a stiff, fecal-scented breeze. The sunlight there was painful, penetrating.

The window where the husk of the hawk had rested was newly smashed, the glass and wood having given way to a jagged, man-sized hole. The sweater, corduroy suit, and a pair of tattered briefs were carefully folded and arranged on the floor. At the window, he winced into the brightness, which suddenly seemed as doom-laden as the night. He called to the flood, calling for Ricky. There was no reply. He leaned out the window as far as he could. There may have been a faint, distant splashing, a tiny break in the seamless carpet of the flood. He could not be certain. When he looked again, the splashing was gone. Once more he began to call Ricky's name, louder and louder, over and over. The floor shifted beneath him, The Old Home Place tilting ever so slightly in time to its own crashes and booms.